€1

THE CENTRE OF THE UNIVERSE IS
18 BAEDEKERSTRASSE

By the same author

Fiction

One Foot in the Clouds
Chameleon
The Office

Non-fiction

The Rise and Fall of the British Nanny
The Public School Phenomenon
Love, Sex, Marriage and Divorce
Doctors

Children's Books

Jane's Adventures in and out of the Book
Jane's Adventures on the Island of Peeg
Jane's Adventures in a Balloon
The Terrible Kidnapping of Cyril Bonhamy
Cyril Bonhamy -V- Madam Big
Cyril Bonhamy and the Great Drain Robbery
Cyril Bonhamy and Operation Ping

THE CENTRE OF THE UNIVERSE IS
18 BAEDEKERSTRASSE

Jonathan Gathorne-Hardy

Hamish Hamilton
London

First published in Great Britain 1985
by Hamish Hamilton Ltd
Garden House 57–59 Long Acre London WC2E 9JZ

British Library Cataloguing in Publication Data

Gathorne-Hardy, Jonathan
   The centre of the universe is 18 Baedekerstrasse.
   i. Title
   823′.914[F]   PR6057.A84

   ISBN 0–241–11492–6
Phototypeset in Linotron Baskerville
by Input Typesetting Ltd, London SW19 8DR

Printed in Great Britain by Billings & Sons Ltd Worcester

The author gratefully acknowledges the grant from the Ingram Merrill Foundation of New York which enabled him to write the story 'The Centre of the Universe is 18 Baedekerstrasse'.

For Nicky, with love

Contents

The Man Who Laughed

Jack Kerouac took to the road in 1946 and to print in 1957. As movements go, it all happened amazingly quickly. The little cloud of marijuana was no bigger than a man's hand on the southern horizon. Torremolinos was still a fishing village. A little group of jazz, drug, white-wanting-to-be-black words had started to cross the Atlantic.

By 1969 Kerouac was dead. The words were everywhere. Torremolinos had quadrupled, the Bar Central been rebuilt three times. The cloud of marijuana covered half the sky, blotting out the sun and the chat of drawing rooms, even drifting down the corridors of august public schools – where it slightly sweetened the sour odours of cabbage, polish, urine and boy.

To Newton Abbas, the little public school 'snug in a crook' of the Dorset hills, such changes were as far away when Kerouac was writing as they were when the school was founded in 1898.

1898! Standing at his study window watching young Mark Thompson in the nets, the Headmaster could almost believe that now – Summer 1956 – those glorious golden days had come again. And gold was the word – gold hair, pale gold speckled skin turning to ripe wheat in the summer sun, that clean, muscular, lithe run, clear grey eyes . . . a faint, long-absent glow warmed the old loins for a brief moment, like the warmth in his hand when he pulled on his pipe.

And yet, Mr Wilson narrowed his eyes and at the same time widened his nostrils as if to catch a whiff of the intangible scarcely definable something he was aware of, was it not a return to some still more remote past, so remote that he felt a sense almost of veneration, even worship, as he stared at the youth below? Didn't, perhaps, couldn't you, quite meaningfully, suggest (the words 'snug' and 'crook' had been the Headmaster's) that the spirit of Camelot was alive again down there?

It was this element of chivalry in young Mark Thompson – something shining, exalted, grail-like, something that belonged quintessentially and only to Englishmen of a certain class – that led Mr Wilson to choose him when it surfaced that there was beastliness afoot in Stour House.

'I understand that the House is rotten to the core – falling apart like a rotten apple,' he said. 'You take my meaning, Thompson? I want you to go in there and clean the place up. Can you do it?'

'Yes sir.'

Mark's clean-cut lips and absolutely straightforward honest answer almost caused the pipe to ignite again. At the same time there was something so simple about the reply that Mr Wilson had to turn away to hide a sudden brimming. 'Yes sir' – what more could you ask for?

Mark Thompson himself had felt a flash of flame which he had immediately doused. He loathed queers. As mouthwatering as the hot-house peach he resembled when he'd first arrived in his Junior House lavender-coloured shorts, he had immediately been subject to the most extraordinary attentions. For a month or so he had reacted with instant and instinctive horror.

But these were senior boys, men of power. Very quickly – and this too seemed instinctive – he learnt the language of glances, blushes, brushed hands, dropped hints, the language of Perhaps. To avoid disapproval and dislike by promising; but never to fulfil – the dangerous strategy of the flirt.

The combination – apparent connivance, sudden furious flushed rejection – drove one or two senior boys to the borders of delirium. There was one almost violent incident behind the Fives Courts. Mark went to Mr Wilson. A promising academic career was cut short two weeks before the final exams.

Mark knew what – or who – was wrong with Stour House. It was the bitch Sprozen, aged fifteen and the tart of the Sixth Form. He was a caricature – great slack mouth, bags under his eyes like scrotums. He seemed to live only for pleasure. They said he'd once been accosted wandering dreamily in the beech-woods by a couple of randy monitors. He'd smiled and simply opened his mackintosh and his large cock was hanging out stuffed through a long, clinging, spongy rubber handlebar grip pulled off an old motor bike.

But Mark's confident, clean 'Yes sir' had a sounder base. He'd been through the fire and emerged unscathed. Two terms before, he had fallen in love. Rowlands looked like a diminutive cherub and smelt of tangerines. Obsessed, Mark followed him at a distance; placed himself where they would meet; the few words he addressed the grubby angel – 'Take your hands out of your pockets, Rowlands', 'Stop scrapping there' – left him dry-mouthed, trembling.

In the second term he managed to get Rowlands moved into the little dormitory of which he was captain. One night, the two other inmates in the San, he climbed into Rowlands' bed. The smell of tangerines was overpowering, like anaesthetic. Unfortunately perhaps, Mark failed to go under. His voice rather thick, clearing his throat a good deal, he talked about the Colts' Rugger XV and the need for a good School Cert. After half an hour he got back into his own bed. It took him three hours to get to sleep. Rowlands, who knew exactly what was going on, was surprised and a little disappointed. He'd expected they'd toss each other off at the very least. He fell asleep at once.

Three nights later, by a prodigious effort of will, Mark succeeded in having a wet dream about the three-foot chart of the female reproductive system hanging in the biology lab.

After two weeks, Stour House was as clean as a whistle. Once again, only just before exams, six promising academic careers were snipped at the root.

Mark's father, who had gone to a grammar school, would have sent him to Eton, but he was still only a hard-pressed employee slowly rising in a large firm of accountants when public school time came round. He couldn't really afford Newton Abbas. It was not until a year later that a series of miraculous deaths brought him, a remote third cousin, the title and a very considerable amount of land and money, even after horrendous taxes.

3

The Headmaster, bluffly obsequious to the new Lord, felt it would be most unsettling and probably impossible to move the boy to Eton now. Especially to Eton. He was a good-looking lad. He frowned at the worried father, pursing his lips. Did Lord Thompson take his meaning?

The worried father started violently. He took the Headmaster's meaning immediately. Lord Thompson's ideas about 'that side' of public school life were lurid to a point of melodrama. Of course, how dense of him, the idea of his lovely son going to Eton was clearly unthinkable.

Indeed it was with considerable difficulty that Lord Thompson even acquiesced in Mark having a crack at Oxford. This was the Sodom among English universities. Not for nothing was it the birthplace or whatever of Oscar Wilde. In fact Lord Thompson had it on good authority that at any one time 80% of the undergraduates and something like 96% of the dons were practising homosexuals.

And his son – glowingly, pinkly healthy, his virility honed and hair-trigger sharp from seasons of rigorous exercise and years of abstinence, bulgy and shiny like some sexual bomb – was at that most dangerous and vulnerable moment in English manhood in that distant period: the year or two before he lost his virginity. Lord Thompson took him for a long ride in the Land Rover before letting him go up for his interview.

So it was that Mark, taut and anxious in any case, having a nervous public pee in the 'Gentlemen' near Christ Church before going back to bed in the College, somewhat over-reacted to the pass made by the elderly man in the faded hound's-tooth Burberry.

It was the merest intimate brush of long and sensitive fingers, a vague fluttering of randy autumn leaves blown from one urinal to another.

Mark lashed out viciously, catching the sodomite a corker on his withered cheek.

'I hope that will teach you to keep your filthy hands to yourself next time,' he said, watching the Burberry writhe feebly on the damp tiles.

The next morning, suffering severely from bruises and the aftermath of the College port which had really led to the unfortunate indiscretion, Professor Drew, recognising Mark the moment he entered, held his handkerchief over the plaster on his face and tried to shrink behind the Senior Tutor.

But some minutes later, realising his assailant had failed to recognise him, he was perched well forward.

'Did you say you enjoyed – were – was it *rugger* you said? I'm afraid I didn't quite catch what you said.'

Oxford and Christ Church consolidated and added to what had been begun by Newton Abbas. On Saturdays Mark went beagling. They said he was a cert for a rugger blue. Finally, in his second year, he was elected to the Bullingdon.

Simon Hamilton said while the Club had dinner in his rooms – 'D'ya know old Ma Feather's place? Waller, he's in the Guards, they all go, took me. We're going at the weekend. Why don't y'join us?'

Ma Feathers finally reassured Mark he was totally, 100% normal. Rowland and the wet dream hadn't quite succeeded in doing this (the reproductive system, although in all essential respects quite remarkably like that of the human female, had in fact been that of a vole).

Mark grew increasingly embarrassed by his father. His ferocious denunciations of homosexuals, for instance (buggers, queens, pansies, poofters). These had accompanied Mark for as long as he could remember. Really, it was quite absurd. A slightly contemptuous tolerance was the line.

When a poet from Cambridge called Gitt or Gatt came to address the Aesthete's Club he was thrown into Mercury. Mark joined his plastered Christ Church friends. But this was an Oxford *tradition*, like punting on the Cherwell or Commem Balls. That Gatt or Gitt was supposed to be as queer as a coot had nothing whatsoever to do with it.

In the Long Vac of his second year he borrowed Simon Hamilton's flat in Lennox Gardens. He'd got onto some sort of list and went to dances and cocktail parties.

The party at which he met Tina North was not one of these. Mark knew no one and realised as soon as he had forced his way into the crowded cellar that his blazer and tie were wrong. He stuffed them behind a curtain.

Although Tina North was standing at the other side of the cellar waiting for some boy to return with her wine, Mark noticed her immediately. She was tall, with long golden hair and very full lips half-open over lots of large, even teeth. She was wearing a sort of shift, pale blue, made of gauze.

Tina felt his eyes and looked up. She thought at once: How good we'd look together. She smiled and was amused to see a deep blush cover the good-looking if faintly porcine face across from her. On an impulse, she beckoned.

Mark, when he'd finally struggled to her, saw she was barefoot.

'What's your name?' said Tina, smiling at him with all her marvellous, crunchable teeth.

They danced. Tina clung very close at once, as though she'd suddenly grown all over him, willowly but definite, and she was swiftly rewarded by that manifestation which always made her think it was as if men liked dancing with huge torches in their trouser pockets.

'What do you do?' croaked Mark.

'I'm a painter,' murmured Tina, her blue muslin the colour of morning glory, as concealing as mist. 'What about you?'

Mark, already in love with her, thought of his beagling and his rugger and the Bullingdon and his blazer stuffed behind the curtain. He swallowed. 'I'm a poet,' he said.

She came back with him that very night. This was unheard of in Mark's circle. Her sudden cry as she came reminded him of a hare that had been caught against a fence when they were out one Saturday morning.

Watching him dress in Simon Hamilton's military little bedroom with its sporting prints, watching him yank his Y-fronts over his protuberant rugger-playing buttocks, Tina said – it was something she'd slightly got into the habit of saying recently – 'You're the first man who's made me feel like a woman.'

Mark glowed.

'I'd love to read your poems,' she said, the water from her bath slopping over the top.

Mark managed to control his razor in its downward sweep. 'They're at Oxford,' he said. 'I'll get them today. I may have to stay the night.'

'Yes,' said Tina. 'Leave me a key. I'll get some of my things too.'

On the lurching train, Mark despairingly crossed out his fifteenth opening verse. His father's favourite poet was Longfellow. He'd given Mark a 'nice' edition in floppy green leather.

> In the autumn, over hillsides,
> Running with his beagles fast,
> Went young Simon Dingley bravely,
> Went he swiftly, heart beats beating. . . .

Once again he stared out of the window, words sluggishly changing places in his head.

It was the sight of Christ Church gate that rescued him. That chap they'd thrown into Mercury. Intense anxiety made his thoughts violent – make the bloody fairy pull his bloody weight for once.

The young man in the bookshop was infuriating in his ignorance.

'I want a book of poems by Gitt – a modern poet,' said Mark briskly.

'Gitt? We have no poems by anyone of that name.'

'Could be Gatt – Gitt or Gatt.'

'No. Not him either.'

'Well even Gett. Good heavens, it's your job, Gitt, Gatt or Gett. Haven't you heard of any of them?'

'I have not,' said the young man, exasperatingly calm. 'I read a good deal of modern poetry and I don't think anyone of that name, or names, exists.'

'You must have,' said Mark. 'He may be American. He's at Cambridge. He came over two terms ago and got thrown into Mercury - Gatt.'

'I think you may be thinking of Thom Gunn,' said the young man.

'That's the chap,' said Mark. 'I knew it was some sort of firearm.'

The young man didn't even flicker. 'That will be twelve and six, sir,' was all he said.

Mark set to work that very morning. It was quite easy, even fun. Many, indeed most, of the poems were incomprehensible – often because Gunn had made simple,

7

sometimes foolish errors of syntax, simile or subject matter. For instance there was a poem about a snail hunting. Who ever heard of a snail hunting, hunting, moreover, 'in a wood of desire'? Mark cleaned up these errors and was able to improve this poem – and others – out of all recognition. Even so, it was a gamble. But he had a feeling Tina wouldn't have heard of Gunn.

He was appalled to find that Simon Hamilton's flat had been transformed. Hunting prints, trophies, shoe-trees, riding crops and the twin hairbrushes of a civilised life had been swept away. Drapes were everywhere, huge swathes of material over which someone had randomly sploshed colours – mauves, purples, blues. About thirty pots of assorted poster paints were arranged at the foot of an easel. Tina's paintings were everywhere.

'It's marvellous, you've made it lovely,' said Mark, trying to remember when Simon had said he'd be back. 'What is . . . are . . . those?'

'That's some tie-dyeing I did,' said Tina, 'and those are my paintings.'

Mark looked at them earnestly. 'I think they're lovely, marvellous,' he said. 'Really marvellous.'

'Did you get your poems?' Tina slid her long arm round his thick waist.

'Yes,' said Mark. 'Look, I've just got to get my clothes.' Supposing she did know Gunn's stuff?

He meant new clothes. He'd realised his entire wardrobe was now useless. Luckily she'd confused it with Simon's and shoved all the clothes she could find on top of the tallboy. He went out and bought three pairs of jeans, some shirts, a pair of espadrilles, a jean jacket. Some instinct told him to keep it small.

He was right. Tina was deeply impressed. 'Is that all?'

Mark nodded.

'You can *really* just get it together and roll,' she said.

That night they read some of his poems. Tina had hauled the mattress off Simon's bed and pulled in the one from his spare room. She curled beside him while Mark, too nervous to read, opened his notebook for her at one of the transformed poems.

The Beagle

The beagle pushes through a green
night, for the grass is heavy
with water and meets over
the bright path he makes, where rain
had made the earth wet. He
moves in a wood of oak and birch,
his rump twitching
as he hunts. I can tell
they are at work, drenched there
but eager, smelling something.
What is their quarry?

Tina read two more poems and then looked up at him.

'You're a genius,' she said, 'a real genius, Mark.' She
thought: It's perfect. A poet, a painter – he'll take me on the
road and then someone else turns up. Fleetingly, she allowed
herself to think of Ned Buckley.

Mark looked down. Her large, rubber lips were almost
black in the shadows; but the surfaces of her big, flat, wet
teeth caught the candlelight and glistened.

He came to realise over the next ten days that they had
virtually nothing in common.

Tina got up late, eating her yoghurt lying dreamily amongst
the churned sheets on the mattresses. There was a second
yoghurt which was rubbed into her face and neck in her
sessions at the mirror. She spent hours in front of the mirror,
brushing and rebrushing her long gold hair, massaging, clean-
sing, eye-lining, tweaking, peering, poking, stroking, looking.
She did several self-portraits of herself.

She had an edition of Rimbaud which she carried about
with her and put by her side of the bed at night. There was
a marker at page four. Mark never saw her read it.

She adored her brother. Dickie, at seventeen, two years
younger than Tina, was having an affair with an American
called Ned Buckley. Mark realised, with an inner gulp, that
he would somehow have to wrench his instinctive disgust at
homosexuals yet further round – from contemptuous tolerance
to actual approval. Since Dickie was apparently queer, he

imagined Ned Buckley was too. He managed to convey the question.

'Oh you mean, is Ned a *faggot*? Oh no, not at all – I think, I expect he makes it with both sexes, whom he likes, which I think is absolutely right. It's odd about Dickie though – he doesn't usually dig whites. He digs spades. I *long* to meet Ned – but he's rolled it to Tuscany with Dickie.'

Make it, faggot, dig, roll it – for whole paragraphs, days, she spoke – when she did speak, which was rarely – a language Mark found completely incomprehensible.

Her diet too – years ahead of her time – was inexplicable. She seemed to survive – or rather, expect them both to survive – mostly on yoghurt and lemon pips. Bowls of wheat germ. Molasses. Raw things. Used to a rugger player's 5000 calories or so a day, Mark was frantic with hunger on this poet's fare. He used to slip out and wolf down hamburgers, bars of chocolate, hunks of bread.

Tina didn't notice. She hardly seemed aware of him at all during the day. Even at night there was something odd about her awareness. Mark was astonished by her excitement, at the pleasure of the long lithe-limbed girl writhing beneath him – a pleasure which Ma Feathers' girls, for all their skills, had never really been able to simulate. But despite her pleasure then, or when she arched over him in the summer darkness, eager, her hair slithery and silken across his chest and shoulders, he never felt it was really him, Mark Thompson of Newton Abbas and Christ Church, she was engaged with. He was just an instrument, a method.

Once he realised he was not after all in love, Mark became increasingly bored. At the same time he felt humiliated. He was terrified of being found out by either side. If any of his Oxford friends rang up he put them off. He hid his copy of Gunn's poems, which he'd almost finished transcribing, under a floor board in his 'studio' (the spare room). He was almost sure Tina's paintings were rubbish. Pure affectation. But perhaps they were modern art. He praised them abjectly.

His nights with Tina were not just to satisfy desire. They had to redress a balance. A certain ferocity entered his love-making.

It seemed a sort of solution, therefore, when some days

after getting a letter from Dickie she said she'd been asked to stay in the south of Spain by an American called Alan Wilder and would he like to come.

'Won't he mind?'

'No. I've asked him.'

'*Asked* him? How?'

Tina indicated Simon Hamilton's telephone.

'Good Lord,' said Mark. 'Isn't it very expensive to ring Spain?'

'I don't know,' said Tina, sounding neither guilty nor even interested. 'They certainly take hours to connect you.'

Packing took Tina a whole day. Her luggage consisted of a trunk, four large suitcases, the easel and a long roll of canvas. Even so, there was no room for the poster paints. Mark managed to cram them into his own modest grip.

Not aware till he collected them that he was expected to pay for both their tickets, Mark was intensely irritated to find that her luggage was enormously and expensively overweight.

'Do you really need all this, Tina?'

'Yes, I do.'

He was trying to calm himself sitting beside her in the plane, when Tina suddenly said, 'You know we're completely free, don't you?'

'*Free?*' said Mark, instantly fuming again.

'I mean, we like making it together, okay – but if you want to make it with someone else, like you just take off. And me.'

'Yes,' said Mark, gathering the gist. He felt relieved.

Rage returned when they landed at Gibraltar soon after four o'clock. As they came down the steps from the plane, heat rolled over them like . . . like . . . like what? Despite himself, Mark struggled – blankets? Open oven? Whatever it was, by the time they'd crossed the tarmac he was sweating. He took off his jacket.

The luggage came through a flapped opening and trundled along a ramp made of metal rollers. Mark's grip was among the first and he seized it to stow his jacket. He'd need all his arms, all his strength, for Tina's wardrobe.

He opened the grip and then stepped back with a cry. Something frightful had happened. It looked as if a huge multi-coloured bird had been bludgeoned to death and then

11

been stuffed hastily and bloodily among his clothes. Closer inspection revealed that, subjected to the unpressurised hold of their Viscount, most if not all of Tina's paints had exploded inside his suitcase. 'For Christ's sake Tina! Look what your paints have done.'

When Tina saw the carnage, she giggled. 'Oh lovey, I am sorry.'

Mark shook her off. 'Look at my clothes. They're ruined.'

'Alan's maids will see to them.'

Somehow, with a little surly Gibraltese assistance, he wrestled Tina's trunks and cases onto the top of the bus. It grew slightly cooler once, crucifix swinging above the driver's head, they started to move.

As if to placate or camouflage itself from the ferocious sun the grass had turned the colour of sand. The narrow road followed the coast past a succession of small, dingy, grey beaches licked by little glassy waves. There was a sign – Malaga 124 km.

Mark was still too irritated to take much notice. He tried to calculate how much Tina had cost him so far. She was asleep, her lovely head heavy on his shoulder. He couldn't think why he had come out with her. About £400.

At Torremolinos, pouring with sweat, he got Tina's luggage off the bus. They took a taxi.

'*Churriana por favor*,' said Tina.

Alan Wilder lived in a large house on the edge of the village. At sixty-four, twice divorced and now alone, he was a tall, balding American with thick-lensed glasses on a flat face like a moose. He'd shared a book shop in Paris in the twenties, once lent Auden £40 at an opportune moment in the thirties, 'liaised' in London during the war. Trends, 'new' writers and artists, titles, London clubs – he got it right about 60% of the time. He liked to have six or seven people to stay and then for their marriages to break up, or someone to run out of money; or to get them drunk and watch the ensuing scenes.

As they followed the two servants, staggering under Tina's luggage, across a small courtyard, Mark had the impression they were entering an institution – or perhaps an embassy.

Beyond the second door, they crossed grass, avoiding the

sprinkler. At its edge, cross-legged, was a plump figure in an orange kimono, with an orange face and henna-red hair. She was rolling a colossal cigarette, the size of a sausage.

'Hi – I'm Anna.'

'Hi – Tina.'

'Mark Thompson. How do you do.' He was not going to say hi.

'D'ya want a joint?' Her accent was a curious flat amalgam of English and American.

'We'd better see Alan,' said Tina. 'Where is he?'

'His study probably. See ya.'

'See ya.'

But their host met them at the top of the stairs. He had a loose shambling walk, one shoulder advanced as though preparing for an attack.

'Good to see you Tina.' He held her in a momentary embrace.

'This is Mark.'

'Pleased to meet you Mark.' The hand was loose, large, warm and dry. 'D'ya have a good journey? Your room's down here.'

They followed the big figure down a long, wide, tiled corridor, past doors and bare walls. Halfway down, Alan stopped at a round table protruding out of an alcove. It was covered in a dark red velvet cloth which reached the ground.

'This might interest you, Mark,' he said. 'Eighteenth-century Andalucian. Pretty big piece. That rug's fixed. In winter, they'd put a brazier of charcoal inside and sit with their knees in to keep warm.'

Mark looked interested. 'Must be heavy,' he said.

Their room was long and high, rugs on the red tiled floor, heavy Spanish furniture, a long mirror on the wall beside the brass bed. The high door had, like all the rooms off the corridor, a curved glass fanlight above it.

'Take a bath,' said Alan, indicating a door to the left of the bed. 'We'll be eating on the terrace half nine or ten.'

'Mr Wilder.' Mark walked over to him and gingerly began to open his grip. 'We had a slight accident . . . Tina's paints . . .'

Together they inspected the clotted mess.

13

'You sure have,' said Alan. 'Give it me. I'll have Maria deal with it.'

'One moment.' With difficulty Mark extracted a zipped plastic folder, now streaked yellow and green.

'They're his poems,' said Tina. 'Mark's a poet.'

Alan fixed Mark with his pale, magnified eyes. 'I'd be interested to read them sometime. I'll show you the library. I think you'll find things in it that will interest you.'

Mark lay on the bed, listening to Tina running one of her deep baths. Very soon he fell asleep.

He awoke to find the room transformed. Once again the swathes and drapes, the tie-dyeing, the portraits of Tina's toes and hands covered walls and furniture. There was a candle in a saucer beside the bed, casting just sufficient light for Tina to see her face in the mirror.

She stopped brushing her hair when she felt him stir. 'Mark, something really great has happened. Guess what – Ned Buckley's arriving tomorrow.'

'Who's he?'

'You *know* – I told you. He's been with Dickie. Isn't it fantastic?'

'I don't know. I've never seen the, even met the blighter.'

Tina turned away irritably. 'I do wish you wouldn't.'

Mark, at once irritable himself, got off the bed. 'Wouldn't what?' he said. He knew she meant use words like blighter, which in fact he'd only just managed to substitute for bugger. But why should she, of all people, who never opened that Rimbaud, tell a poet how to use the English language? 'Wouldn't what?'

'Nothing. Forget it,' said Tina. She gazed deeply into the mirror, soothing herself, brushing her hair. It was uncanny. Sometimes, it might have been Dickie gazing back at her.

At dinner, Mark had Alan on one side, Anna on the other. Next to Anna was Tom, her husband. Small, with a four-day beard, he said nothing the whole meal.

Alan addressed himself to Tina. Occasionally he swivelled deliberately towards Mark.

'What College you go to, Mark?' He had looked the Thompsons up in Debrett before Mark and Tina arrived but he wanted more exact placing.

'Christ Church.'

'Do you see anything of Isaiah Berlin? I remember him way back.'

Mostly Mark let Anna's talk flow over him. She spoke the same language as Tina, but with an even larger vocabulary. It seemed a language particularly suited to long rambling tales which didn't require listening to.

Maddened by hunger, Mark was in any case incapable of listening. Fortunately, the food was plentiful – a huge pile of yellow rice with bits of meat and fish in it. When he'd shovelled in about a kilo he began to revive. Anna was describing some interminable, threadless trip across Morocco. He glanced past her at her husband. Tom was staring vacantly out into the warm Spanish night. His hand rested, palm up, relaxedly open, on the marble table beside his empty and still clean plate.

Anna interrupted her narrative. 'His fix was too big. He'll eat later.'

'Oh,' said Mark.

'As I was saying,' Anna went on, 'there was this chick who'd had too many downers – no, wait – that was the other one – *this* chick was having a benny hallucination. Well benzidrine, you know, it can be great, but she was really freaking, wow, like you know . . . .'

Suddenly Mark realised what it felt like. It wasn't an embassy, it was a school. He'd just arrived at a new school. This was its jargon. If he had been going to stay, he'd have had to have learnt it. But as he wasn't he'd be damned if he would – chick, downers, bloody rubbish.

He did, however, discover the meaning of one of the words. After the coffee had been cleared away, Anna began to roll another of her enormous cigarettes.

'Let's have a joint,' she said.

Mark realised it was some drug he vaguely remembered reading about. It was meant to rot your genes or something. When Anna, after an amazing and elaborate parade of rolling, sealing, shaping, tipping, finally lit the big cigarette, took a series of shuddering inhalations and passed it on to him, he handed it back to her.

'I don't think I will,' he said.

15

Anna, holding her breath, had gone purple in the face. She gestured away from her with her hand. 'Pass it to Alan, Mark,' said Tina.

Alan put it to his lips and passed it to Tina. Her reaction was a variant of Anna's: a gulping of smoke and then holding her breath. Oddest was Tom's. He expelled his breath and then, deflated, forced out still more puffs of air, wringing himself empty. Finally he fastened his mouth onto the cigarette and began to breathe in through it very slowly. In in in in in in – it went on for minutes. The joint, sausage-fat, sausage-long, glowed against the darkness of the vast garden beyond him. He won't have a gene left, thought Mark.

Now came a pause, Anna holding the joint in her podgy fingers. 'Not bad grass this,' she said. No one replied.

The second time round, Alan passed it untouched to Tina. 'Come on up to the library Mark,' he said, 'I've some things I think you'll appreciate.'

As they left the terrace, Mark heard giggles ripple round the table. He wondered if they were laughing at him, the new boy who'd refused the ritual.

The library was a long room with low marble tables in front of broad sofas and large armchairs with white covers. Every wall had shelves full of books. Alan pressed a switch and a block of these, illuminated from above, sprang out at them.

Mark tried to think of something to say; but 'what a lot of books' didn't seem sufficient from a practising poet.

However, it was the comment Alan appeared to answer. 'Yeah – it's quite a collection now. I started way back in the twenties in Paris.' He shambled ahead of Mark towards the illuminated shelves. 'I thought you'd like to see my collection of modern poetry.'

A feeling of immense fatigue came over Mark. The covers, the meaningless, unknown names, blurred with Alan's deliberate, ponderous monologue.

And then all at once it was as if one of the books had shot out of the shelf and thumped him violently between the eyes. Mark stared horrified. The trap had been sprung.

'What?' he said. He must divert Alan's attention.

16

Alan was handing some volume or other to him open at the flyleaf. 'Of course I've got most of Wystan's early work.'

Mark glanced down and saw 'To a friend in need from a friend in need – Wystan Auden'. 'Very nice,' he said. He handed the book back, meanwhile edging round to interpose himself between Alan and the shelves.

But it was too late.

'Ginsberg of course you'll know,' said Alan. 'But what about this guy Gunn? Do you have any views on him?'

'Not really,' said Mark. 'Well, yes actually. I met him once – briefly. In fact he's been an influence.' He'd destroy everything in the morning. Burn it all.

'Is that so?' said Alan. 'I'd certainly appreciate it if you'd let me read some of your work sometime.'

'Well – it's very experimental at the moment,' said Mark. 'It's at the start.'

'Sure, sure; take your time.'

'Tina told me Ned Buckley was coming tomorrow.'

'Yeah, and we may have some trouble there,' said Alan, momentarily deflected. 'About six months ago his wife Donna left him. Married five years. She's shacked up with the guy who runs the Bar Central. You can see her there any time. Long pale hair – white, platinum. I didn't know to warn him off or not,' said Alan, who was looking forward to the encounter.

'What's he do?'

'Ned? You don't know him? Ned's a poet too. Maybe one evening we could have a reading – whataya say?'

Christ, thought Mark, not answering, it's a bloody nest of vipers. Gunn himself might turn up.

Drawn back to the wretched subject, Alan leant heavily forward and pulled a small book from a lower shelf. 'Whataya think of this guy Santorini? Gabriel Santorini?'

'I haven't read him,' said Mark.

'They call it "Discrete Poetry", like there's "Concrete Poetry" I suppose. He writes a poem, then cuts it up, shakes the words up and spreads them out in lines. I can't make a thing of it, but he's well thought-of in the States. Here – might interest you.'

'Thanks,' said Mark.

17

'Use anything you want from the shelves.' Alan put his arm round Mark's shoulder, walking him out.

'Thanks a lot,' said Mark.

The joint had a strange effect on Tina. Her love-making was even more prolonged and passionate than it had been in London. Yet he felt she was less aware of him, farther away, than ever before. It was just another elaborate lonely ritual that had to be followed through in order to reach a particular state.

The solution of his major worry came to him with the dawn. It was so simple, but so complete it allowed him to fall asleep again.

He was first down to breakfast, though Alan appeared as he was finishing, carrying a pile of mail. Mark asked if he might have a room to work in, and was there a typewriter.

'Sure – use my old Remington. And you can write in the gazebo. That's right on up the stairs you take to your room. Hope the work goes well.'

Mark locked the door of the gazebo, spread his poems on the table, selected his favourite and typed it on the Remington. He took Tina's nail scissors and cut the poem into words and phrases, put these in his sponge bag, shook it and then emptied it out onto the table. He made an anagram of the title, and then arranged the words more or less at random on a page and painstakingly typed the whole thing out again.

The Gleeab
night, that they are at work
and birch, baying through a
quarry? but eager, drenched there,
he hunts.
The bright path twitching as
the gleeab pushes or the grass is
with water I can tell.
He moves in a heavy
wood of oak and meets over
his rump smelling something.
Where rain made green
earth their what
he makes, wet.

18

It compared well with the poems in *Sempo Eadem* by Gabriel Santorini. His were rubbish; so was Mark's. He was fairly sure that all trace of Gunn had now been eradicated.

After some thought, he took out the word Gleeab. It had a Lear or Carroll ring. Instead – a trick of Santorini's, many of whose poems were titled with single letters, numbers or nothing – he called it '?'.

Mark worked furiously all morning. The gazebo was really a wooden room built on one side of the roof. From it he could see the whole two-acre garden; paths winding between flower beds and shrubs, the little groves of trees which broke it up – young eucalyptus, full-grown chestnuts, ilex. There were one or two palms and clumps of avocado with their dark green, glossy leaves. At the far end he could see the sun flash on the surface of a swimming pool. Immediately below, at the end of a eucalpytus avenue, was a secluded square of grass enclosed by a hedge, itself surrounded by tall bamboo rising, feathery and graceful, almost to the roof.

It grew hot in the gazebo. Mark worked on, sweating, bare-topped. There was no knowing when the Headmaster might not ask to see his poems or suggest a reading to the assembled crackpots. He worked through the afternoon while the rest of the household slept. Tina had embarked on a marathon of preening. He left her lying on her back on their bed, two lint pads soaked in yoghurt on her eyes.

By five o'clock he was exhausted. But three-quarters of the poems had been translated and the rest he could do tomorrow. There remained one last task.

He buried Gunn and the original transcriptions deep in the centre of an unidentifiable but painful thicket. Then he sauntered the length of the garden to the swimming pool.

For the first time since their arrival he felt moderately relaxed. After a swim he lay in the shade of the bamboo surrounding the pool. Three careful days and he would be the glorious gold that had carried Mr Wilson back across the centuries.

Ned Buckley arrived that evening. It was something of an entrance. They were on the terrace having drinks and rather spasmodic talk before supper. Tom had clearly overdone his

19

evening fix again – whatever a fix was – and stared glassily out into the garden.

And suddenly – there he was among them, like Jesus with the apostles or something in a pantomime.

'Ned!' cried Anna, waddling importantly over to him, her flat fat bare feet thudding.

Alan came lopsidedly after her. 'Good to see you Ned. D'ya have a good journey? Let me introduce you '

Ned held up his hand. 'There's one introduction you don't need to make,' he said. He walked up to Tina. 'You must be Tina,' he said softly. 'Dickie's told me such a lot about you. Yes – as I thought, your hair's a lot like Donna's. A lot like. I'm very pleased to meet you at last, Tina.'

He held her hand for several seconds. Tina was blushing. Mark had never seen her blush. He felt a stab of jealousy.

Ned held everyone's hand for several seconds. He held Mark's for what seemed like minutes.

'Dickie's told me about you too, Mark. I know you haven't met him, but you will. You write po-atry. So do I.'

Ned was about thirty. He was shorter than Mark, slightly plump, a square, tanned face covered in freckles, narrowing to a pointed chin and a sharp little nose. His hair was fair and curly. He had intensely blue eyes which he fixed unwaveringly on Mark, his nose twitching as though he were sniffing him.

'Good to meet you,' he said finally, his voice soft, the American accent smoothed from years rolling round the shores of the Mediterranean. His lips were dry, a lighter colour than his face. Mark thought he felt a barely detectable squeeze before the freckled hand had let him go. He found he too was blushing.

Ned spoke the same jargon as Anna and Tina, only with even greater expertise – digs, spades, chicks, hips, grooves, kicks, cools and greats flowed from him with careless ease. It was as if, Mark decided, the head boy had returned from a victorious away match. Ned sat between Alan and Tina, addressing them in turn.

To Alan he talked names. He seemed to know everyone. You name them, Ned knew them. 'Ginsy' had sent a personal message; Neal Cassidy, Greg Corso, Bill Burroughs, Luc

20

Carr. Mark gathered they were writers mostly. Nodding without listening to Anna, he followed the list apprehensively.

It was Alan who brought up the dreaded name. 'Mark here says this guy Gunn's pretty good. Isn't that so Mark?'

'Yes,' said Mark.

'Do you know Thom?' asked Ned.

'Well he's an acquaintance more than a friend.'

'He's a great guy,' said Ned. His eyes were fixed on Mark, very blue, knowing, the little nose sniffing again.

But it was onto Tina he turned the full force of his attention. He talked to her about Dickie. He'd brought a letter from Dickie. He said what they'd done, where they'd been, how often they'd wished Tina had been with them. Tina listened, her mouth slightly open. When Ned turned to talk to Alan, she kept her large kohl-rimmed eyes fastened to the freckly back of his neck.

Mark wanted to force them apart, drag Tina over to him. He began to loathe Ned. Yet when Ned looked across and involved him for a moment – 'You'd've really dug that Mark' – he felt Tina's envy and approval of the new if temporary favourite, and was grateful to Ned.

Anna had put herself next to him again. Very close next to him. Mark felt her thick calf press against his. He moved his leg away. After a while, the calf followed him, and he suddenly realised Anna was attracted to him. It occurred to him that the blatancy of Tina's fascination had made Anna feel that he was, as it were, becoming vacant.

He moved his leg again. He was virtually sitting sideways on his chair. Anna was describing another journey. Her life seemed to consist of these huge, goalless trips, in different countries and with different people, but all somehow the same. Mark began to feel she had got inside his head and was trampling his brains.

The drama of Ned's arrival meant they didn't eat until 10.30. It was nearly twelve by the time they finished. Anna started to produce her rolling equipment, but Ned forestalled her.

'Pass me the skins, Anna. I scored in Tangiers.'

He took a long time preparing it; shredding, tweaking, loading, rolling. His fingers were plump and generously freckled. He lit it, inhaled in a series of sharp, noisy gulps and passed the large cylinder to Alan, who gave it his perfunctory peck and passed it to Mark.

Mark took it, hesitated, aware that Ned and Tina and Anna were all watching him, then put it to his lips, sucked in the fragrant herbal smoke and, as he'd seen the others do, held his breath.

The effect was quite swift and not totally pleasant. It was as though a number of nerve ends were snipped in his head, detaching him; at the same time cotton wool got into the cortex. Then nothing. I'm immune, thought Mark with relief. Next time it came round, he tried unobtrusively to imitate the carp-like gulpings of Anna and Ned and held the smoke down longer.

All at once, he found he was laughing. He wasn't sure why. It was as if he'd been seized with laughter from outside; it shook him in violent spasms. He got his breath and then, helpless, was shaken by laughter again – the more so when he tried, choking, to explain to Anna, also laughing, what it was that had made him laugh.

After that the night for Mark deteriorated rapidly. He couldn't grip time. Things didn't happen – or did so very slowly. Yet he looked round and Alan had gone. A record played. Cortex was now total wool. Anna next to him was describing a trip across the Kalahari Desert.

Mark was astonished to suddenly hear his voice say, 'Let's have another joint.' It was the first time he'd used their jargon. It sounded completely artificial, even mad.

The result of this smoke was to give him a raging thirst. He drank three tumblers of red wine, but it made no difference. The thirst had become an integral part of his throat.

Doors kept opening and people appearing on the terrace and then going back into the house.

He could see Tina's teeth gleaming. The whole of her gleamed. He wondered if she would go off with Ned that very night, in front of everyone.

More doors, more people on the terrace. No guitar. Mark felt slightly sick. Ned was talking about sex.

It was like Ned talking names – you name it, Ned had done it. Done it, had it, had it done to him. He was telling them all, intimate, frank, sincere, how when he first had orgasms he used to laugh. This helpless laughter, like he just couldn't help it, he just dissolved. He had to stop it, control it. Chicks didn't like it. Kind of insulting if you laughed and laughed when they came and you came.

'What about men?'

Mark was appalled. It wasn't just that his voice sounded unnaturally loud. He'd meant it to be a sneering, queer-bashing question, an insult. But it had come out all coy and flirtatious and insinuating – more like an invitation.

Ned took it like that. He looked straight into Mark's eyes, his own twinkling, his nose sniffing, mouth smiling. He paused, then said, 'They said, "Just dig that laugh man".'

Everyone laughed. Mark felt he was going to faint. He felt brittle. His arm would break like ice if he just tapped it on the back of the chair. He managed to stand up and somehow got across the terrace.

Behind him he heard Ned saying, ' . . . had this great British ass on him'. The terrace laughed. They're talking about me, thought Mark.

He was sick in the bidet in their bathroom, but it made him feel no better. He lay naked under the sheet in the hot darkness, paralysed, spinning.

He imagined Tina was now in bed with Ned. But after several hours he heard the door click, and rustling as she undressed at the end of the bed. Mark felt relief, gratitude, desire.

As she slipped beneath the sheet next to him, he put his arms round her and started to pull her towards him. Tina struggled to free herself. Mark held her firm – they sometimes had mock fights like this.

'I want you.'

'I *don't*.' She sounded furious. She pushed him violently away with her knee, leapt out of bed, seized something from its end and slammed the door behind her.

Mark wanted to follow, but he was still paralysed. He thought, I've driven her into his arms. He lay in a state between trance and doze; finally, at dawn, he slept.

The joint or kif or whatever it was, though still evident,

23

had sufficiently relaxed its grip by eleven to let him go groggily down to breakfast.

Tina was the only person there, toying with a few lemon pips. After a long silence, when he'd finished two oranges, three bowls of coffee and several rounds of toasted Spanish bread, Mark said, 'Where did you sleep?'

Tina didn't answer. Head down, she was eating within a tent of hair.

'I suppose you slept with Ned?'

The tent whirled open. 'It's none of your *business. Actually* – no I didn't. But if he wants me I will.'

Mark stood up. Should he be angry? or cry?

'Please Tina. Couldn't we somehow . . . I don't know – why don't we go up to bed – now?'

Tina stood up so violently that her metal chair crashed backwards onto the terrace. She jumped down onto the grass and ran towards the garden. She ran gracefully, her golden hair tumbled and streaming, her short nightdress pressed flat against her by her speed.

Unnerved by despair, Mark was unable to follow. She vanished into the maze straight, with purpose. She probably knew Ned was by the pool.

It took him two hours to complete the poems. The sun blazed vertical but a minute breeze made the gazebo just bearable. The tall bamboo stems swayed, clacking and knocking gently together.

Mark crumpled the last of the Gunn transcriptions into a ball and carried them over to the window. He felt a definite sense of achievement. He looked out over the garden, the sun hot on his bare shoulders. Santorini's poems were no better. Often they were worse. And he prefered his own title – *Sepom* by Mark Thompson. He'd publish. Become famous. But it wouldn't do to have the chaps of the Bullingdon find out. A pen name. *Sepom* by Ark M. Sponsmoth. A transatlantic ring.

The present, with its torments, returned painfully and instantly at the sight of Tina and Ned Buckley strolling towards the house under the eucalyptus.

Mark shrank against the window of the gazebo, keeping one horrified eye on the couple below. They were close, but not quite touching. They walked into the middle of the grass

24

square immediately below him. As they turned towards each other he saw that Tina's vast, red, ravenous mouth was half-open, her eyes closed. Ned's sharp little nose was quivering. Mark sank to his knees to avoid seeing them kiss.

He crawled into the middle of the gazebo before he stood up. He was shaking. He wanted to hurl the table down on them.

Halfway down the stair he stopped hopelessly. What was the point? She was determined to go off with Ned. The only thing to do was to get them away. Not to witness the humili-ation. Tell them they must leave.

Mark hurried down stairs and along corridors and knocked at the door of Alan's study.

'Yeah?'

Alan was lying on a couch, a book open and face down on his chest. He looked as if he'd been asleep.

'Sorry to disturb you Alan,' said Mark. 'I was wondering if there was a car I could borrow. I want to get into Torremo-linos to get some clothes.'

There was truth in this. Maria's efforts to clean his clothes, though admired by Anna, had, in Mark's view, only been partially successful, leaving them as if the victims of some particularly vague and loony experiment in tie-dyeing.

'Sure, Mark, sure.' Alan lumbered across the room, removing a key from a ring as crowded as a medieval gaoler's. 'Take the Seat. It'll be on the street outside the big door.' He put a paw on Mark's shoulder. 'Stay out to lunch if you feel like it. La Fonda opposite the Bar Central does a good paella.'

Driving down the dusty road through olives and patches of withering maize, Mark reflected on that paw. It had been friendly, fatherly, almost a pitying gesture. Observing this blatant, public cuckolding, no doubt they all pitied him.

The horrid scene was still so vivid to his eye that he felt he had to have a drink at the Bar Central. It was crowded but Mark was almost sure he recognised a figure prominent at a fringe table. On an impulse, emboldened by misery, he went over. 'Excuse me, you don't know me – Mark Thompson – but I think you must be Donna Buckley.'

25

'Sure am.' Pale pink lips smiled automatically in a pert, pretty, golden face. 'Pleased to meet you Mark.'

'Alan Wilder, where I'm staying, said how marvellous your hair was – and he was right.'

'Thank you.' Donna shook her tiny, perfect head at him so that the white, startlingly white waterfall falling straight down her back shifted and spread. 'That was real nice of Alan. He always dug my hair.' She moved magazines and café flotsam. 'Say – sit down. Have a drink on the house.' She clapped her hands at the bar and added over her shoulder, 'It's not Buckley any more. Henderson. He's the guy runs this place.'

'Actually, Ned arrived yesterday night as well.'

'Je-sus Cher*ist!*' Donna spun round and threw her cigarette violently out into the road. 'You don't say? You mean that faggot's made it back to the coast again? I might've guessed.'

'Faggot?' said Mark, obsessed, having momentarily forgotten that aspect of Ned. 'It's girls he seems to – er – dig.'

'Don't you believe it,' said Donna. 'I was married to the creep for five years I should know. Ned's 88.8% faggot. What he really dug was making it with me and *another* fag. And he liked me to *watch* him and well, I guess, just applaud.'

'Oh,' said Mark.

'Yeah,' said Donna. 'And does he keep up that phoney poet scene?'

'I think so.'

'What a joke,' said Donna. 'That's only because of all this beat stuff. Nine years ago he was going to co-produce a musical on Broadway. Ned would eat shit if he thought it was chic.'

Conversation languished and Mark soon left. But he bought shorts instead of long trousers. In particular he bought bathing trunks that were really no more than a fist-sized bag for genitals, a vivid blue sheeny-textured codpiece.

He found that the next convenient (that is cheap) flight to London was in three days' time. On an impulse, he didn't book it. Perhaps she would come back to him.

They were all drinking on the terrace when Mark came down in his new shorts.

It was impossible to tell how far Ned and Tina had gone.

Tina was dressed in one of her short white drapes, indistinguishable from a nightdress. There was something feverish about her, her teeth flashing, her laughs too loud. But Ned seemed to have distanced himself from her slightly. Or perhaps it was just the way he held himself; like many smallish men, head up, chest up, braced to extract a few extra millimetres.

He was talking to Alan, Tina listening, but when he saw Mark he came over and put his hand on Mark's shoulder.

'Where'd you get to, Mark? I looked for you all over, with Tina. I wanted to see your work – if you'd let me.'

Mark, not thinking, on automatic, gave him a full Thompson, M.J. smile and then, almost bashful, lowered his head and let the smile go secret. 'I went into Torremolinos,' he said. 'I had to get some clothes.' He paused, then looked up and smiled full at Ned again, but a frank, honest, involving smile, edged with tenderness.

'I met Donna, Ned,' he said. 'I thought she was – well – great.'

Ned twitched his jaw muscles. He looked into Mark's eyes. 'I knew she was here,' he said. 'A great chick. The greatest. I . . .' he looked away, speaking very quietly ' . . . haven't felt . . . not that is . . . not since. . . .'

'I understand,' said Mark.

Ned looked at him and twitched again. 'I believe you really do,' he said. 'I'm . . . sorry. . . .'

'You don't have to be,' said Mark. 'I understand.'

This crucial exchange, of rather obscure meaning to Mark, brought them next to each other at table. Several times Ned's leg brushed accidentally against him during lunch. Each contact brought a shiver of gooseflesh, but Mark forced his leg to remain where it was.

Alan was explaining that he had to go to Granada that afternoon for two or three days. He was picking up some old friends – a sculptor and his wife.

'Antonio normally does the driving, but he's sick. I'm sure sorry to have to leave you.'

He meant he was extremely sorry to have to leave at that moment. A very pretty little situation was building up. He didn't want to miss a second.

Mark nodded, abstracted. He was listening to Ned telling Anna and Tina how he'd left Italy.

'I liked it there. Plenty oh plenty. It was a groove. But one afternoon I just found I'd got a few things together and rolled – I didn't give a damn where – anywhere – but, you know? – I just wanted to get to Malaga, to *be* here, right *here*. You know.'

Anna knew. 'There was this time Tom and I made it from LA to Mexico City – no pack – some grass – I had a roll. . . .'

When Alan left after lunch, however, Mark felt a sudden chill. With no Headmaster, disgusting things might happen. How could he keep the pupils apart, on his own?

In fact things began to happen quite soon, though not in the direction he most feared. Tom, who seemed to have over-done his morning fix, went glassily to bed. The rest of them went up to the pool. Ned lay in the shade of the bamboos. His tan was really a *pointilliste*'s trick – a million freckles. Tina, heavily oiled, and Anna lay under the full fury of the sun. Mark alternated.

After fifteen minutes in the sun he felt on fire. He stood up and walked slowly round the pool. He was very conscious that Ned's eyes were fixed on the taut, bulging, brilliant blue bobbing blob of his codpiece.

The water was cool and clear. A tiny frog swam frantically to escape his approach and then dived to the bottom.

He lay down in the shade. There was nothing accidental about the contact of Ned's leg this time. He'd had to cross the entire width of his towel to achieve it. Mark lay rigid, letting waves of gooseflesh subside. He wanted to stand up and kick Ned as hard as he could in the crutch. He tried to sleep.

Each time he returned from the sun or the pool, the surrep-titious contact was resumed. Despite his disgust, Mark did finally manage to doze.

It can only have been a few minutes. He thought he heard someone say his name. When he sat up Ned and Tina had gone.

'They went thataway,' Anna vaguely, plumply, indicated the garden.

'Let 'em do it Mark. Come and sit here.' She gave off a

heavy, pungent, musky odour which seemed to come from a thick oily unguent she was slowly rubbing into herself – probably the source also of her curious marmalade colour.

Mark did not answer, but set off at a run into the maze of little hedges, flower beds and trees. He did not mind how obvious it was. He had to keep them apart.

Away from the sanction of the pool, the codpiece, bounding up and down between his legs, seemed totally obscene.

Ned and Tina were walking slowly side by side. Ned was gesticulating with his stubby, inexpressive hands.

'Hi Mark. We thought you were asleep. Isn't this just the most fantastic place you've ever seen?'

Mark stood panting. He was still overwhelmed, made speechless by the relief they had not been holding hands. Tina was looking at the ground or at her lovely long hand-like feet.

'Say Mark,' said Ned. 'Could I see some of your writing now? Tina's told me a whole lot about it.'

'All right,' said Mark.

They walked in silence towards the house. As they were about to enter it, Tina suddenly turned and ran back towards the garden. Mark stopped, half-turned, but Ned put his arm round his shoulders and gently pushed him forward. He did not speak but smiled at Mark, his blue eyes pricking him all over: cheeks, lips, chest, codpiece, cheeks, chest again – prickle, prickle, prick, prickle. Mark wanted to lam into the solar plexus. He tried to loosen his fist.

In the gazebo, he began to worry about discovery. The large ball of crumpled Gunn transcriptions lay where he'd dropped them in shock. While Ned read, Mark flicked it behind a flowerpot with his toe.

Ned read in concentrated silence for ten minutes. Every so often he looked up, fired his eyes at Mark and formed his pale lips into a silent whistle. At the end of it he stood up and came purposefully across the gazebo, his face clearly showing 'a new respect'.

'Could I take these away with me for a while, Mark? This is the real thing. I think it's really great – the way you're not hung up on grammatical constraints – incredible.'

Mark dimpled, shrugged modestly. 'I don't know,' he said.

As they went out, Ned looked him straight in the eye. 'You've got class, Mark.'

After supper that night, Mark again smoked pot (or was it grass, hash, tea, kif, dope, slop, slap, shit – God knows why they bothered with words at all). His head rapidly filled with cotton wool. The pattern was becoming familiar. A burst of hysteria. A fiery thirst, which wine could not touch – though a great deal of wine was nevertheless drunk. If the words had made sense they would have been personal abuse about him. Reality at pinpoint.

Ned talked and talked. 'My dead brother was in the corner of the room. There was light all round him. I said – "Bill". He disappeared. I have these visions.'

Someone – Tina? – said, 'What are you going to do?'

'I don't know. I just go along. I dig life here. Here. Now. Being with all of you.' He looked up and round and found Mark. His expression said – 'You understand.'

People were leaving. Soon it was just Ned, Mark, Tina. Mark felt terrible – breakable, dizzy, very tired. He'd barely slept. But he had to stay. If he left, they'd go to bed together. At half past two he heard his distant voice say, 'Let's have another joint.'

Tina had gone.

Ned and he were walking in the garden. 'Dig that moon,' whispered Ned. He was holding Mark's hand very tight.

The thick hot blanket of pot-fog that now encased Mark probably saved Ned from serious injury. Ned's tongue was enormous and tepid. It completely filled Mark's mouth and throat. He was aware he was being kissed – silly dainty word for this invasion of butcher's meat, this taste of old harbour. He felt a sluggish, murderous fury. But it was the invasion and fury of a dream. He could hardly move his limbs. He just managed, choking, to haul himself free.

Ned was trembling. He reached for Mark. Mark held him off. Suddenly Ned began to speak.

' . . . and meets over his rump,' he said urgently, 'smelling something.' He paused, the gibberish hanging over them. Then went on in a soft sing-song voice—

' . . . his rump smelling something
    where rain made green

30

```
                 earth their what
                 he makes, wet.'
```
'What?' said Mark. 'What are you talking about?'

'One of your pomes,' said Ned. 'I knew at once what you meant. Mark – have you ever thought – would you ever ball it with a man?'

There was a long pause. Mark didn't think. He was waiting for someone else to answer. Finally he heard his voice say, slowly, lingeringly – 'Perhaps.'

He turned and ran off up towards the pool. He heard Ned chuckle and set off heavily in pursuit. But Mark was one of the fastest wing-threes in the Oxford Reserve XV. For a fortunate instant the fog lifted, clouding his senses no more than the high moon did the vast, cicada-resounding garden.

But it was not as light as day. All at once Mark heard behind him a sharp yell of pain. He looked back. Ned was lying motionless, flung flat out in one of the flower beds.

Mark put on a spurt. How strange it was to race down these still, moon-muffled paths – a wing-three-quarter with a nightdress pressed flat against him by his speed.

The drug struck him again at the top of the stairs. He lurched down the corridor, panting, once again feeling sick.

Tina was in their bed, but stretched out at the farthest edge, lying in a 5 inch-wide band down the entire length.

Mark knew better than to touch her. Swaying, he pulled off his clothes. He lay under the sheet, his eyes shut, the cicadas in his head.

He wasn't asleep. Nor was he awake. It was that same unpleasant, trance-like, paralysed state of the night before.

It meant – minutes later or hours later – that he heard the click of the door. He reached out. She'd gone.

He was still unsteady on his feet but could not have been more than a minute behind. The corridor was empty.

Mark, naked in his urgency, tip-toed along the warm red tiles to Ned's room, two up from theirs. Very slowly he depressed the handle and then gently pushed.

It was locked. He put his ear to the panels and listened. Surely those were springs creaking, moans. He stood back – the fanlight above the door was feet out of reach.

He looked desperately up and down the corridor. In the

dim light from the moon, he could just see the big eighteenth-century Andalucian table protruding out of its alcove.

It was extremely heavy. Crouched in the hot darkness of the velvet table cloth, his arms encircling the thick central leg, Mark strained to get it off the ground. Sweat poured down his back and chest. The table tilted from side to side. Very gradually, it began to rise.

Mark stood gasping. Then took a short step to his left. At once there was a sharp crack as the table struck the wall of the alcove and another as, reeling back, Mark drove it into the opposite wall. Quivering with the effort, he slowly lowered it to the ground.

He crawled out and carefully lifted the velvet cloth up on top of the table to enable him to see.

It took him five minutes, pausing for rests, to stagger with his monstrous umbrella down to Ned's door. He lowered the table and, his stomach now gripped by apprehension, clambered on top of it.

Ned lay on his side in the middle of the large bed, his face turned away, his curls pale in the moonlight. He was quite alone.

Twice more that night Mark made the terrible journey. At the end of the second, he had to leave the table halfway up the corridor.

After breakfast he stationed himself in the gazebo – a vantage point over the whole garden. Tina was sunbathing on the concealed lawn. If she moved, he'd follow.

He was interrupted, dozing, by Ned knocking on the door to return his poems. Ned had a large plaster over a bump above his right eye. He held out the sheaf of poems. 'I think this is some of the greatest stuff I've read in years, Mark . . . Greg . . . Allan . . . grammatical hang-ups . . . rump. . . .'

Mark didn't listen. He was suddenly exhausted. He thought, this absurd situation has got to stop. I can't take any more of this.

When Ned had finished, Mark made some modest disclaimer, then leant out of the window so that Ned had to lean with him. They looked down.

After a moment, Mark said gently, 'Why don't you take her away with you, Ned? You want her.'

Ned gave him 'with new respect' and 'you've got class' in one long, blue, glistening beam.

'I didn't mean this to happen, Mark. It's just – well, Dickie partly – but I haven't felt like this about anyone since Donna. It's as big as that. But what do you feel about her?'

'I love her,' said Mark. 'But I shall tell her I don't. She wants you – not me. She must be free.'

'But it's not as simple as that,' said Ned. 'Remember last night. I want you too, Mark. I think we could – like make it together, Mark.'

Mark looked soulfully out over the garden – out over rugger fields and Fives Courts. 'I know, I know,' he said.

But this was no smitten stripling of eighteen. 'Christ how I want you.' Ned's voice had gone thick. 'D'ya know Dickie went to Greece two weeks before I got here. I haven't had. . . . D'ya know I get a hard-on every time I look at you?' To Mark's horror Ned seized his hand and pressed it to his trousers, where he could indeed feel the hard-ridged evidence of this revolting effect.

He tried to free his hand, but Ned held fast, unstoppable. 'We could all three make it together. That way you could still have Tina. Whatd'ya say Mark – a *partouze?*'

Once again he dragged Mark's hand towards a now discernible bulge. 'Go on Mark, you're trembling. Give, man, give – you want it as badly as I do.'

Mark was trembling. He thought – no, felt and saw rather than thought, a savage image – one grab, a violent twist and wrench and I could yank the whole thing out by the roots.

He pulled his hand away from Ned's, and took two hasty steps to the window.

'You may be right. It's true I. . . . The thing is,' said Mark, 'it's a difficult decision. For me I mean. If I didn't have to think of you and Tina. Look Ned, if you promised not to – er, make it with Tina here, I could sort of concentrate on you – do you see what I mean?'

'You mean make it with me here – first?'

'Perhaps,' said Mark. 'Possibly. Yes – possibly. But could you say you won't – here with her I mean? Then I can – you know.'

'Okay – sure – I see that. But remember,' Ned turned at

33

the door, his eyes blue pinpoints, sniffing. 'Every time I look at you. . . .'

Having extracted something that could be considered a promise, Mark temporarily relaxed. But when he learnt after lunch that Ned and Tina had gone for a walk he set off at once to find them.

Why should Ned keep his promise? Provided Mark didn't find out, he had nothing to lose. As for Tina, she'd do everything she possibly could to seduce him – crawl in front of him, ass up; arch up, thighs open, beseeching; lick me; anything, everything.

There was no sign of them in the garden, but it would have been easy enough to hide.

It occurred to him that the promise not to sleep with Tina 'here' might have been given literally. Some sleazy, stained-mattress hole in Torremolinos wouldn't count. Was her Dutch cap in their bedroom?

He was pulling out drapes and knickers when Tina herself came in. She stared at him, her eyes dark. She came slowly across the room and sat on the bed. Suddenly she put her face in her hands and burst into tears.

'Oh Mark, Mark – what am I to do?'

For a moment he weakened into hope. He sat beside her and put his arm round her thin, shaking shoulders.

'Come back with me. Let's go back to London together – now, this afternoon.'

'But you don't love me.'

'No.'

'Well then.'

How could he explain he'd discovered that jealousy was a far stronger emotion than love? That she obsessed him totally – far more even than their first two days together? That his desire to see her, to be with her, to know where she was and what she was doing was the most intense thing he had ever felt?

It could be narrowed down, it had an essence. His jealousy had retreated and concentrated until it centred only on Ned and Tina making love in that house.

'You're quite free.'

'Yes, but it's you that he loves,' Tina burst out. 'He's told

34

me. He wants you as well. I think he wants you more than he wants me. He says you want him too – do you?'

'Perhaps,' said Mark. 'Would you mind?'

'Well, I'd rather – but I'd do *anything* for Ned. *Anything* he wanted.'

'Look,' said Mark, 'I'll try and help you. But would you do one thing for me? I can't concentrate if I keep on thinking you and Ned are about to make love. Would you promise not to do it while you're here, in this house?'

'Oh Mark – I do like you. I'll try not to hurt you. I promise not to do it humiliatingly.'

This double assurance should have calmed Mark, and in a way it did. Yet any time that afternoon and evening he was with one of them and they left, after a few moments Mark was jerked to his feet and followed, feverish, secret.

The nightmare returned with darkness. Several times while they ate, Ned guided Mark's hand beneath the table. The only way he could endure it was to smoke hash. He called for sausage after sausage. Ned supplied them like a middle-aged man getting an adolescent girl drunk. Mark felt the dope crashing into his nerve centres, smashing up synapses. He thought, I'll produce monsters.

But the need for paralysis was paramount. At first his disgust and at the same time terrified fascination with Ned made it almost impossible not to react violently. The easiest and quickest and cleanest solution to the whole mess would simply be to kill him. Then he thought, why can't the faggot go and rub himself off on someone's knee like an Alsatian? And gradually the terrible thing beneath the table, the terrible events almost but not quite perpetrated there, receded. They were happening below him, to someone else; dwarfish, insignificant twitchings; ants in fog.

He smoked far too much. Tina left early. Mark realised it was so that he could have his talk with Ned. Everyone had gone.

'Take a walk?' Ned was standing beside him.

'I can't,' said Mark. He was made of glass or ice again. Glass. 'I feel terrible. I think I'm going to faint.'

'You're stoned, man,' said Ned. There was a slight edge to his voice.

Mark vaguely remembered being helped to bed. There was no Tina. Someone had undressed him.

An hour, or perhaps several hours, later he was all at once awake, alarms wracking his weary body. He suddenly knew, without a doubt, that Ned and Tina were making love next door but one.

He dragged himself out of bed and stumbled naked into the corridor. Ned's door was locked.

The table weighed twice as much as the night before. His shoulder was slippery with sweat when he finally reached Ned's door.

The moon was not so bright, but he could see that Ned was alone. He inched his way back.

An hour or so later he was compelled into a second journey. This time, as he staggered and nearly fell, the heavy velvet cloth flopped off the table top and enveloped him. He was in total darkness, stifling. Crash! Crash! went the table as he cannoned from one wall to another – Crash! Crash! Crash!

If Tina had been there, he thought, looking down on Ned's solitary form, she would have heard that noise and hidden under the bed. It was impossible to see if Ned was awake.

Further journeys with the table were impossible. He was beyond shame. He had to find where Tina was sleeping.

The house was quite different at night, either pitch dark or lit by a feeble, illusion-creating moon. Mark groped his way down unfamiliar passages, opening doors and listening, feeling for steps.

Suddenly, somewhere on the opposite side of the house, a door opened ahead of him.

'Who's there?' whispered a dim figure.

Mark stopped. 'It's Mark,' he whispered back. 'Is that you, Tina?'

'No – it's Anna.' She advanced closer, and Mark saw she was wearing one of her kimonos. He was very surprised to see her. The household had long since shrunk until as far as he was concerned it consisted only of him, Tina and Ned. 'What are you doing?' he whispered.

'I thought I heard something,' whispered Anna, now rather close to him. 'It sounded a lot like someone was moving furniture.'

36

'Yes,' whispered Mark. He took a step back. He was very conscious suddenly that he had no clothes on. Anna had become aware of this too. Her voice took on a cooing quality.

'I like you a lot, Mark.' She took a gliding step towards him. 'Ever since you came here you've been growing in my mind like a flower – spreading through my mind. I've needed someone a long time. There's been a vacuum Mark – an emptiness for a long long while.'

'What's wrong with Tom?' Mark stepped back again.

'Tom!' said Anna sharply. 'Tom's got so much junk in his system he can't hardly function any more. He couldn't get a hard-on to save his life.' She feasted her eyes on the glowing muscular figure like a vision before her and her voice cooed softly again. 'We ought to make it together Mark – you and I. I need you badly Mark.'

'I can't, Anna,' said Mark, backing away. 'I don't want to. Not now. I'm trying to find Tina.'

Anna had a theory about herself. Despite a good deal, even a great deal of evidence to the contrary, she believed that her sexual powers were magical. A man had only to sleep with her once and, at some deep level, and often despite those appearances to the contrary, he was enslaved to her forever.

She had a sudden feeling, so powerful was her desire, that she had only to touch Mark and the magic would start to work at once.

She grabbed for him, held his hard, hot forearm for a moment, then he had wrenched himself free and was running away from her. Anna gathered her kimono high above her waist and with surprising swiftness set off in pursuit.

Mark ran down the front stairs, darted through the room that led onto the terrace, up the back stairs, along the corridor. He locked his door and lay panting on the bed.

This is farcical, he thought – or would be if it weren't so painful. Farce is other people's pain.

A few minutes later he heard someone try the door. There was nothing very subtle about Anna. After a pause, the door was shaken violently. Mark lay with his eyes shut. Finally he heard her pad flatly away.

He could do no more. Let them fuck if they wanted to.

What did it matter? He sank into the trance state which brought no rest but was as close to sleep as he could get.

But one last, strange thing happened that night. As dawn was breaking he opened his eyes as though someone had called his name. There, behind the fanlight, he had a sudden intense vision of Tina, her face haggard, extraordinarily vivid. He closed his eyes, opened them. It had vanished.

He got up late. It had got to stop. But after breakfast he could find neither Ned nor Tina.

At once agitated by the usual but ever fresh, ever sharp suspicions he roamed the house. There was also the additional hazard of Anna whom he felt was quite capable of straightforward rape.

He found Tina in the gazebo. There was a canvas on her easel at which she had taken a few desultory swipes. She was leaning out, looking over the garden.

'Sorry Mark – do you mind if I'm here? Do you want to work?'

'No. Go ahead.' On an impulse, taking advantage of the new friendliness, he said, 'Where are you sleeping, Tina? Are you comfortable?'

'It's okay. There's a little room at the bottom of the stairs coming up here.'

'A very odd thing happened in the night. I had a sort of hallucination. I thought I saw your face above the door of our room.'

'Actually it was me,' said Tina, after a slight pause.

'It *was* you. What were you doing?'

Tina blushed. 'I thought you and Ned might be in bed together. Listen Mark, have you had your talk with him yet?'

'I can't find him. He seems to have disappeared.'

'He's gone down into Churriana.'

It suddenly occurred to Mark, as he walked towards the three shops in the little village, that Tina must have gone up to the gazebo for the same reason as he did – because it was the best place from which to spy.

He found Ned buying razor blades and toothpaste. 'Hi Mark – not working? Hold these while I find my pesetas.'

Outside the shop, Mark said abruptly, 'Look, you've got to take Tina away. The strain is getting too much like this.'

38

'Okay okay – but what about you? And us?'

'I'll come later. You go first.'

'You won't,' said Ned. He stopped and looked at Mark, sniffing him. 'Oh what the heck. You might at that. You do just what you want. I sure do wish we'd balled just once, Mark. The other night. And I *know* the three of us could really make it, go really high.'

'I think I ought to wait and thank Alan,' said Mark. 'After that.'

'Oh Alan – yeah,' said Ned without interest. He just doesn't have any regard for the common decencies, thought Mark.

Ned put his arm round Mark's shoulder as they walked back. Its hot weight made him shudder. Ned made him feel physically sick. His stomach knotted. Yet he couldn't quite pull away; even the reverse. His very repulsion had an element of attraction, a mesmerising, exploratory element which drew him back, as a child, fascinated, picks up the pale yellow coil of its own shit.

Ned drove down to Torremolinos after the late lunch to try and find 'them' an apartment.

Mark went to his room for a siesta. It should now at last have been possible to relax but he felt tenser than ever. This was the last act. He was in sight of victory, but the juggling had to be kept up to the very end. He felt as though he had been beaten up.

After a hot restless hour he decided to swim.

Tina caught up with him in the garden. She too hadn't relaxed.

'Ned said you were coming too, Mark. Are you really?'

'I might.' He looked at her distressed, strained face and suddenly took pity on her. Astonishingly Tina, cause of all his suffering, was suffering herself. 'I had to tell him that. He wouldn't have gone otherwise. No – you two go alone.'

'Oh Mark – I'm so glad you're here.'

They spent the declining day – still very hot – beside the pool. Mark and Tina, allies now in his final humiliation, lay side by side slightly apart from Anna and Tom. Anna, squatting in the middle of a large, dirty bath towel, was once again applying her unguent, this time in lavish palmfuls. From time to time she gave Mark long, lingering looks. It was clear now that the unguent was also in fact a stain. From her glowing orange, Anna was changing before their eyes to a deep, chunky-cut Tiptree.

During supper the nightmare resumed and became reality.

There was an excited, almost hectic atmosphere. Ned had found a 'great' apartment. He informed Mark and Tina together. He seemed to regard the three of them as a unit already. He sat next to Tina and opposite Mark. But his sharp blue eyes darted between them. Each received secret smiles. His team.

Tina was flushed, tense, laughing too loudly. Several times she looked desperately across to Mark. He avoided her eye.

Anna had come to a decision. She would leave Tom. Chuck him out on his arse. She had felt her magic increasing all day. Mark had now grown in her to such an extent that he filled her completely. She sat herself next to him. Her narrative power had never been so strong.

And Mark – Mark nerved himself for the final battle; listening, watching, keeping it all whirling in the air.

When it became time to smoke Ned produced his Moroccan kif. It seemed to Mark that he rolled joints the size of cucumbers.

He knew why he had become stoned the night before. He hadn't drunk enough wine. Wine was the antidote to pot, kif, hash, dope, junk and shit.

There was no single incident, but gradually the evening grew sinister. Mark was suddenly aware that Ned and Tina had formed a plot against him. He saw them whisper together, both look at him and then quickly look away. He wouldn't let them be alone. If necessary, if his poor beaten brain would allow it, he'd stay up all night.

Everything became remote. He bobbed about above the table, aware of minute voices.

Then he was yanked back. Tom's head was a mass of black, dead veins. The smell of Anna's unguent was overpowering, choking him; she roared at him out of a concentrated essence of the whole of the Middle East.

The mechanics of the plot became evident at two o'clock or three o'clock, when Tina said she was going to bed. After a while Mark followed, pretending he wanted to pee.

Her room was empty. So was Ned's. So was 'their' room. When he came back he saw that Tina was hiding behind the curtains. He could see her long thin feet.

Anna and Tom had gone. Ned stood up as he approached. He looked at Mark, not speaking, sniffing, then took his hand and led him towards the garden.

Three minutes later Tina came out of the curtains and ran lightly after them.

Moments after that Anna bustled out onto the terrace, took a swig of wine from a bottle on the table, and followed them all into the moonless dark.

At the swimming pool Ned stood against the balustrade and gently pressed on Mark's shoulders until he was kneeling. He swayed on his knees. He felt completely detached. He thought, this is the position of interposition.

It didn't taste of anything. It was all texture – soft, smooth, oily, the texture of glistening. After a while it made him gag. He turned his head and spat.

He was high above looking down on the extraordinary scene. The suppliant on his knees; the other man standing rigid, his arms stretched out, each fist gripping a bamboo stem. All at once the standing man moaned.

It seemed to go on for hours. The little cherry had been dipped in hot olive oil, so that the gagging became more frequent, impossible to stop.

And then, in a convulsion, Mark was choking, and suddenly they all heard – a sound which did, finally, make him vomit, violently and repeatedly; which made Tina, straining to see through the bamboo, clutch her ears, tears streaming down her cheeks, and Anna, hopelessly lost, stop and stand listening, her magic momentarily but completely draining away – they heard floating out into the night above them, high above the garden and the trees, on and on, uncontrollable, the high, wavering sound of Ned laughing.

The Picnic

'Mamma had better come in the front with me,' said my uncle, 'she's still bigger than any of us.' He laughed and, catching his eye, I laughed too. Just thirteen, I had not yet learnt to evade the demands which my uncle's sense of humour made on all those near to him. 'You can go in the middle with your mother and Frances,' went on my uncle, 'and perhaps you could get in the back with the children, Miss Norma.'

'Into the back, children,' said Miss Norma as though his instruction had somehow not applied to her. She opened the door at the back of the shooting brake and Simon, eight, and Tessa, nine, scrambled in.

'Bags I the cushion.'

'Bags *I* the cushion.'

'I'm oldest.'

'*I* shall have the cushion,' said Miss Norma. She manoeuvred her long legs through the door and began to arrange herself precisely. A taut middle-aged woman, she had been with my uncle and aunt ten years, filling a combined role of nurse, governess and secretary. Her favourite garment was a mackintosh and even on this hot cloudless July morning it lay neatly folded beside her. On top of it was a blue bag containing letter-writing materials, knitting and her book. My uncle looked at his watch. 'What *are* those bloody women doing?' he said. He put his arm through the window and pressed the horn. Then he limped round to the front of the car and shouted towards the house, 'Frances! Rose! Frances!'

Looking through the window from my seat in the middle I could see my aunt Frances and my mother coming slowly round from the back of the house, each carrying a basket and a rug, my mother also a wireless. They were laughing. When my uncle saw them he shouted again: 'Frances, it's after a quarter to twelve.'

Unhurriedly they came through the gate and approached him. My aunt aimed her sharp nose and fine pointed face up at him and said, 'If you'd come and help carry the lunch instead of standing there bawling we'd be at Farnham by now.'

Without answering, he took the basket and rug and half-ran round to the back of the car where he thrust them on top of Miss Norma and the children.

'Take the rug, Simon,' said my uncle, 'come on, quickly, quickly.'

My aunt climbed into the driving seat and my mother climbed in beside her. So heavy that he tilted us all towards him, giving the car a list, my uncle put his foot on the running board and spoke through the window.

'Frances, darling, hadn't I better drive? Mamma always likes coming in the front with me, and there's no room for her in the middle. She's still larger than any of us.' He laughed and looked round for the applause of his unwilling and only audience. I smiled without looking at him.

My aunt said, staring straight ahead: 'James likes to think he's still eighteen and nothing's changed since 1910. Your mother's now a very small old lady of eighty-one.'

'We can change when we get there,' said my mother soothingly.

To cancel any effect this might have had my aunt snapped, 'Do get in, James. Really, you're behaving as if you were in the army.' And then, as though alarmed at having touched on the forbidden topic, she turned round and swept non-existent dust from the leather beside me, making it comfortable. 'Come on darling,' she said to her husband, 'you can drive when we get to Farnham. There's something I want to talk to Rosie about before we get there.'

'Fair's fair,' said my cousin Tessa from the back, as usual re-arranging events so that they should not disturb her. 'It's enjoying itself,' she would say as a chicken squawked and flapped, seized for strangulation, 'that noise means you're tickling,' and then would hurry away before she could be proved wrong. But this 'fair's fair' could hardly have been a gloss on the altercation of her parents. The small-arms warfare of their marriage crackled around us as incessantly, and was as little regarded, as the distant thumps from the battle school or, later on, the noise of the flying bombs spluttering overhead on their way to London – echoes of the real war. The car raced up the drive between the walnuts, away from the farm. Left at the gates into the lane, the sun flashing through the windscreen and making my aunt pull down the sun-shield. Swish past the grasses almost touching the car on either side, their feathery reproductive systems swaying in our wind.

We were off for the day. Going for a picnic. We were going – where were we going?

I leant forward again, carefully, so as to avoid my uncle's arm.

'Where are we going, Frances?'

'Langham Bridge,' said my uncle promptly, 'we can all look for mice.'

'Mice!' said my aunt, 'James ought to have married a mouse. I thought we might go to the sea. We went to Langham Bridge last time.'

'That means sea defences,' said my uncle, 'and Mamma loves looking for flowers at Langham Bridge. Anyway I wasn't with you last time.' It was true. Debarred by his leg from the army, he flung himself into unspecified war-work in Cambridge and London. He was seldom with us. This was something of an occasion. 'Besides,' said my uncle, 'I expect Robert would like to look for mice, wouldn't you?' But I was saved an answer. We were arriving at Farnham, my grandmother's house, and as the car stopped she stood up from the seat beside the front door. Everyone got out.

'Hullo Ma, how are you?' Affection made my uncle bluff. He kissed her perfunctorily on the top of her head and stepped past her, heavily, onto the flower bed. 'See that verbena shoot's taken all right.'

'Yes, isn't it splendid?' said my grandmother. 'Hullo, Rose, hullo Frances, how lovely to see everyone. Darling Robert. Now I *think* I've got everything. Cigarettes, matches,

45

handkerchiefs, spectacles.' She began to flap the pockets of her cardigan and rummage in her bag. My grandmother was a negative pole to her possessions and they flew from her continually into distant corners. 'Spectacles, spectacles, spectacles,' she said, 'where are my spectacles? Robert, be an angel and see if they're in the drawing room. On the table beside my chair or else among the papers on the floor.'

When I had kissed my grandmother, her grey hair had been level with.my chin and my arms had met easily across her back. Yet it was true that she had once been very large. There was an oil painting of her at the Big House done when she weighed sixteen stone, sitting on a sofa. Both were covered in patterned cotton and it was difficult at first glance to tell which was sofa and which my grandmother. She moved impetuously, almost running, as though she had still not quite got used to being so much lighter. As a result she frequently fell over – 'taking a tumble' she called it – and when this happened everyone looked very worried and said, 'You'll hurt yourself badly like that one day.' 'Nonsense,' my grandmother would say, enjoying the fuss, 'I've taken tumbles all my life.'

Simon appeared in the doorway. 'Granny's found her spectacles after all,' he said. I followed him back through the hall and out into the sunlight.

'So sorry, Robert darling,' said my grandmother, 'they were on the seat all the time, where I'd been sitting.' I went and put an arm on her shoulder.

'Doesn't matter. How are you, Granny?' At once she seemed to shrink a little, putting on the crumpled face appropriate to her condition.

'Well, *not* too well. I was telling Rose. I had a bad go with my heart and had to sit up all night. But I'm better now. I'll just have to take it quietly today, that's all.'

'Now come on Ma,' said my aunt briskly, 'you get in the front. Where would you like to go?'

'Well, what about Langham Bridge?' said my grandmother. 'It's so lovely at this time of the year, and we might find a fritillary. But I don't mind a bit. Anywhere would be lovely.'

'All right, let's go to Langham Bridge then,' said my aunt, by stating the decision making it her own. 'You drive, James.' Doors slammed. We moved off, under the pines, left at the

46

lane and then down past the Maltings to the signpost – *Langham 4 mls*.

All at once my grandmother gave a high, sharp yelp, as though she had been stung. 'Stop! Stop! James!' she cried. 'Quick – back there.' We all swayed forward as the car stopped.

'I think I saw a *paparva angemone*,' said my grandmother, 'back there.'

'Well done Mamma,' said my uncle. 'We'll have a look.'

'*Do* be quick, James,' said my aunt, 'we'll miss the news.'

'Won't be long,' said my uncle airily, staring past her to reverse, 'this may be rather exciting.'

They both climbed out and walked up on to the shallow bank beside the road, then along its top, my grandmother stumbling eagerly ahead, my uncle behind smoothly limping. After a moment they stopped and both bent down.

'Look at them now,' said my mother. Two bottoms, outlined against the flat green field beyond the bank.

'You can't tell them apart,' said my aunt, 'exactly the same.' Two large bottoms, aristocratic English bottoms – distending the tweed, filling the trousers. Turtle-like, they supported our world, inscrutable, implacable even, like the appearance of all authority. Yet kindly, too; their reverse a lap. Particularly could I remember my grandmother's lap, on to which, like an explorer attaining a plateau, I had often struggled when a child, and upon whose soft prominences my uncle, though it was hard to imagine, must once have reposed. Perhaps even now, bent close together, two beaming faceless faces, they responded to each other, remembered that distant contact.

'It was only a stunted *paparva rhoeas*,' explained my uncle, as though we had all been waiting impatiently for the result.

'Still, interesting, James,' said my grandmother, peering at a tuft of small green leaves with roots, held in her earth-covered hands. 'The last time I saw one I was staying with Simon in Scotland.'

'Oh yes, interesting,' said my uncle, passing her a cigarette as the car started.

The River Langham, shrunk to a stream and overgrown at this time of year, ran between woods on one side and water

47

meadows on the other, bending with the same gentle contours as one of the many tresses of weed waving on its surface. To the right, parallel to the meadows, the ground rose and turned, beyond a straggling line of trees, into common, covered in gorse, bracken and bramble. My uncle drove over the bridge, then immediately turned left off the road, bumped a few yards over the grass, and stopped.

'Look at the gorse,' said my grandmother, in the momentary pause, 'isn't it glorious? When we were children we used to say, "when gorse is out of bloom, kissing's out of tune".' She laughed.

The two children ran towards the river. My grandmother and uncle began to walk towards the nearest tree, she resting her arm in his. Miss Norma made the most of carrying mackintosh and bag.

'You can't swim till after lunch,' shouted my aunt in her high, discipline scream, as she and my mother unloaded the back.

'Will you bring the other basket, Robert?' said my mother.

I sat on the hot damp grass and took off my sandals, then followed them. Bird song, the smell of the grass, the clack of plastic cups in the heavy basket.

Miss Norma shook out her mackintosh, then one by one arranged the rugs into an island, on one end of which my grandmother sat down heavily, becoming a mountain. Cities formed of plates and grease-proof paper packets.

'James, go and see those children don't swim,' said my aunt.

My uncle looked at his watch. 'Damn, we've missed the news,' he said. 'Still, we can get the headlines at two o'clock.' He walked towards the children, suddenly stopped, shouted, 'Tessa! Simon! Your mother says you're not to swim,' and, perhaps distracted by a mouse, veered left to a large clump of grass, which he began to peer into.

'And how are you, Norma?' said my grandmother.

'Quite well, thanks m'lady. And how have you been keeping?'

'Well, *not* too good,' said my grandmother, crumpling again. 'Rather a bad go with my heart. But you can't expect everything at my age.' Then, her duty done, she turned to the two mothers. 'Frances, wine! How wonderful. I haven't drunk wine for years. Australian – they say it's very good.'

'Children, James,' screamed my aunt. 'L-u-u-u-u-nch!'

The island had been devastated by the attack; packets of sandwiches lay split asunder, egg-shell debris was heaped in a cup, a tomato had been squashed in a rumpled valley. Simon was teasing an ant in the grass, Tessa flicking grape pips at him.

'Shut up, Tessa.'

'Well shut up yourself with that poor little ant.'

'Have some more wine, Mamma,' said my mother.

'Oh dear, that will be my fourth glass,' said my grandmother, 'but it's so delicious.'

'Go on,' said my mother, pouring. 'Good for you.'

'Well, perhaps just a little.' She was lying stretched out, looking almost abandoned, her fine grey hair a little disarranged – a mountain levelled by the assault. Every few moments she gave a great yawn.

'Now,' said my uncle, 'time for the news. Hush, children.' He frowned at the wireless, turning its two knobs as though manipulating some highly complex and delicate instrument, which only he could manage. 'Hush.'

' . . . is the BBC Home Service. The time is two o'clock. Here are the news headlines for today, Friday, July 2nd.

'The following communiqué was issued by the War Office at 09.07 hours this morning. Axis forces have repulsed an Allied attack launched on Tobruk in the early hours of yesterday evening. A counter-offensive by bombers of the Royal Air Force is still continuing. . . . Casualties are at present not known but are feared to be heavy. . . . the Prime Minister will make a statement this afternoon. . . . In the north-west. . . . The Prime Minister. . . .' My eyes, followed by my mind, began to wander. The sun flashing on something a mile away, making the distance molten, warming my feet. The faces of the grown-ups. Three hairs stuck to my grandmother's forehead. She must be sweating; incongruous with that old, wrinkled, dry-looking face.

Click. 'That sounds bloody serious,' said my uncle, turning off the wireless; 'a breakout at Tobruk. We may have to

49

evacuate Heifitz now. It may mean falling back all along the line.' He stared grimly at imaginary maps.

My aunt looked at him coldly and seemed about to speak.

'Now, Frances,' said my mother.

'Really, James?' said my grandmother in a worried voice, 'that sounds terrible. What will we do?'

'We could pull up the 7th I suppose,' said my uncle.

'Would that help?'

'Might,' said my uncle, 'it will have to.'

'Oh dear,' said my grandmother, 'let's hope it does. Poor Ralph's boy is out there, you know. That's Jack, his eldest by Penelope. He was a dear little boy. I wonder how Penelope is now.'

My aunt stood up. 'Rose and I are going for a walk,' she said; 'will you be all right, Mamma?'

'I feel rather tired today,' said my grandmother, 'I may go and look for some flowers presently.'

'Why not have a little sleep?' said my mother.

'Well I don't want to, but perhaps I ought to. Yes, I think I may just doze for a while.'

'We'll probably be over there on the edge of the Common if you want us,' said my aunt to Miss Norma, 'sunbathing.'

My uncle, who had been staring at his fingers and angrily pulling them one by one, looked up sharply at this word. 'Sunbathing!' he said scornfully.

'Well we're not going to help Tobruk by sitting in the shade,' said my aunt, and she walked briskly away, followed more slowly by my mother.

My uncle looked after them for a moment, his face blank, then rose to his feet. 'I suppose no one would like to come and help me look for flowers or water rats?' he said. When neither Miss Norma nor myself moved he turned and began to limp away towards the river. 'Or shrews?' he said to the air in front of him.

'Poor James,' said my grandmother, 'no one is interested in his mice. If only. . . .' She did not finish her sentence, but turned to watch Simon running across the grass towards us.

He was small for his age, with short fair hair and an eager pointed face, silent but active, perpetually alert to the need of 'keeping his end up'. He was holding a handful of yellow gorse flowers; 'Granny, does it matter if you eat them?'

'I shouldn't think it would hurt,' she said, taking one. 'Don't eat too many. Aren't they lovely? Do you know what our old nanny used to say?'

'What?'

'When gorse is out of bloom, kissing's out of tune.'

'I know. You said that when we got here.'

'Did I? Oh dear, I expect I'm beginning to repeat myself. Like your great-grandmother used to. Anyway, they're lovely.'

'Now let your grandmother sleep,' said Miss Norma, with an air of coming to her rescue; 'run away and play quietly.'

'I'll just sleep for about twenty minutes,' said my grandmother with one of her huge yawns. 'Aaaah, aaaaaah.' There was a silence while we watched her lie back, settle herself and close her eyes. Miss Norma reached into her bag, took out her knitting and began to arrange it with large semaphore gestures, as if starting to eat unwieldy blue spaghetti, her book on her lap like a plate.

'When can we swim?' whispered Tessa.

'In ten minutes when you've digested your lunch,' said Miss Norma quietly.

I lay back and stared up into the leaves of the tree, which gently moved, although there was no wind, alive. A dead branch was lodged directly above my head. If it fell . . . I moved sharply and heard Tessa giggle.

She and Simon were sitting close to my grandmother's head. Simon had a long piece of grass with which he lightly touched her forehead; each time he did so she raised her arm and brushed it away. When he stopped, Tessa whispered imperatively, 'Go on, do it again. She thinks you're a fly.' Suddenly, still not waking, my grandmother gave a moan, moved her arm indefinitely above her head and then let it collapse across her face. Tessa and Simon giggled. Miss Norma looked up.

'Stop it, children,' she hissed, 'behave yourselves or you can't swim.' Simon stood up and went and lay on his face near my grandmother's feet. Tessa glared at Miss Norma, and then, with mincing face, parodied her knitting. After a moment Simon went 'psst', beckoning her over, and they lay side by side staring up my grandmother's skirt, began to smile, then stuffed their faces into the grass, shaking uncontrollably, silently. What could they see? Her long grey knickers? Some animal? '*And from his queer abode came forth giant toad, a toadess in a bodice.*' Simon launched a spear of grass; another and another and another. Groping for a weapon, Tessa found a small flint, threw too hard so that it landed on my grandmother's chest. But she was properly asleep now, breathing fast and shallow, almost imperceptibly; the stone flake did not move. Pause for giggles.

'You may swim now,' Miss Norma said in a low voice, and the children leapt up and raced for the river, their laughter loud.

I stood and looked down at my grandmother; her lined, kind face was half-hidden by her arm, her legs in thick brown stockings stuck straight out. 'Does her good to have a good sleep,' Miss Norma whispered. 'Yes,' I whispered back, then stepped over her and ran obliquely across the meadow towards the river. Just where it curved right nearer to the Common, I turned and looked back. The oak rose like a giant umbrella above the two women; my grandmother a mound, Miss Norma a pillar, eyes on her book, hands in her knitting.

The river was hardly more than a foot deep, five yards wide, and so thick were the weeds growing from its muddy bottom that it looked more like a luxuriant extension of the meadows. I walked slowly, feeling lonely. If only the other two cousins, Harvey and Jane, would come back from their aunt, then I would have someone to talk to. I took off my shirt to subject the spots on my back to the sun, stepped carefully forward through the cool grass, then suddenly stiffened, motionless as a savage, at something ahead on the far side of the river, which might have been a heron. But five crouched strides showed it to be a post. Alone, alone, a boy alone. Taking hold of a grass, I unsheathed a pale stem; a telescope of grass, for in that was another stem and in that a further one, white and shiny: '*and the Prince did drink of the finest wines and eat thereof the most delicate grasses*'. I put the grass into my mouth and began to chew.

All at once, from among some gorse to the right, came a

high laugh and then voices. A savage again, I dropped to my knees, and crawled slowly up towards the sound.

'Pass me the oil, Rose, could you?'

They were lying side by side in a small clearing surrounded by gorse, both naked except for their knickers. My aunt's large, dimpled thighs, the colour of butter milk, passed me close where I knelt concealed. She took the oil, filled the palm of one hand and began to cover herself, dealing with her voluminous and freckled bosom thoroughly but rapidly, as though in the bath.

'Did you hear the commander-in-chief after the news?' My mother was lying face down, her broad back uppermost, also glistening.

'I know,' said my aunt. 'I wish he wouldn't. It only over-excites him and then he feels frustrated and gets angry and miserable. I think the thing is, you see, he knows he'd be so fearfully good at it. He would too. I think it's terrible for him. I keep on trying to think of things he could do.'

'What happened when you suggested the Home Guard?'

'He flew into a rage and said it was just a lot of old men playing at soldiers.'

'And yet I sometimes feel he secretly longs for invasion.'

'I know.' My aunt giggled, resumed her lathering, the pinched anxiety of her face relaxing. 'You know he cleans all the guns once a week and has now bought enough cartridges to kill an army.' She lay back beside my mother and aban-doned herself to the sun. A butterfly fluttered by in tattered flight, seemed about to alight on her knee, then fluttered off.

'Ma was in good form at lunch,' said my mother.

'Strong as a horse,' said my aunt.

'But then suddenly so frail it makes one's heart bleed. I dread the winter for her.'

'I suggested to James we might get her a winter house on the south coast,' said my aunt, 'but he so hates the idea of her dying that he can't really talk about it.'

'Of course when she is ill she just wants to be at Farnham. We'll just have to pray and pray she gets through this winter.' They were silent, and very cautiously I began to crawl back-wards. Knees in agony, but slowly in case the Germans heard.

53

They didn't, or not until I'd reached the river, when laughter came from the gorse again.

I, too, longed for invasion; so that we could all defend the farm house, firing from the windows, the Germans falling in swathes upon the lawn, leaning low from my galloping horse and gathering my mother in my arms, saved in the nick of time. A tree bending over the river had folded its wooden lips over a rusty strand of barbed wire once nailed to its trunk. My grandmother's wedding ring had to be cut off when she was forty-two because the finger had swollen all over it. I couldn't understand about her – was she ill or not? Sometimes they said 'strong as a horse', sometimes 'we must be thankful she's alive'. My father's story of old Dr C's instructions – 'when her ladyship yawns, give her the whisky,' how visiting him at Eton she had suddenly sat down in the Hall and, yawning and gulping, gulping and yawning, drunk quarter of a bottle watched by his amazed house-master. The problem of her sleep. She said she only slept two hours a night or not that. Yet when I stayed at Farnham, sleeping in the room next to hers, she often woke me up and kept me awake with loud snores.

There could be no doubt about her sleep when I reached the picnic tree again. Miss Norma had gone, and the two children were running round and round in a narrow circle which included my grandmother and involved jumping her. 'We're playing jumping the hump,' said Tessa. I watched them fly over, yellow soup plates spinning in front of my eyes from the sun.

'Be careful you don't wake her,' I whispered.

'Oh it's all right,' said Tessa. 'She's *deeply* asleep now. She doesn't even respond to the fly-grass.' It was true she lay very still, seemingly undisturbed, but it would be like her to suddenly grab one of them by the leg, to be pretending.

'I can do it hopping,' said Simon, 'look.' He stood close, hopped, over-balanced, and only prevented himself sitting on her by hopping back again. 'I *could* do it. Wait a minute.' If he landed on her stomach all her food would spout into the air from her mouth. Poor Granny.

'Try jumping her longways, I said. Tessa considered it.

54

'That would be too difficult,' she said, 'for Simon anyway. He's already dropped a sandal on her.'

'She didn't mind,' said Simon aggressively, 'otherwise she'd have woken up.'

I turned and walked away into the sun towards the river. Hours of afternoon still to be used up. It might be nice to paddle. Behind me they began to jump the hump again.

At five o'clock, as though a bell had been rung, everyone began to gather round the tree. The two mothers from the gorse, my uncle with large dripping plants in one hand, Miss Norma, unchanged by exercise, upright on her mackintosh. The children, at last tired, leaning against the tree. We looked at my grandmother.

'We must wake her,' whispered my aunt, 'it's time to go.'

'Yes,' said my uncle, 'yes I will. I want to show her this water crowfoot.' But no one moved. We stood lethargic, caught in the amber of the early evening, invaded by the stillness of my grandmother's sleep.

'She can't have had a good night,' said my mother, 'she's slept all of two hours. Very good for her.' Simon was looking at everyone in turn with his black eyes. Miss Norma held up an envelope and stuck out her thin pale tongue. Unbelievable it should be wet.

'Do wake her, James.' My aunt moved restlessly. My uncle turned reluctantly towards her and stepped backwards close to my grandmother.

'All right,' he said, 'in a moment. It's so good for her. Just one jump first – come on, Tessa.' He held out his arms to his daughter, and pushing herself off the tree she ran a few steps and leapt up at him.

She leapt too hard. He held her for an instant then, beginning to fall, thrust her away from him. It looked as though he would land plumb on his mother's chest, but with a great effort, though brushing her, he managed to bring his bottom down with a thump on the far side. Then, in one slow, ponderous movement, he turned a complete somersault, to end up facing us, his thick hair wild, the plants still clutched in his left hand, an almost fatuous look of achievement on his face. 'Sorry to wake you, Mamma,' he said, 'Tessa knocked me over.'

He had, however, not woken her. She lay motionless, her arm outstretched where the movement of his acrobatic had flung it.

My uncle stared at her and then scrambling to his feet he went and knelt by her head. He seemed to bend over her for a long time, concealing her with his bulk, doing something to her. At last he stood up.

'James!' said my aunt. 'James, what's wrong? What's happened? What's the matter?' At the sound of her high voice, the expression of surprise faded from my uncle's face. He suddenly looked imperious.

'Frances, take the children to the car at once. Rose, clear up the picnic things and follow her.'

'But James . . .' said my aunt.

'At once, Frances,' said my uncle, 'that is an order. Children, go with your mother.' No one moved. '*At once!*' shouted my uncle.

Confusion. My mother's face went very red and she started to grope among the picnic things. Simon burst into tears and ran sobbing to his mother. 'I didn't mean to, I didn't mean to,' he cried, 'she's asleep isn't she? She's still asleep.'

'Your grandmother isn't very well,' said my aunt. She took her two children and began to walk to the car.

'She's *deeply* asleep,' said Tessa, as they walked away.

'Leave those, Rose,' said my uncle, 'we must all go at once. No, Norma, you stay here beside. . . . Can you stay till I get back?'

'I'll do my best, sir.'

'Good girl,' said my uncle, and looked blankly for a moment at his mother lying on the rug. Then he tapped Miss Norma lightly on the shoulder. 'Good girl,' he said again. 'I'm relying on you not to do anything foolish, Norma. We must all keep our heads.'

Turning he began to limp with lopsided briskness towards the car. I followed and somehow, in the photograph which is my memory of this final scene, I am the most significant figure. I am at the back of the line straggling across the grass, carefully keeping step with my limping uncle, wearing the expression I had so often practised for just such an occasion, an expression suitable for death.

56

Mothers

There was a baby in our street that used to cry at night.

It's extraordinary the noise of a crying baby; not particularly loud or powerful but so high and thin. It has an ultrasonic quality, a quivering which penetrates bricks and bedclothes and sleep.

It certainly set me quivering. Beastly bloody mother, I thought, if I could get at you you'd catch it.

The sound went on and on in the still bleak winter nights of our suburban street. I used to wonder if all women, even at fourteen like I was, had special tuning forks which responded to that quivering. I thought of us all lying awake – our different emotions.

Christ this house smells awful. It's drifting down into every room. It's that painter's fault. The windows are painted shut, sealed. Those corpses Christie walled up. Didn't they smell in the street? You can't hide something like that – even a mouse under the floorboards will stink a house out in the end. Like now. Like then. Men are revolting. Imagine screwing those corpses; and for how long? Till the flesh came away on him? Did he secretly smell his fingers as I used to see Terry do?

My own baby was born when I was twenty-four. From the first her crying filled me only with rage; a cold, calculating, murderous rage. Several times I nearly killed her.

How flat it sounds. It was a savage marvellous pleasure, clotted, mouthwatering: little red screaming hideous face, then – wham! wham! wham! wham! The first time I broke three ribs, falling out of her cot, careful to shut it properly next time.

57

Don't think I didn't love her. I kept her so clean, her little pink bottom, her perfect miniature cunt. She came into bed with us, edible, smelling of pee. We talked together, she and me. I have lovely long pale breasts, heavy and creamy, the shape of enormous tears. I fed her fourteen months, couldn't stop.

People seem to find it hard to understand. I don't see why. It was completely automatic. Did you ever see that old French film *Nous Sommes Tous Assassins*? I can't really remember it, but the point was how the squalor and poverty of his life, the whole family of thirteen in one room, about 1922, getting up at four to go to work, drove him mad. It was the endless crying of the new baby set him off. He tried to kill it. He was horrified. There was this scene, her visiting him in the prison – him gentle and contrite. Then the baby starts to cry. It won't stop. Suddenly he goes mad, shaking the bars, screaming with rage, trying to get at it to kill it.

It was like that with me. One moment we'd be playing and laughing; the next, she'd start to cry. I'd feel the switch go inside me.

I'd go all cold at first. 'So *that's* how it is, is it?' I'd think, 'Watch it! You'll catch it – you know what's coming your way if you go on.'

She knew all right, little contorted back-to-just-born face, screeching crunched up. I'd wait, letting it build up. I could feel it – oh delicious – something being drawn and drawn across a very tight string inside me so that I'd be quivering, and then I'd let it all out in a long hot shuddering flow and really lam into her. Ribs aside, did you know you almost can't break a baby's bones. They bend. A greenstick fracture – evocative title.

Oh I know *why* I did it. Terry made me go to the doctor after a bit, and he sent me to a psychiatrist on the National Health. Sweetman – like a used car salesman. But analysis never stopped anyone doing something they wanted to do, did it? You just know why you want to do it.

My baby crying was me crying. The rage was the rage I'd felt left crying for hours when a baby, when a child, left crying in rooms too far to be heard, in prams at the end of the garden. She must have seen the pram shaking. Rage at my mother.

The pleasure bit was because I liked to hear my sister being beaten, I was jealous of my younger sister. My mother used to beat her next door. I'd listen to her screaming and enjoy it. Beating my baby I'm listening to my mother beating my sister and getting sexual pleasure from it.

I used to masturbate when I was fourteen, listening to that baby crying in the night in our street. Funny how easily you forget pleasure. He made me remember.

There's a lot of pleasures mixed up in it. The crying's a pleasure too. 'You'll stay there till you've cried yourself out,' my mother would say. Now that's orgasm talk – cry yourself out. 'Having it off.' 'He licked me right out.' I can remember after a bit listening to my crying, and being so sorry for myself I'd cry even harder, and love myself and cry on and on – and gradually it all ebbed away and I'd feel all limp and relaxed and go to sleep with the lino cool on my hot cheek.

Anyway, come off it – don't we all? Don't millions at least. You can tell by the expressions. 'You'll catch it' – it's a game, playful. 'I'll give you what for.' How come – 'what for'? Obviously the children had done nothing. 'What for?' 'I'll give you what for?'; it was for the adult's pleasure of course. Millions of them for centuries.

Anyway, it's natural enough. It's a sodding awful noise so shut the fuck up or I'll give you one ('give you one' – see? A gift). Excuse the language but that's what comes if you marry below your class, as my father used to point out.

No, Sweetman did more than just show me why I did it (if it's not all a load of crap). Terry was what my father called lower-class. He was weaker than me, but in the end he hit me. I'd hit Angie and he'd hit me, the place was a shambles, a battlefield.

Since Terry went I've often put her in the top room, so's not to hear her. I'm frightened of what I might do.

But – of course – I *can* hear her. After Waterloo the stench of the corpses spread out like a vapour. They could smell it five miles away, inside their houses. The sound of her crying is deafening in this house sometimes. I catch it even crouching in the cellar, thin and sharp – it really gets my gristle, as if she were tugging me up against my will, by a thread on my nerves, winding me closer, sweating with excitement, swallowing, raging, panting up the stairs, deafened, quivering, itching for a back-hander, a full-blooded shoulders-open swipe, knock the living daylights out of her. . . .

But Sweetman made me try not to – see what I mean? Before I'd hardly even try. When it's over I can't believe it's happened. I forget it, put it right out of my head. It's like we were two people – like she was. One a murderous screaming screw-faced shrieking little beast; the other my sweet pink hot soft-bellied tiny edible button mushroom.

And it was Sweetman discovered my mother used to beat me. It had always sort of comforted me she beat my sister and not me. I was describing one time listening to my mother beating her, how her screams got so high you couldn't hear them, made me tingle.

Sweetman suddenly said, 'How old would you be at this time? About?'

I said, 'I was exactly four. I know that because my sister was being beaten for being greedy with my 4th birthday cake.'

Sweetman said, 'But your sister wasn't born until you were five years and three months old.'

There was rather a long silence. Then Sweetman said, after he had waited for me to say something, I'd gone all cold, 'It was you your mother was beating, not your sister.'

I tried to prove him wrong. The thing was, I could still *hear* it being my sister even though I realised it was impossible. I still do now, this second.

When I beat my daughter, I'm my mother beating me. At the same time, my daughter is my mother. I'm getting my revenge. The screwed-up screeching face I glare down at is the contorted face I used to stare up at terrified when I was a child. So Sweetman said, or rather got me to say which is his method of speech.

I don't suppose anyone but my sister and I saw her looking like that. She had a round face with pink cheeks and china blue eyes - beautiful little pools at which her tall thickly clustered lashes had come elegantly, swayingly to drink. She was a miniature china doll, a child.

Our father absolutely adored her. He worshipped her. She

was perfect. He used to wrap her up and then unwrap her when they came in from being outside and wrap her up in her indoor things. He used to take her her meals in bed. He used to *put* her in places, like a precious object – near the fire or against the light where it would catch her halo of doll's-gold hair, always this silly expression on his face.

I used to think – when he lies her flat at night her eyes tilt shut and stay shut till he sits her up in the morning. God knows what they did in bed. Certainly not fuck. Perhaps he polished her.

She was completely cold. She felt no emotion at all. Except irritation, and then rage, that we were not dolls too. I remember watching her bath my sister once. It didn't look as if she were bathing anything alive, a person. It was as though she were stirring a bundle of sticks.

My father was steeped in class up to his eyeballs. He wasn't even a proper solicitor, just the head clerk. His one act of rebellion was against fresh air. The house was always stiffling - she being 'delicate' of course.

But I think he thought her miniature perfection, her tiny red cherry-pip sized dot of a mouth, her round blue-pool eyes, having bumps for breasts and a china cunt were all evidence of upper-classness, as though she came from the Queen's doll's house or something.

But I don't think she was upper-class or anything like. How could he have got that in his position? The upper classes don't belt people like she did, do they? They pay people to do the belting for them. I don't know. We were both too young when she died to take in that sort of nuance.

I was twelve and a bit when she died, my sister just seven. She caught pneumonia or something, it was before antibiotics. Or perhaps it was cancer. We were never told.

Our father went every day. One night we heard him crying in their bedroom. Everything in the house seemed to wait.

Then he came and said we were to go to the hospital with him. Everyone was very kind. He took us to her room and then left us both there.

You could tell she was dead – mostly from the way the grown-ups were carrying on. But she was a waxy colour and you could see someone else had put on her rouge. We were standing very close to the bed staring at her, holding hands. Feeling rather frightened in case after all she should wake up, I slowly reached out and pinched her cheek. It was cold. The pinch stayed for ages. She didn't move.

'She's really dead,' I whispered to my sister.

We looked at each other and then we began to laugh. We laughed and laughed and laughed and *laughed*. The more we tried to stop so's they wouldn't hear, the more we laughed. I pinched her again. Helen pinched her. I wanted to dance round the room screaming out my laughter.

When we came out we were very red in the face. Our cheeks were wet. I kept on choking. When I choked, Helen began to choke too. I'd slightly wet my knickers.

I could tell our father was pleased at our appearance because he put an arm round each of our shoulders to make a picture for the nurses. But when he went off with them to discuss arrangements, he turned and made a 'Sssh' gesture with his fingers.

We soon found he refused to believe she was dead. He had her brought back and laid out in their room. He sat next to her for hours, like you sit with people who are ill. At night we could hear the murmur of his voice.

He made us sit with her too.

'Your mother would like you to come and sit with her for a while,' he'd say.

We sat in silence, sometimes smiling at each other. We didn't scream with laughter any more, but we each had this lovely bubbly laughing feeling inside. Those are the two things I remember best: that free happy warm safe feeling, we've escaped! we've escaped! That – and the smell.

The smell. It was July. Blazing hot. Our father thought she'd caught a chill, that had started it he said. He didn't just shut the windows, he hermetically sealed the place up. He stuffed rags and rolled newspapers in all the cracks.

She started to go bad so you noticed after three days. The face got all mottled – yellows, purples. I remember, handkerchief over my nose and mouth, watching a big blue-bottle disappear up her nostril. Some black oozings came from the corner of her mouth.

It was almost unbearable. It's the most *visible* of all the smells - yes, it is like a vapour. 'Corruption' doesn't really get it. There are no comparisons so you can't describe it. Except by its effect. It's a cloying gauzy ectoplasm going down your throat – makes you choke and want to be sick. You can't get away from it.

When they finally took it away, for days afterwards you could smell the corpse all over the house.

I can't get away from it now, I'll have to get the man in to open the windows – sealed in like this in August – he needn't go into the top room or anything. . . .

Even in the cellar I smell it. Like crying, it can get through floors, doors, bedclothes, sleep.

Except the baby doesn't cry any more in our street now. It's so quiet, so silent in our street at night, so quiet, so terribly terribly sad.

Peiter and Paulina

About 115 years ago in Denmark the beautiful Countess Paulina Vind-Frijs died in great agonies while giving birth to her first child, a boy.

Shortly afterwards her horror- and grief-stricken husband Svende, who had spent most of the few intervening days sitting beside the plump, fresh little mound of his young wife's grave and had refused even to look at the son whom he considered responsible for her death, himself vanished. A note indicated suicide.

Little Peiter was left in the care of his grandmother, the Dowager Countess Frederikke, an elderly woman even then, matching in years the century. So too were his estates. These were extensive, including plantations in the West Indies and a fine town house in Copenhagen.

For the first months the baby had his Russian mother's delicious India-rubber stub of a nose and her *orecchiette* ears, those tiny crimped whorls of Tuscan pasta, delicate, charming. Then the nose slowly grew pointed, the ears flat. His hair had always been and remained his father's, a glowing powdery gold, the colour of gorse blooms.

His grandmother observed these developments with irritation. Not that her son Svende had been ill-looking. With his high flat cheeks, his scimitar mouth and flaming hair he had been almost magnificent. But he had been pious, silently critical, a prig and a bore.

She had infinitely preferred his twin brother – a perfect demon. No one could control Jens. He had been forced to flee Denmark years ago for killing a man in a duel. It was rumoured he led a scandalous life of concubines, gold and

65

slaves in Africa. He had never communicated. The old Countess knew she would never see him again. She hoped the rumours were true.

But in the beautiful Paulina her son Svende had brought back from Russia – a bride twenty-three years his junior – she had seen signs, during the year she had known her, of promise. Not just the life and laughter of youth; something more – a kind of manic frivolity, the foam and froth on some real inner wildness.

'You have your mother inside you,' she would say to Peiter. Her little grandson didn't know what she meant. Nor indeed did the Countess; at least, she didn't know if it were true. But she knew you could bring things about by saying them. For the same reason she would say, 'You were born for love.'

Did she mean inside him as his mother's matrioshka dolls were inside each other?

The Castle of Øorneredein in remote Jutland was fifteen kilometres from Lemvig up a winding driveway through the thick forests of the vast Vind-Frijs estates. The castle was decorated in the fashion common all over Europe at the time. Heavy brocade curtains with tassels, looped round and held back by braided golden cords, had their rich purples and dark greens glowing in miniature in the thick velvet or satin padding of forty silver photograph frames, and reflected in enormous mirrors in whose dark, steely depths could also be seen the innumerable objects which jostled all round and often hid the photographs on the tables, pedestals, pianos, spinets and cabinets, commodes, escritoires, chests, caskets, coffers, desks, dressers and chests of drawers which crammed the lofty rooms.

Many of these photographs were of Peiter's father, but there were some of Paulina. The Countess Frederikke saw no reason to hide these. She wanted him to remember his mother. When she had all Paulina's dresses and effects removed, it was only to a large attic room easily accessible by a winding stair from the briefly used married apartments.

Peiter, free to roam where he wished, discovered these, and the attic above, when he was six. In the attic was the matrioshka doll. But there were other dolls, Russian dolls with wooden limbs and china cheeks, brought by Paulina in

66

the hope, perhaps, of one day having a baby girl. And as though obedient to her wish, as if it were still caught in the long tresses of real peasant hair the dolls were adorned with, Peiter used to play with them, dressing and undressing them and talking to them in an invented Russian. Later still, he enjoyed putting on his mother's dresses and buttoned boots, her hats and bonnets, and gazing at himself, turning this way and that, in an old mirror which he leant up against one of the trunks.

It was to this room of childhood fantasy, for some years neglected, he ventured on an inspiration one hot summer afternoon when he was fourteen. He had always been physically advanced for his years, and his pubic hair almost formed a complete, solid, red-gold wedge. Peiter slowly pulled off his breeches and pants and dragged his shirt over his head. He looked at himself standing naked and then, with a deft movement, brought about a transformation. As he had thought, by tucking himself sharply in and pressing his strong smooth thighs close and hard together he could produce in the almost watery reflection of the ancient mirror an appearance, in this detail, not unlike that of the sixteen-year-old servant girl Anna he spied on washing herself in a tub in the old laundry. As he stared and stared, Peiter felt himself stirred by a curious emotion, half love for himself, but half love for, desire for, this dim detached embodiment of his imagination.

But in fact love, if this were love, had entered his life long long before this; at least there had been laid down at a very early age deep, hardly choate memories which years later, like thick mud at the bottom of a pond, were to be churned up to enrich and to colour in a peculiar way his first experiences of physical love when eventually they came.

By chance a peasant woman of the village lost her own first, new-born baby just a day before Paulina died. The Countess Frederikke sent for the woman, one of the Plejt family, and inspected her. The large white breasts with their hard, prominent, dark brown nipples almost like acorns, were distended with milk. She was fit and strong, and her high Slavonic cheeks and slanting Mongolian eyes showed that in the remote past one at least of her forebears must have come out of Russia; this was all to the good. It was well known a wet nurse passed her characteristics on to her charge.

So Aisë Plejt was engaged and for twenty months Peiter sucked nourishment from those splendid breasts. When he was finally, lazily weaned, the Countess kept the woman on, despite a certain slatternliness, as nurse proper.

Aisë Plejt told him the stories of her childhood, just as her mother had told her and her grandmother told her mother. Tales of werewolves who came out of the forests and carried off little boys, of mermaids who swam up the fjord and stole the heart of the good man, of the maiden found in the glacier, as pink and as fresh as when she'd fallen in a thousand years before, and what happened when the youth fell in love with her. . . . 'And is it *true*?' Peiter always asked her, clinging tight. 'Things happen which you cannot always explain,' said his nurse, her arms about him and herself moved because of the belief and emotion she could conjure up. After these stories she let him sleep in her bed, partly because he was frightened, partly because she was lonely without a man.

But above all Aisë Plejt had a quality of calm and placid acceptance; there was something almost simple about her. It was this, as well as the comfort and pleasure it gave her, which let her allow him to hang so long and so greedily upon her nipples, nor did she object when, as if sensing that the secret of life lay there, he plunged beneath the bedclothes and explored in the hot, mushroom-smelling darkness. She minded not at all even when, in pursuit of his explorations, he pulled her flannel nightdress high above her waist. And night after night Peiter would return to this enchanted spot as if burrowing into the moist, friable earth of Piedmont, deep down to where the earth is warm and the delicate truffles gestate, and would often fall asleep with his golden head lying on the dark soft fronds of her abundant bush.

There was Amelia, a little older than him, his chief play-mate at the village school to which he went each day until he was ten. (Even at that age he preferred the company of girls.) After school, on Saturdays and Sundays, she would come and play with him at Ørneredein. They would play mothers and fathers in houses made of cases and trunks, or sheets off a bed, or in the hayloft. After 'supper', they would go to bed. 'Now you must go jig-jig like grown-ups do,' Amelia would say, making him lie on top of her.

All these things, the sight of himself as Anna, of himself wearing his mother's clothes, his grandmother's bony embraces, the soft pillow of his nurse, Amelia – and many others, the long swinging pizzle of the stallion, his kittens, Christmas – each became another block in that inner structure of love which, unconsciously obedient to the old Countess, he was slowly constructing.

This task – along with others related to it – she took up in earnest on his tenth birthday.

Aisë Plejt was sent back to the village. The Countess engaged a tutor, a thirty-two-year-old Frenchman, M. Roger Blois. An amiable, intelligent young man of slightly feline appearance, he had at once commended himself to the Countess by giving Byron as his favourite author. Together they worked out a programme: Byron, English narrative poets, some nineteenth-century French authors (Stendhal, Baudelaire) to stimulate the imagination; Voltaire, Les Philosophes, St Simon, Laclos, Mme de Sévigné and other seventeenth- and eighteenth-century French authors likely to educate him in reason and worldliness.

M. Blois secretly added lectures in anthropology, which fascinated him. In particular it was the amatory behaviour among primitive peoples recently explored that fascinated him. He recounted the tales of Richard Burton, his gaze fixed on the face of his good-looking pupil. Sometimes he would read accounts of still odder practices in remote jungle communities, accounts veiled, for decency, in Latin. At these times, translating for Peiter's benefit, M. Blois's slightly slanted eyes glowed green and he looked like an animal about to pounce.

Peiter really preferred the activities of the afternoon. Then he learnt to shoot, went fishing and sailing; he learnt to dance, and once a month an elderly man came all the way from Copenhagen and stayed for three days to teach him the foil and épée, the art of pugilism and how to handle duelling pistols. None of these last, it was impressed upon him, were mere sports or recreation.

Of all these pursuits, Peiter liked shooting best. He loved

to go fowling, to squelch out in the early evening upon the marshy fields by the Nissuus Fjord where it met the cold grey vastness of the North Sea. Here from mid- to late March came the geese on the journey north to their summer feeding grounds. The sodden grass would be squashed flat for 200 yards around, smeared and coloured with the pale grey-blue messes like thick worms of squeezed-out oil paint where the birds had come the night before. As the light faded, Peiter would grow more tense, crouching alone, roughly concealed by the low sea bank. At last he would hear the rhythmic honking and whistling and wheezing and such a concerted beat of myriads of heavy wings that the air, the very ground seemed to shudder in time to it. And then suddenly he would see them coming in off the sea, slowly, inexorably, only twenty feet above the ground, so many that fear clutched at his heart; it was an army, a host, it could overwhelm him by sheer weight and momentum of feather and flesh. Then they were upon him, twice his long fowling piece flashed and – with honks and whistles and a noise of fear-hurried wings that was deafening – the whole throng had wheeled and made off, leaving him to take the two dead birds back on the long ride home, looking forward to the warmth and food and his grandmother's praise.

It was she, the Dowager Countess Frederikke, who was the chief figure in his education, just as she was its sole architect.

The old Countess could remember back to 1812 when the castle establishment had been double what it was now. She could remember forty indoor servants and thirty outdoor ones. The outdoor servants – the grooms and gardeners, the gamekeepers, coachmen, herdsmen, woodsmen and the rest – were paraded once a month, along with the men of the indoor servants – the butlers, footmen, under-footmen, valets, porters, scullions, bootboy; all were dressed in the russet livery and it was twelve-year-old Frederikke's belief that, if called on, they would go to war on her father Count Frederik's behalf.

It was in these vanished days of splendour she still preferred to dwell. In fact she really preferred the seventeenth- and eighteenth-century France of her reading, and as she had grown older what she had read and what had, to a certain

70

extent, among one or two great houses, still existed when she was young, had melted and fused together and become a glittering multi-coloured prism through which she viewed the present and transformed it.

It was this transmuted world, a world she promised he would enter when he was eighteen, she described to her grandson. She talked about the winter balls at the Royal Palace, when the sledges hissed to a halt and footmen sprang forward to remove the heavy, glossy white furs from the duchesses and princesses beneath them. She described great hunting parties that went on for weeks, mock sea battles fought for the pleasure of the court and assembled aristocracy on the Sound in front of Elsinore, gambling parties where entire estates changed hands in an evening, banquets where glistening confections of sugar spun seven feet tall were wheeled in, pink and green sugar fashioned into grottoes, mountains, meadows, with rivers and waterfalls of ice, clear as crystal or delicately tinted, over which trembled spun sugar dragonflies suspended from invisible springs. . . .

But above all she spoke of love. The only point of this world and its balls, its parties, its banquets was to facilitate, to act as the theatre for, romantic passion. That was the sole aim and chief pursuit of the princes and princesses, the barons and baronesses, of all the handsome men and beautiful women who peopled it.

Caught by her elaborate tales, gripped by the vitality with which they were told even though he often scarcely understood them, Peiter began to be puzzled as to his father's role in all this passionate intrigue. He found himself unable to phrase the question exactly, did not, indeed, exactly know what it was he wanted to ask. But he could not help being aware how boringly reliable and solid his father was whenever the Countess referred to him, how tiresomely dependable, how Christian, how virtuous – how unfitted for the real business of life, which was love.

Hitherto, he had always accepted without question that at some distant period his father had just 'died'. But now, so stolid, solid and dependable did the Countess Frederikke make him seem, it became totally uncharacteristic to just go

71

and die like that – indeed the peak of unreliability. When? How? What of? Why?

The Countess explained in response to confused questioning that his father had killed himself, stricken with grief at the death of his beautiful young wife. It had astonished her then, and it astonished her anew. Astonished her and pleased her. It was as though the frightful event of Paulina's death had been required to release within her son Svende her own tender and passionate spirit. And this, too, Peiter somehow instinctively grasped, this inner beauty. To 'die for love' – his father had reached, in one bound as it were, the heights.

'All love is tragic,' said his grandmother, her knuckly old hand gripping his shoulder and staring out over the endless forests of the estate.

'Do you know the Spanish *Copla*? What a people for love! How does it go?' The Countess, who had often visited her mother's Spanish relations when a young girl, put on the harsh, nasal voice she remembered from Andalucia.

> En la orillita del mar
> Suspiraba una ballena
> Y en sus súspiros decía
> 'En amor hay siempre pena'.

'It means,' said the Countess, ' "On the edge of the sea a whale lay sighing. And among its sighs it said – 'In love there is always pain'." You see,' she went on, sighing herself, 'love always ends. Marriage kills it, jealous wives or husbands put an end to it. In the end, if nothing else does so, it dies of its own accord. That is why there is always a sort of melancholy hovering round the edges of even the most passionate love.' She felt the words swelling inside and bursting like so many bubbles, spreading a deeply pleasurable sadness.

The young boy nodded, catching her sadness. But his own held no pleasure because her words made him think of Aisë Plejt and how she had left him.

The news about his father had a profound but only slowly evolving effect on Peiter – as though deep structures and foundations inside him were shifting and loosening and dissolving away. It was an unformulated awareness of this, as well as the sly Anna (the girl knew quite well she was being watched and by whom), that drew him that hot summer day, and many days thereafter, to the attic room where Paulina's clothes lay strewn about from other, similar games of long ago.

The Countess was not an idiot. She knew perfectly well that the last time a mock sea battle had been staged on the Sound had been over 190 years ago. Duelling had been forbidden in Denmark eighty years before Peiter's uncle Jens had, alone, momentarily and disastrously revived it.

Her inventions were in part deliberate. Aside from educating and changing Peiter, she wished to change her own past. Her youth and marriage had been without love and with insufficient temptation, and both these deficiencies she now supplied in abundance.

And who was to say which was more 'real' – the present, much of which was ephemeral, or the past out of which the present had grown and which contained its essence?

In any case the Countess, like most people, was perfectly able to hold in her head and believe two or three or as many completely contradictory descriptions and explanations of reality at the same time as she wished.

In 1884, when Peiter was fifteen, his grandmother appeared one day, flushed and excited, fluttering a letter. She had received unexpected news from Copenhagen and was going there at once. But she had decided to spend part of the year there anyway, perhaps as much as, well – the Countess hesitated – well, four months at least. Still full of vigour, she missed the entertainments of the season. Why, a new theatre, the Royal Theatre, had been completed ten years ago and she hadn't been to it once. There were old friends to see. Also the administration of the young Count's affairs and very considerable fortune had led her to neglect a small but charming property of her own a few kilometres outside the city on the road between Charlottenlund and Joegersborg.

Peiter missed her, but continued his studies with M. Blois and found solace as usual in shooting and fishing and sailing, and in firing his duelling pistols at little targets which his grandmother, when she watched, called 'those husbands'.

When Peiter was sixteen the Countess returned briefly from the start of the Copenhagen season to supervise the loss of his virginity. Establishing first that her journey was necessary, she then asked him if he found any of the girls who worked in the castle attractive. Somewhat embarrassed, Peiter mentioned Anna.

The Countess Frederikke felt she could remember the days of the *droit de seigneur,* but unconfident as to its currency she dispatched her most trusted manservant – the discreet, persuasive and authoritarian Jakob – with Rijks-dollars. Pink of cheek and plump of bosom, the healthy young girl – now eighteen and for whom it was not in fact the first time – was brought that night by a back stair to the old nursery, where Peiter still slept, albeit now in the large bed.

After that Anna came to his bed on many occasions. And not only Anna. The dispatch of Jakob had been quite unnecessary. Count Peiter's beauty had long been famous in the village. Almost any of the girls would have welcomed a child by him – just imagine the flow of Rijks-dollars *then*. And some of them had still more wonderful dreams. 'Bed him, wed him,' the old proverb had it, and was, like all proverbs, about half-true. Curiously enough, none of the girls ever became pregnant.

Two years later, on his eighteenth birthday, at the midwinter height of the season, the Countess gave a ball for him at his house in Copenhagen. Still nearly as active at eighty-eight as she had been twenty years earlier, she asked everyone. The Prince Royal came with the Princess Louise and said that for far too long had the Vind-Frijs house stood silent. Sledges hissed to a stop at the imposing steps of the front entrance. There were sculptures of ice four feet high. It was all just as she had described and just as she had promised.

However, the evening was nearly a disaster. The young Count Peiter behaved at first impeccably, bowing, dancing, responding as years of teaching had accustomed him. But as the champagne, to which he was not accustomed, began to bubble in his veins, two fiery spots kindled on each high cheekbone. So – this was the city of love, the city he was to conquer. Emptying his seventh goblet, holding it out to be filled again, he realised he hadn't known what beauty could

74

be. Love now meant one thing only to him. At 2.30 in the morning, considerably flushed, he made a suggestion to the ravishing sixteen-year-old daughter of the Baroness Ingeborg von Westenholz which caused that delicate creature, who looked as though she had been spun out of something ethereal, to turn as pale as tissue and faint dead away. The Baroness sought out the Countess Frederikke and whispered furiously in her ear. But they were old friends. When they saw across the now emptying ballroom (their tête-à-tête was interrupted every moment by guests saying goodbye) that some young officers who had befriended the boy were helping him discreetly from the room, it became clear it had been the champagne. The Baroness promised neither she nor her daughter would say a thing.

From the ordinary bourgeois girl of Copenhagen right up to the heiress of the noblest aristocrat, the idea of seduction before marriage was quite unthinkable. It is difficult to convey the magnitude of the horror to children born of later generations. A girl who succumbed would have been cast from her home in disgrace – sent to languish for ever with some remote aunt or forced into a convent.

'But grandmamma,' cried the bewildered youth, his head vibrating, 'but you said. . . .'

'I know I said,' said the Countess impatiently. 'You weren't listening. I was talking about *after* marriage.'

'Do you mean the unmarried girls of Copenhagen never allow themselves a lover?' said Peiter, more and more astonished. He felt that a new species, completely different from the one he knew, had been sprung at him out of the blue.

'Never,' said his grandmother firmly. 'Don't you realise these girls have been betrothed to their future husbands from birth often? This is invariably so with the aristocracy. And virginity is prized. It is only a few years – I can remember it vividly – since sheets were hung from the windows and left waving in the wind for a week, the great splash of bright scarlet blood, the glorious oriflamme of virginity, proclaiming to the world the bride's spotless purity.'

This practice had last been heard of in the twelfth century, and even then the accounts are dubious, but for a moment, in the Countess's mind, the streets of Copenhagen flapped with a mass of linen as though an armada of ex-virgins was about to set sail.

'Of course everyone knows young men must . . .' the Countess waved her long, much spotted hand in an expressive gesture. 'The girls of the lower classes are quite different. The lower classes, from this point of view, I'm afraid I'm putting this coarsely but that is an old woman's privilege, you can regard as your brothel. And there are those too. I noticed you were friendly with Captain Stiernholm of the Second Brigade. Ask him, or any of the other officers. There are actresses. For all I know, those of the Royal Theatre – but it is so new. Certainly those who disport in the Tivoli Gardens. And there are certain young women who – how can I describe them? Not necessarily well born, usually not, but beautiful, intelligent, cultivated – what the French call the *demi-monde*. You may have to share their favours, but they won't give them unless they like you and you will scarcely be aware you have companions equally honoured. I understand one Cléo de Mérode has recently arrived from Paris and is very charming. I must. . . .'

The Countess's voice faded away and she sat musing, planning. Peiter waited, listening to the throbbing of his heart.

'But it is with the married women of the aristocracy you will principally consort – and where the rules are strictest. The prime rule from which all others flow is discretion. To be openly discovered or to flaunt an affair is completely forbidden. Honour then compels the husband to expose the scandal, and even divorce, though he of course is behaving in exactly the same way. Scandal or divorce are social death. Everyone will know what is going on; no one will mention it. You will both of you be asked to stay a week or two at some country estate. Her husband will not be there. But your bedrooms will be quite separate. You must return to yours at 6.30. Or, your heart at the moment free, you may be suddenly smitten on such a visit. During the evening you will come to an understanding and arrange for some sign which means you can come to her bedroom that night. Do not,' said the Countess, with the sudden giggle of a girl, 'choose the signal arranged by the Countess Raben-Levetzau. She left a plate of sandwiches outside her door. Von Eckardstein, the

German diplomat, who was also staying and is extremely greedy, passed them on his way to bed and gobbled them up, much to the Countess's consternation.'

His grandmother gave Peiter numerous lectures in similar vein. She also arranged that he should be apprenticed, so to speak, to Cléo de Mérode. The lovely Parisienne, then at the height of her beauty, was perfectly willing to have as her pupil the young Count, so good-looking and so rich.

Within a few years Count Peiter had conquered Copenhagen. At least half the married women in his circle were mad for love of him. Not that he confined himself to a particular circle. Among the artists and writers who assembled at Cléo de Mérode's apartments was the leading actor at the Royal Theatre – Angers Noegler. Through him he was introduced to the actresses there and the whole world of the Tivoli Gardens – a world whose great advantage was that it could accompany him home.

But it was indeed, as his grandmother had foreseen, principally among the young – and often not so young – wives of his own class that his major campaigns were waged. He became adept at the delicate language of elliptical notes, pressed fingers, dropped fans or glances, sighs; he could sit at breakfast – oh, the piquancy of it! – next to the woman in whose passionate arms he had passed the last six hours and when that night – having parted dangerously, at the last moment, too late for either to have bathed – still hovered palpably between them, and do no more than politely acknowledge her as a fellow guest: 'Such a storm! Did you hear that rain? Might I have the toast?'

It might be thought such pastimes would not be enough to occupy all the energies of a healthy twenty-four-year-old. But pursuing his seductions, arranging and then repaying his visits, diverting the sudden suspicions of husbands, evading detection, soothing the fury of the rejected and the torments of the jealous, Peiter found he scarcely had a moment to himself.

In particular, as time passed, it was the possessiveness of the jealous with which he had principally to contend. So much so that, unable to disentangle himself, he was often in a position of having to visit three or four young women in the course of twenty-four hours. He was fortunate here in possessing an unusual stamina. This hunger was not the least of his attractions.

After a year, Cléo de Mérode returned to Paris. Peiter accompanied her and, in his six-month stay, acquired a certain sophistication which stood out in some sections of Copenhagen society that were, if the truth were told, rather provincial.

More potent was the fact that Peiter was never for very long in love. Pursuing with ardour and hope, once he had attained his object he would soon start to withdraw. Instead of discouraging his conquests this distancing seemed only to excite them. They longed to explore and possess and, abandoning what had in any case only been a formal resistance, they strove in time-honoured fashion to hold tight to what they quickly sensed was trying to escape them.

Peiter was not particularly happy in this increasingly frenetic existence. Riding through the empty streets of Copenhagen at four in the morning, the cold of his saddle would bite with pleasing sharpness into the warmth of his loins. His horse's hooves would echo against the sleeping houses. The city streets had recently been converted to electricity and the new lamps cast a harsh acid light, more efficient but less romantic than had the widely spaced globes of glowing gas hanging like so many moons along the pavements. And already as he rode slowly on, clop, clop, clop, clop, Peiter would feel with despair, like a disease – the image of the girl he was about to see irresistibly replacing that of the one he'd just left – desire stirring him again. Was it this that compelled him on, just this?

Or was it more profound? M. Blois, long since departed to France, had once described to him an idea of the Chinese. Everyone was born half of some perfect whole. The object of life for both men and women was to find that other half. And Peiter did indeed sometimes think that the solace and peace he felt each first week or two when he believed he was in love was that of a wound being healed, a limb put back. Then an irritation there, a hard projection here – once again, it was the wrong limb, the wrong half.

Or was it, he wondered, that the very essence of his nature

was not love *but the search for love*? It was as though, not sufficiently mindful of the end she sought, his grandmother had too firmly imprinted the means.

She may even have done it on purpose, for herself. Even though she was now over ninety, long past the age when people find such matters almost without interest, even distasteful, she wanted to hear every detail of his endless escapades. Her husband had been virtually incapable of being either a lover or a husband – only once, in fact, a night upon which her twin sons had been conceived. The Countess Frederikke was an example, like some old priests, of how long the sexual imagination will survive, especially if vicariously stimulated, if it is not properly fed during the years it most wishes to be satisfied.

She revelled in his effortless, almost arrogant avidity. 'So,' she would croak, propped up in her large bed, her huge eyes gleaming yellow under the many-folded lids like gems gleaming and bulging out of old wrinkled leather pouches, 'so – *tell me*.'

In 1895, she too being – it always came as a surprise, like a trick – ninety-five, when Peiter was twenty-five, she died.

It was late August and they were together at Ørneredein. There were now no close friends left; relatives were distant and much younger. The funeral was attended by the castle staff and Mr Linde, the family lawyer.

Everything was left to Peiter, as he had expected; as was indeed by law enjoined. But he was surprised to learn she had left her own property near Copenhagen outside the family.

'I understand it was in repayment of some debt,' said Mr Linde.

'I would have paid any debt of hers,' said Peiter, a little hurt. But he understood now why she had always been evasive when he had mentioned this property. He had never seen it, feeling too irritated by the mystery with which she enjoyed surrounding everything to please her with the effort.

He had loved his grandmother, but she had been too old for him to feel pain, or even grief. He felt a sense of release.

Four nights after the funeral he was standing naked, about to pull on his shirt, in the old married apartments – which he had converted to his own use some years before – when

79

he was suddenly seized by a violent shivering and began to pour with sweat. He thought, I'm going to have a fit, just had time to blow out the candle and fell in a swoon across the large bed.

He came briefly to the surface some two hours later, possessed now by a ferocious fever. In his turmoil, he had an hallucination there was some girl with him. He just managed to drag himself, burning hot, under the linen sheets and sank back into confusion, dreams, unconsciousness.

He awoke to find it had not been an hallucination, except that the girl he had imagined to be with him was in fact himself.

For a long while he lay staring at the complex aerial geometry of the flies above his head as he had when ill as a child. He felt very weak, but the fever had gone. He felt no surprise. This was what he had been promised, or been awaiting, all his life. 'Your mother is within you.' He now realised he had always known she would one day surface and transform him.

Half an hour later the mirror hanging above the chest of drawers – and the actual sight was indeed extraordinary, shocking, almost frightening – showed the face of a young woman with milk-white skin and thick black hair. No one stood beside him; he reached out (and tiny, tentative fingers reached towards him) – it truly was a mirror, not a window in the wall. Looked at closely, examined, the face was not really like that of Paulina, but the charming little nose was Paulina's, as were the crumpled, crimped *orecchiette* ears.

The knock at the door sent her hands flying across her breasts, her heart beating.

'The Count is not well. I will look after him.' Paulina's voice was high, lively, carrying, imperious. She knew they would suppose some city girl had arrived during the night, as had happened two or three times before. She ran lightly across to the door and turned the key in the lock.

She looked at the bed, half expecting to see a body where the sun fell across the sheets, then on an impulse she went to his nightshirt, draped it round her shoulders and skipped upstairs to the attic room.

It was curious, after all those years, to stare into that long

80

mirror leaning against the trunk and see once again through the dust motes her girl's body reflected in its dreamlike wavering depths. But the clothes now fitted her perfectly. Paulina tried on dress after dress, picking up capes, hats with ostrich feathers, turning this way and that before the mirror. How funny the old-fashioned dresses looked, with their bustles, their tight lacings and trimmings and silk flounces.

During the morning she became rapidly used to herself. It seemed, as it were, quite natural. But, although still not exactly surprised at the extraordinary thing that had happened to her, this late birth that had flung her out in, as far as she could judge, something like her twentieth year, Paulina did increasingly begin to worry about the predicament she was in. Was it permanent? If so, they would ask her where the Count was. They might accuse her of a crime, of murder – but where was the body? What would she do for money? Where to live? She wondered to whom she could turn for help and found herself thinking of the old nurse Aisë Plejt.

By evening Paulina had become ravenously hungry. She rang the bell and asked for some chops and vegetables, and for a bottle of claret with two glasses, to be placed on a tray outside the door.

During the night the fever again attacked, bringing wild dreams and once more a vague, semi-conscious awareness of violent shivering and copious sweating, but when he woke in the morning Peiter was himself.

He collected up the clothes Paulina had flung about the room and then, in some perplexity, went out, locking the door behind him. He explained that his friend and himself were the victims of an influenza. They would take meals in his room. Did he wish Dr Hohn to be called? Peiter only just managed to check himself saying that if he told Dr Hohn what had happened the doctor would certify him a lunatic and have him confined.

He sent, meanwhile, Jakob into Lemvig with a message to telegraph to Copenhagen. The house was to be prepared, including the guest apartments, for the imminent arrival of himself and his cousin Miss Paulina Hansen (the name was that of some remote relations). It was possible Miss Hansen would arrive alone, in which case she should be made welcome.

The next day, a Monday, Paulina could hardly contain herself; to stay for hours in the bedroom was intolerable. She felt possessed by a surging, almost manic energy. Wearing Peiter's yellow silk dressing gown, she sallied down the corridor to the bathroom – acknowledging the curtsey of a chambermaid on the way – and ran a deep bath. In this she examined herself minutely all over for the first time.

In the afternoon, still just too nervous to brave the indoor staff in the clothes of the 1870s, Paulina managed to get out on to the roof, where the outside staff watched those same clothes blowing in a mild breeze.

On Tuesday, Peiter decided to gamble that these bizarre alterations to which he was already becoming accustomed, indeed beginning to look forward, would continue as regularly as they had begun. Nevertheless, he started for Viborg at dawn in the phaeton, changing horses at Skine, and reaching it at nine o'clock. The train reached Aarhus at eleven, the ferry took four and a half hours to Kallundborg; there was a maddening wait for the train to Roskilde, and another for the connection to Copenhagen, but at ten that night, to his intense relief, Peiter was clattering up to the fine steps of the Vind-Frijs town house.

He informed Wedel, the highly discreet German who ran his establishment, that his cousin had been delayed. She would arrive late that night and he would let her in himself. He would be absent the next day and Wedel was to see she had everything she wished. And he thought after all, said Peiter, that Miss Hansen would prefer the Blue bedroom adjoining his own rather than the sumptuous guest apartment already prepared. Wedel bowed. Women often arrived in this way and not infrequently preferred the Blue room.

Next day Paulina felt free for the first time. She set off after breakfast in the brougham and by lunch time had spent about a thousand Rijks-dollars (or two thousand Krona) on clothes and jewels. She experienced for the first time the novel and stimulating pleasure of male heads turning when she passed.

But at the end of the first week in Copenhagen an incident

82

took place which made Peiter realise that he and Paulina could not, so to speak, continue living together.

Although now early September, the Prince and Princess Royal were still in their château near Charlottenlund, for some reason delaying a departure that normally signalled the start of the season. Quite a number of people, however, had already returned to the capital from their summer residences, among these a company of strolling players from Italy trying to revive the traditions of the old *Commedia dell'Arte*, who had come for the past two years for a spell in the Tivoli Gardens. Sophie Visone was twenty-seven, a leading actress with the company. From her there arrived on verbena-scented paper a note expressing a willingness to resume a liaison begun the previous winter. Sophie Visone was tiny, passionate and as highly coloured as a raspberry, with red hair unusual in Italy, rouged cheeks, magenta lips and skin the colour and texture of custard olive. Restless from unaccustomed nights alone, Peiter invited her to a *dîner intime*, saying regretfully he would have to ask her to leave at a quarter to twelve, since he expected a visitor to discuss an important business venture.

The evening was everything they had both desired. When Sophie, still flushed and glowing, laughingly accused him of being about to entertain one of her rivals, he was able to deny it with such sincerity that she retired delighted.

She realised as Peiter's brougham started to drive her away ten minutes later that she had, without being properly aware of it, been nursing a smouldering fire all summer which had now, on the instant, been blown into a fierce all-consuming flame. She stopped the brougham after a hundred yards, dismissed it and walked back to stand on the pavement opposite his bedroom windows, not with any suspicion she was deceived but to feast her eyes upon them and, perhaps, by chance, catch a last glimpse of her lover.

To her astonishment, horror and fury she saw a feminine form flit across the gap between the curtains!

But was she correct? She had to make sure. Her little but exquisite frame shaken by the pounding of her heart, the actress ran to a secret side door frequently left unlocked (Peiter had forgotten he had told her about it) and hurried through the warm, silent house. Reaching the door of the young Count's bedroom she bent her head, only to find her vision blocked by the key. She raised her folded fan and poked its thin ivory handle into the lock.

Sitting naked on the end of the bed, Paulina heard a soft thud as the key landed on the carpet. She turned her head, saw what had happened, and immediately imagined she could see the bright eye of some curious or lascivious servant.

The sight of another beautiful creature perched almost on the very spot where but moments before she had writhed in ecstasy, was too much for Sophie Visone. An horrendous shriek – famous for being audible well beyond the foyer when delivered full blast upon the stage – shattered the summer night; shriek followed shriek as Sophie beat a furious tattoo with fists and feet upon the door.

The scene that followed was also equal to something from the *Commedia dell'Arte*. Light flooded the corridors as startled domestics came running from the depths. Paulina darted through to her room and hurriedly put on one of twelve Belgian nightdresses she had purchased a few days before. Then she strode out to do battle.

When she appeared, the enraged actress made as if to spring upon her, and had to be physically restrained. Paulina explained to Wedel that his master had had to go out and ordered him, so commandingly that it never occurred to him to disobey, to remove Signora Visone immediately. Kicking and cursing and screaming, the unfortunate woman was carried ignominiously from the house.

But it was not just because she would be a source of difficulties and embarrassments that made Peiter see he would have to set Paulina up on her own. It would have been impossible for her, as a single girl, to retain the reputation her rank demanded and yet also lead the life upon which she, like him, was determined. But, clearly, she could not marry. As far as he knew she had no particular talent as an actress. About the only avenue left was that of the *demi-monde*.

Peiter rented a sumptuous apartment in a fashionable part of the city. Almost immediately they were plunged into a life for which the previous five years – tangled, frantic, dramatic and exhausting though they had seemed – now appeared but an apprenticeship, a rehearsal for this prolonged climax.

Peiter knew a restaurant where if you ordered half a dozen oysters they brought you seven; if a dozen, fourteen. The tables were separated into alcoves, hidden by domes of frosted glass elaborately patterned. Here young women of the *demi-monde* were wont to come alone, to sit in an alcove and wait for neatly folded *billets doux*. And here came Paulina, treated with particular deference since Count Vind-Frijs had had a word with his friend Adolph, the Head Waiter. Within five minutes she was in receipt of an elegantly written note from Captain Anders de Bülow.

This was the first of many escapades. The young men (and some not young) of Copenhagen might have been so much dry tinder simply waiting for this vital, fiery spark. Paulina's success was as widespread and seemingly as instantaneous as a prairie fire. Endowed with a knowledge of men and of how to please them quite astonishing in one of her years, she captivated by her skill, her liveliness, her abandon, and kept what she had caught by her independence. It did not matter that she frequently rejected or dropped; nor that she clearly had other lovers – for whose company she would often abruptly leave at inconvenient hours. Of these, one who was known (though usually so skilful at deception) was Count Vind-Frijs, who several times was seen slipping out of her apartment in the morning – just as she had been seen dashing into his house late at night. No one believed for a moment they were distant cousins, as the Count had tried to put about.

Peiter's own career continued as before, though this suspected liaison (it was noted how careful they were never to be seen in public together) cost him some terrible scenes. Paulina, too, had sometimes to endure veritable typhoons and hurricanes of jealousy, since although the knowledge of each other's existence did not deter her lovers it did not prevent them being extremely jealous. And these explosions were the more perplexing and difficult since, like Peiter, it was an emotion she found absolutely incomprehensible.

But there now entered an element of recklessness, almost defiance, into Peiter's progress. This was made easier because, remembering aspects of their common education, they often assisted each other in their adventures.

On several occasions Paulina saved him from what would have been highly embarrassing and possibly scandalous discovery. Once, for instance, just before midnight, when he was about to leave the matronly but still very attractive Countess Castenskjold, her husband returned unexpectedly fuddled and unexpectedly early from a regimental dinner. On his way to bed, he unfortunately heard a male voice coming from his wife's bedroom. After trying the locked door, he demanded to be let in.

'Delay him five minutes,' whispered Peiter in the bathroom, to which they had both retreated, 'then say your new lady's maid has been helping you undress and is hanging up your things.'

'But he'll search,' replied the Countess in a low, distraught voice.

'Do as I say,' whispered Peiter, and he ran across the carpet and disappeared into the deep wall cupboard which contained her dresses.

The Countess turned on the bath, shouted to her husband to wait a minute, pretended not to hear him and, when he threatened to break down the door, she dropped the key several times and then had difficulty with the lock.

Count Castenskjold was ready to murder fifty lovers by the time he'd finally been let in. Imagine his surprise when there came, muffled but unmistakenly feminine, a call from the clothes cupboard.

'Which gown does your ladyship wish me to put out for tomorrow?'

The Count's surprise was only surpassed by that of his wife. 'I tried to tell you it was only Clara, my new maid,' she said, almost fainting with relief. 'Don't bother now,' she called to the new maid. She'd no idea her sweet Peiter had such astounding histrionic gifts.

But she began to tremble again when Count Castenskjold strode to the door and pulled it open. But what he saw – no doubt some cunningly draped back, half-lost amidst her dresses – evidently satisfied him.

'I must beg your pardon, Madam,' he said. 'I was mistaken.'

But now the most astounding thing of all took place. The

Countess had started forward to embrace her lover and congratulate him, when the door of the cupboard flew open and out tripped a black-haired girl of nineteen or so, whom she'd never seen in her life before. She was wrapped in one of the Countess's cloaks and carried a rolled-up bundle of clothes in her arms. She gave the Countess an enchanting smile and ran from the room. The cupboard itself was entirely empty.

Paulina, in any case more headstrong than Peiter, also became more and more reckless. She liked to dress as a servant and go to the taverns round the port. She found a relish in those hot, noisy, crowded, sweat-smelling dens, filled with smoke, where smoking oil lamps cast shadows luridly upon grimy, sweating walls, where men could grow dangerous as well as lustful on drink, where humanity was raw, close, frightening, desperate, alive. Certainly the danger was real enough. And here Peiter several times helped her. Three gin-filled sailors had finally, very late, trapped the provocative, self-willed servant girl in an attic hole under the roof. They would have raped her. Suddenly the little door, a hatch, behind which she had retreated snarling, burst open and out sprang a furious, powerful young man, nothing but a sack round his waist, who sent them reeling with expert blows and vanished into the night.

Paulina shared Peiter's past and remembered his thoughts, and he did hers – but each considered the other as quite separate, as indeed they were. Yet which did he or she 'prefer'? If the alternating state could have been at last frozen, upon which side would either have had it fixed?

As well ask which part of your own nature do you prefer. Those parts *are* you. But this existence, this whole which depends on all its parts, was much sharpened in their case. Peiter felt he needed Paulina, Paulina that she needed him. Together they were complete – as complete as they could be. Each shared an impossible dream to be both at once. And in fact their feelings about the other half of themselves were the closest either had ever come to love. She looked on his photograph, he on hers, with desire.

Few people really wish to change places with someone else *for ever*. They can say they do because it is impossible. Were it suddenly to be made so, they would find they had grown an obstinate fidelity to their own selves and would shrink in terror, as long-married couples suddenly draw back on the edge of an affair.

Nor is sensation, for instance, susceptible to calculation. Peiter, piercing to the hilt, nearly delirious with needle-sharp pleasure, no more thought of Paulina than she of him when, sporting on seas of delight, still swept by its voluptuous waves, she lay at last panting on the shore, wanting nothing else, unable to imagine anything more exquisite.

And physical feelings – pleasure or pain – cannot be remembered with any force or sense of reality. Were it possible it is likely few women would have more than one child.

Yet it often occurred to Paulina that – putting aside the question of preference as impossible – she and Peiter were in a unique position to find out at last what exactly were the precise differences between men and women. But the more she tried to analyse them – or deduce them from her adventures – there seemed at bottom very little difference. Whenever she thought she had found one, invariably something happened that proved her wrong.

For instance, she remembered one of M. Blois's anthropological lectures. There was a tribe – the Maurapas or some such name – who characterised the male sexual instinct as something quite apart from the man, not remotely under control. They likened it to a man standing naked in a river, whereupon his penis, like a fish, somehow quite under its own volition, would dart off now to strike here, now bury its head there, now leap upon the bank.

Paulina took this to be a real difference in the world of sexual passion, the principal world of her own and Peiter's experience. She certainly thought it explained one of her odder experiences.

One evening a shabby man servant arrived at her apartment and begged leave to deliver a message from his master. He understood she was one of the most celebrated young women of – the servant paused. His master begged her to excuse the expression – of pleasure in the whole city of Copenhagen. Would she do him the honour of visiting him, in consideration of a small sum?

88

Ordinarily, Paulina would have sent such impudence packing. But the small sum mentioned was so staggering – more than enough to buy a fine racehorse – that she agreed to accompany the manservant, curious to see who could afford such an amount and what they would expect for it.

The manservant drove an equally shabby coach out north-west of Copenhagen, to an area where there were numerous villas, and one or two private palaces. It was through the gates of one of the most imposing of these that they eventually arrived. More and more intrigued Paulina recognised it as one of the residences of General the Baron X. . . . She had supposed the old hero dead at least twenty years before.

Holding a lantern above his head, the servant conducted her through a palace which, although it had once been magni-ficent, had clearly not been touched for almost as many years as that. The dark, damask curtains, like resting tents, were ripping from their own weight; dust puffed up lightly with each step through the lofty, crowded and silent rooms. She noticed once, when they paused as the servant opened two vast double doors, a little circle round each foot of a charming German Biedermeier chair, a little rim of fine sawdust where a wood beetle had been able to bore undisturbed.

At length they reached a wing which showed signs of resi-dence. Here she was shown into a low-ceilinged rectangular room, lit by candelabra along the panelled walls. At one end, five foot logs burned on a large fire.

Here the servant asked her to undress. When Paulina hesi-tated, he said, 'It would be a great service. I can assure you, madam, you will come to no harm.' There was an almost pleading note in his voice. But she had already decided to continue with the adventure and, taking off her clothes, laid them neatly on a low chair clearly placed for the purpose in the middle of the room.

A door now opened at the end furthest from the fire and an extremely old man hobbled in with the aid of a stick. He was followed by the servant carrying a tray. She could see plainly, for the old man was quite naked, that he must once have been large and strong and had now considerably shrunk. His skin, the dirty grey colour of thin gruel, hung shrivelled and loose, especially at his buttocks. In their deep sockets, each huge eyeball was hooded from above and pouched from below so as to resemble that of a chameleon.

He stopped some way from her and fixed these great eyes upon her rounded, youthful, beautiful body as she stood, quite unselfconscious, her pearly whiteness glowing in the light from the candles and the leaping flames.

Paulina, looking back in her turn, could now see that the servant's tray, made of black lacquer, was piled high with fresh cream cakes. The whipped cream bulged half an inch thick between the halves.

Having gorged his eyes on her, the old man suddenly reached out one boney quivering hand, picked up a cake, and threw it at her. It struck her softly on the knee and fell to the floor. The old man gave a little gasp and threw another cake, which went wide.

He now threw all the cakes, one by one. He seemed to grow increasingly excited because the cakes began to fly wildly all over the place, hitting the ceiling, striking the floor, one even shot over her head and she heard it land in the fire with a faint hiss. But a good number struck the amazed Paulina, exploding quite harmlessly like fairy grenades and leaving, as upon some exquisitely sculpted peach, their vague rounded outlines in minute specks and blobs of cream. And each time one of his tiny cannonballs struck home the old General gave that same little gasp.

When the cakes were finished, the Baron, panting with effort, trembling and shaking but showing no other indication of either agitation or pleasure, slowly tottered from the room, assisted by his servant's hand.

This man returned a few minutes later carrying a pile of hot, scented, dampened flannels for Paulina to wipe away the traces of cream and a large warm towel with which she could dry.

She accepted a glass of red wine, refused the money, and soon afterwards was driven back across Copenhagen.

This and other experiences almost as extraordinary for a while convinced Paulina that M. Blois's metaphor, or rather that of the Maurapas, was true. These male fish could entertain, indeed crave – and so explain – the most bizarre aberrations; desires which seemed to bear no relation at all to their often distinguished and fastidious possessors.

And yet Peiter had experiences which were in their way just as surprising.

There was, for instance, the Baroness Lippe-Detmold, about twenty-five, who had a long but strangely compelling face like an extremely sensitive and refined goat. She was clearly attracted to him and yet always cold in his arms. One evening – only a month, in fact, after Paulina's visit to the old Baron X . . . – Peiter and the Baroness Lippe-Detmold were to go with some companions to the opera. They were late. Their friends called from the hall that they would miss the opening. And suddenly, her fine face alight, the Baroness seized Peiter and pulled him into her bedroom. Quivering all over, one hand behind his neck, the fingers of the other trembling at his buttons, she fell back upon the bed. The more urgent the shouting, the more her ardour increased until, when they heard the exasperated crash of the front door as their friends left, she became completely transported.

Every woman, Peiter maintained, was like a darkened room in which there was a secret switch which, fumbling, a man had to find before the light came full on. This was the Baroness's switch and for a while – until as usual he tired – his life was all operas and plays of which he saw only the last two acts, or boat trips to Malmö or Landskrona where they always missed the boat.

That little difference which Mme de Sévigné wished to preserve, where was it? Paulina wondered. Then one day she thought she'd discovered what it was. She fell in love – and both their lives changed for ever.

Captain Jens Westergaard was a tall, darkly handsome young man whom she encountered one May evening towards the end of the season in the Tivoli Gardens. He had answered the request of an acrobat and, with some courage, had allowed himself to be wheeled in a barrow along a wire stretched fifty feet above the ground. He noticed Paulina by the warmth of her applause (she had wanted to volunteer but had not quite dared). He bought her a glass of hot chocolate. She invited him back to supper. Instead he took her to the Fugmann in

Kongens-Nytorv, then one of the most elegant and expensive restaurants in Copenhagen.

Within four days Paulina felt more passionately about him than she had ever felt about anyone or anything before. And now she thought she had at last discovered the difference between men and women – something so obvious that she had always known it and about which people often joked. Women longed for marriage and men were terrified of it. She had often thought about marriage before, of course, but as something in the future. Now she wanted Jens to propose to her every day.

She desired Jens with an intensity which sometimes made her feel physically sick. But he was the first man she'd found attractive whom she refused to make love to. At the same time, she dismissed all her other lovers and admirers as it were on the spot, by word or by note, in the course of a single day. She said she never wished to see any of them again.

And Captain Jens loved her as much as she did him – it was not lack of love that prevented him marrying her, of that she was quite certain. He had some highly important job in the Danish Secret Service. Most of his work took place at night and he would have to tear himself away at ten or eleven-thirty, often as a matter of urgency, to meet returning agents, to work on cyphers, Paulina understood, or perhaps it was interrogation or maps. She did believe him – but she also thought he was married. He was returning to a wife. Jens vehemently, tormentedly denied this. He swore, with tears in his eyes, that there was no wife. But, there was, something had happened it was true, he couldn't explain, like a ghost . . . and Paulina indeed felt haunted by this mysterious past which disturbed the present; and yet she felt pity, too, because the pain Jens felt, his torment, was over her, for her. She clung to him before he went; then ran to the window to watch which direction he took. It was always towards the Ministry.

Paulina felt now for the first time the terrible torment of jealousy. Every day saw her become more obsessed with what Jens did when he left her. She felt her life was being poisoned. Peiter was the one person who could have helped her. But now, also for the first time, his interests were, not exactly in

conflict with hers, but suddenly far too strong to be subordin-
ated to hers or to be postponed.

He had first noticed the Countess Christina Danneskjold
because she had arrived so late – well after midnight – at a
ball given by the Prince Royal to celebrate his birthday, 17
May.

'Look,' said his friend, pointing at the beautiful young
woman standing irresolutely in the doorway.

When he saw her the strangest thought flashed into Peiter's
head. He found himself thinking: That is the girl I am going
to marry.

She was tall, with high Slavonic cheekbones, a wide,
upward-curving mouth, a straight somewhat pointed nose,
and cascades of curly, golden hair; a gold that was not the
rich Danegeld gold of Peiter's, but a colour that was nearly
too fine to be a colour, the purest, palest of gold, the pale
pale gold of primroses.

'Can I be of assistance?' asked Peiter, bowing low.

'My coach broke down,' she said, smiling at him. 'You
may protect me till I find the Baroness Rosenörn-Lehn who
was to introduce me.'

'We will be safest in a waltz,' said Peiter, transfixed.

They danced every dance together till dawn – the Baroness
Rosenörn-Lehn having long since retired exhausted to bed.
How swiftly love flares up when the fuel has been long stacked
and never ignited. Peiter felt more and more extraordinary
as they danced. So light she was upon his arms, so perfectly
in step, it was like dancing with himself.

'Why have I never seen you before?'

'I have been in Paris, in Rome. Then just under a year ago
my guardian who was also my grandmother died; this was at
the time of my, my, my marriage' – and here she faltered so
that Peiter should know, and how his heart leapt, that her
marriage wasn't happy – 'just about the time I got married.
My grandmother asked me before she died to wait a year
before I entered society. But my husband is much occupied.
I felt I was dying of boredom. Baroness Rosenörn-Lehn,
entrusted with my introduction, agreed we had waited a
respectable interval. . . .'

So engrossed were they in each other's company, they did

not even introduce one another until Christina was about to depart. He asked if he might call on her the next day and she gave him directions to the district outside the city where rich folk had villas and châteaux. He was invited to tea. Her husband would not be back till late.

It was along the road which runs from Copenhagen to Elsinore beside the Sound. At Charlottenlund he took the road left as he'd been directed. This led through thick woods towards Jœgersborg. Her house was on the left, just beyond Bernstorf.

During that afternoon and evening their intimacy deepened and he learnt her story.

Her father was a Danish nobleman who had been obliged to flee the country many years before. He had fled to Africa where he had acquired vast wealth, sufficient for him to travel the world. In 1877 he had met and married a Russian girl, Christina's mother. She had died of malaria in 1884, when Christina was seven, and the father, fearful that the same thing might happen to his daughter, had sent her back to Copenhagen to be under the care of grandmother – the Countess Valborg, a figure in whose vivid description he had no difficulty at all in recognising the Countess Frederikke.

'My grandmother,' said Christina, 'could only spend about six months of the year with me, having some sort of responsibility in Jutland.' But she had laboured to keep the girl's father alive in her – 'You have your father's spirit within you' – and had spun, Peiter had little doubt, the same elaborate dew-spangled webs of romance. In any event, she had sent the young Christina to Rome, and Paris, to continue her education, where she had returned to marriage – about which she did *not* wish to speak – and her grandmother's death. This last had unfortunately taken place on one of her visits to the north, and Christina could not be with her.

Peiter rode back to Copenhagen his head in a whirl. Now, and repeatedly over the following few weeks, he wondered whether to tell Christina that they were first cousins and each time decided to put it off. Marriage – again that hitherto ridiculous word – was not forbidden between such relatives, but it was rare and, he believed, medically frowned on.

Yet this cousinly consanguinity was undoubtedly one of the

reasons for their extraordinary accord. Within a very few days they had become lovers. But this was a love quite unlike any that he had experienced before. He wished to be with her continually; each time he came, he brought her a present, each one more splendid than the last. Once he gave her a small golden goblet that had been in the Vind-Frijs family for 300 years. It was eight inches high, chased with silver and set with six large rubies. No sooner had she seen it than to his horror Christina cried – 'But how strange! It's exactly like one my father used to describe.' Peiter hurriedly invented a set of six, long dispersed.

Remembering his old tutor, he thought that here was that other half he had been born into the world to find. A cynic might have said it was Arabian rather than Chinese wisdom that Peiter demonstrated. The Arabs have a fable about a lovely maiden awaiting the seeker after true love on the other side of the Bridge of Suirat. When he appears she says, 'I am thyself'.

But whatever deep roots that now stirred in him, Peiter longed to marry her, and the more he longed the more desperate did he become. At last was borne in upon him the cruel nature of his situation. Many times confession trembled on his lips, yet how could he expect Christina, sweet and loving though she was, to believe him; and if he convinced her, as of course he could, how could he expect her to tolerate it? Surely she would shrink from him as from a monster. Of what use was the search for love, the discovery of love, if that love could not be properly enjoyed? He felt that his grandmother was responsible for the search, for the discovery and somehow or other for the whole tragic dilemma and he cursed her bitterly.

There were further agonies. Christina did not love her husband – her passion with Peiter proved that – yet she was terrified of him. She drove Peiter out in near-panic at night lest he should be found on her husband's return. Peiter himself, now beginning to experience the fires of jealousy for the first time, longed to wait in the shadows and catch a glimpse of his rival. But there were numerous approaches to Christina's house. Also such behaviour was completely contrary to the conventions by which he had lived for so long and whose momentum still held him.

Christina, on the other hand, would never agree to come and stay with him alone at one of those house parties where it was accepted such affairs could be conducted. Although of course it would have been next to impossible for him to go either, Peiter wished to know why she refused so adamantly in advance. Several times he sensed she was about to tell him something. Once or twice she even began, then turned away with tears in her eyes, half uttering the words, 'You don't. . . .' This mystery, to do he was sure with her husband, increased his suspicion and her fascination.

Peiter and Paulina grew more and more desperate – both more in love, each more jealous. But they were as a result still less able to help each other, their demands pulling them apart at crucial moments.

Paulina had always been wilder, more wilful, than Peiter. Her life had become a torment. Moody, distrustful, sleepless, restless, desirous, chaste, she set countless small traps for Jens, and read mistresses and wives into replies which were only confused and unhappy – and yet were, also, she was certain, guilty.

One day late in June she instructed her groom to bind sacking tightly round the hooves of her horse and have him saddled, ready in the stables that night. When Jens, as usual, kissed her goodbye at eleven o'clock and left for his work, she swiftly wrapped herself in a long cloak and then ran down some back stairs to the mews behind her apartment.

Jens made at first for the Ministry of Foreign Affairs, as always. But when he was well out of sight he turned left and headed towards the Nörrvoldgade. The wide boulevard was by no means empty and Paulina realised her muffled hooves had been over-dramatic, which was just as well since, moving at a brisk trot, the sacking was soon discarded.

When, at the end of the boulevard, he turned towards the Sortedamssö, Paulina's heart, already beating hard, gave a great leap. He was heading for the main road from Copenhagen to Elsinore – that flat Elsinore where the only cliffs that beetle o'er their base are beetle-high and bare mute, amused witness that writers needn't know too well the places where they put their dramas.

Ten minutes more and the signpost said Charlottenlund. At once Paulina was certain. *Jens was married to Christina.* This could be the only explanation of the direction he was taking – no matter 500 other people had villas there as well. And if so, surely at last there was hope. Something could be worked out.

She had a sense of gathering climax, of inevitability, as if the events of the past year were to be at last resolved or, if not, then ended for ever.

She wondered why he had lied to her. Perhaps he was frightened. The thought made her love him all the more.

At Charlottenlund, as she had expected, he left the road and set off at such a pace she soon lost him. No matter, she knew the way as well as he. Better probably, since, sought out by impatient desire, several short cuts had revealed themselves. The beech leaves were still young and small and the high nearly circular moon cast enough light for a lover. Paulina's long cloak, her black hair, streamed behind her as she cantered through the silent forest.

When she reached Christina's villa, the sense of inevitability faltered – what if he weren't there? Perhaps after all she was wrong. The cypher office or interrogation or whatever it was he did might well be set amongst the villas and châteaux of the unknowing wealthy for greater secrecy. But she saw a gleam of white where the moon caught the flank of Jens' horse as he turned it into the stables, and she pulled the other way towards the door in the ivy at the side of the house.

The key was in its mossy crack. Paulina let herself in and ran up the winding stair which led to the corridor outside Christina's room. She was just in time to see Jens disappear through the door, and hear the key turn in the lock, as though he did not wish to be disturbed.

The sight and sound shocked her profoundly. Had they been a couple like so many others, amiable, complacent, but not in any way in love, all might have been well. But perhaps they had both been lying, both Jens and Christina. It became imperative to discover if they were lovers as well as husband

and wife. Paulina slipped along the carpeted corridor and bent her eye to the keyhole.

She could see nothing. The key was in the lock. Still carrying her riding crop Paulina pushed the tip of its horn handle into the hole and gave a sharp push.

Luckily Jens had not heard the key drop. He was standing with his back to the door, slowly undressing in front of the dressing table mirror. There was as yet no sign of Christina. Slowly he stripped off jacket, shirt, boots, trousers, dropping them wearily at his feet. He stood for a moment naked, then sat down and suddenly put his hands on the dressing-table and let his head fall on them, as if overcome with despair.

But at that moment, as a wave of nausea swept her, Paulina realised with horror that she had been out too long. She heard the muffled sound of the stable clock striking midnight. Her time had come upon her. With a sigh, she fell in a swoon upon the carpet.

But this was no longer the rending birth-change it had been at first. It was no more than a few moments, as long as it takes a tadpole to come wriggling from the spawn, a chick from the cracked egg, for a newborn baby to cry.

Three minutes later, Peiter struggled to his feet, pulled off Paulina's splitting clothes, wrapped her cloak about him, and went to the keyhole.

At first he thought Jens was still slumped despondently on the dressing table. But the naked figure he could see was not Jens at all. It was Christina. Peiter pulled back his head and then bent back again. Christina. Christina. Christina stirring.

He stood up and knocked on the door. 'Christina,' he called urgently, 'Christina. It's me. Open the door.'

He heard her turn the handle, then she rattled the door. 'I can't.'

'The key's on the carpet.'

An instant later he was in the room. There was no one else.

'You shouldn't have come. My husband might have been here. I've told you not to come.'

She looked so vulnerable naked he had to force the harshness into his voice. He pointed at the uniform heaped untidily on the floor. 'You mean Jens? He was here. I saw him come in. Where is he? Tell me Christina.'

She looked in despair round her bedroom, as though trying to conjure her husband out of the pictures on the wall, from the patterns in the carpet. Then she flung herself sobbing into Peiter's arms. 'There's no one, no one. Don't you see – *I* am my husband. It's me.'

There is no relief like that of confessing a long-kept guilty secret, unless it be that of suddenly discovering that some situation, or illness, or desire, which you thought was yours alone, is shared by someone else.

Peiter and Christina talked till dawn. Then they fell asleep in each other's arms and did not rise till after eleven. In the afternoon they strolled in the grounds of their grandmother's villa, going over once again what had happened and what to do. As the evening turned to night, they grew more and more apprehensive, but also more excited, both feeling that whatever it was they were undergoing wouldn't be complete, wouldn't be 'true', until it took place when they were together. At five to twelve they were sitting on the bed in Christina's bedroom holding hands. The minutes passed very slowly, and then they heard the stable clock chime midnight.

Nothing happened. Christina remained Christina, Peiter Peiter.

A month later they got married. Several people asked Peiter if he knew what had happened to Paulina. He said she'd gone to live in Paris.

Peiter and Christina never had any children. They seemed all in all to each other – father, mother, son, daughter, brother, sister, lover, mistress, husband, wife. They were one of the few couples in Copenhagen, perhaps the only one, to whom in their long and happy life together no scandal or even hope of scandal ever attached itself.

For some years, as midnight approached, they would look at each other and there would be a slight tension – and perhaps a slight hope. Then gradually they even ceased to refer to the strange events which had brought them together.

By the end of their lives they both really wondered if the whole thing had not been some sort of dream or joint hallucin-ation; or perhaps it had just been one of those 'inexplicable happenings' which, like Aisë Plejt's werewolves, mermaids and swan maidens of so long ago, are supposed both to have happened and not happened, somehow held to be true and untrue at the same time.

The Infant Hercules

When Dorothy Martel's husband was killed in a raid over the Ruhr, she went to live with his sister and her little son David. She also kept on her job as a VAD at the Norwich General Hospital.

Both moves kept her close to Jack – and in various ways.

The VAD job was menial and hard: scrubbing floors, making beds, bathing the men, dressing wounds. But it was war work, carrying on what he had been doing.

And he'd always been close to his sister Jessie, protective, fatherly, even though she was three years older than him. Partly it was her asthma.

'They've only got me really,' he'd told Dorothy, when Jessie's shiftless Welsh husband Danny Hughes had run off. Jack'd helped her with money too; more, Dorothy suspected, than he'd let on.

She hadn't realised how much of her had been Jack, and how much of her was now 'missing presumed dead'.

I'm a word without a sentence, she thought. It wasn't her own idea. There was a popular song at the time.

> I'm a word without a sentence,
> A song without a tune.
> You're my life, my whole existence–
> My love, come back to me soon.
> Come back, oh come back soon.

But in the song he did come back.

For a long time Dorothy secretly thought that Jack would too. She had herself assigned to the ward of the severely

101

wounded. She didn't mind how long she worked or how unpleasant the tasks. She wasn't just carrying on his work; she was tending Jack himself.

And there was Dave. She felt she'd never have a child now. All that side of life was over for her. Dave was the closest she'd get to having one.

And he was half-Jack in a way. Her little nephew, now eight, had the same golden hair his uncle had had (except it was curly), the same sturdy energetic body. He used to show off his boyish strength and was able to lift his mother Jessie clear off the ground – by half an inch.

'He's a proper caution,' Dorothy would exclaim. She thought to herself: He's like a little god.

How the two women talked about him, worried about him, planned for him! Dave's colds, Dave's shoes, Dave eating too much, Dave off his food, Dave standing up for himself in the playground, Dave's being far more like Jack, like a Martel, than his useless Hughes father, Dave's future.

Dave's future – the army, the air force, a doctor, going to London, an MP. There seemed to be no limit, as Jack had said on becoming an officer – no limit; but how to achieve it?

'He ought to go to one of them proper boarding schools. That'd take him to Oxford or Cambridge,' said Jessie.

Strange as the idea seemed, Dorothy agreed. That's what Jack would have wanted for a son of theirs – and would have achieved. But they couldn't possibly afford it. Even with what she got from the War Office, she and Jessie could hardly make do (Jack had been virtually supporting his sister, she'd discovered). She had to help old Mrs Martel as well.

Besides, the two women agreed, they couldn't possibly have sent the little boy away on his own like that – not yet, not at eight or nine – no matter what the advantages.

It was the Station Commander who suggested the solution. He'd kept an eye on the young widow, dropping in whenever he was in Norwich. She'd talked about Dave's future with him.

Wing Commander Henry Edwards had an old uncle of seventy-four, a retired prep school master. Soon after the outbreak of war his old school – Danehurst Court – had moved from invasion-threatened Sussex to the far north – to Westmoreland. He himself had been begged by the Governors to return from retirement and run the school again, for the duration.

As more young masters left for the war, old Stanford Edwards had had to recall from the dim recesses of his memory and the remotest hamlets of England aged colleagues of the past, cobwebbed in retirement. The average age of the staff was sixty-nine.

A sudden crisis just before Christmas had prompted the old headmaster to write to his nephew. Matron had left. It seemed impossible to get a substitute. Any ideas?

The Wing Commander hurried round to the Martel house. Why didn't Dorothy apply for the post? He'd write the recommendation himself. And she could make it a condition – he'd mention that in his letter too, it'd come well from him – that young David Hughes became a pupil – free, or in return for a slight reduction in salary.

The two young women came to their decision after half an hour's excited discussion. It was still war work – teaching was a reserved occupation. Dolly could send money back. Dave wouldn't be lonely. But above all – Jack would have wanted it.

Stanhope Edwards had been prepared to accept this serious-faced, rather silent young woman sight unseen. A deserving war widow; strongly recommended by that sensible chap his nephew; a trained nurse; attractive too. . . . Mr Edwards was not so old that he couldn't appreciate the delicate but definite curve beneath the clean starch, the full young mouth.

For form's sake he made petty demur over young David. Could the little fellow read and write? Shortage of staff. Rather unusual. Then, suddenly nervous lest he frighten this southern gazelle from their bleak northern wastes, he hastened to conclude – but, well yes, he was *sure* it could be arranged, so long as she was ready to take the position. Dorothy nodded, almost too excited to speak. 'I will.'

Stanhope Edwards beamed with relief and looked at his watch. He'd show her round and she could catch the 2.40 to King's Cross. Hope she didn't find them all too much old

103

fogies. Watson-Smith, eighty-three, Latin all forms, had a slight stroke last term, collapsed in the middle of a subordinate clause. But they were a game lot. Had a letter from his sister, with whom he lived; the old boy would be back this term.

So Stanhope rambled as they toured the empty classrooms, ink-stained desks rickety, the last lesson still evident on the blackboard. In the 'surgery', he opened a green metal cupboard and together they looked vaguely at the contents: Dettol, a thermometer, Vick, dressings, tins of Elastoplast, linctus, Cascara, a brown bottle of Gentian Violet. 'I'm sure you'll find all you need here,' said Mr Edwards, shutting the door. 'But this has always been our pride in the surgery. It was presented by a parent some years ago. I believe your predecessor Miss Malster found it invaluable in the rare cases of serious illness.'

Dorothy looked uncertainly at the eleven large, dusty red volumes along a shelf on the wall beside the basin: *Green's Encyclopaedia and Dictionary of Medicine and Surgery*. She suspected a first aid manual would be of more use.

The next two weeks were frantic. Mr Edwards had said, 'Do what you can about uniform.' But Dorothy and Jessie pooled their coupons, determined Dave should have of the best. Dorothy could imagine how humiliating it would be to have the wrong clothes. 'Especially as he won't speak the same as them really,' said Jessie. 'Poor little Dave,' she added after a pause. She knew what they were doing was for his good in the long run, but she often had more than half a mind to keep him by her, her little man. 'I'll be with him,' said Dorothy comfortingly. She remembered her own efforts to subdue the last remnants of Norfolk in her voice when Jack had become an officer and she had had to mix with the other wives. It had taken her months, over a year. Dave would be much quicker. Children always were.

All too soon they were huddled on the snow-sprinkled platform of Norwich station. Jessie held Dave tight, his little golden head over her shoulder so's he shouldn't see her tears.

'Be a good boy.' Dave was far too excited to notice. He chattered all the way to London.

'Don't you want to read your *Dandy*?' said Dorothy,

amused. Dave didn't answer, but climbed onto his seat to look again at himself in his crested cap. It was only with difficulty he'd been persuaded not to travel in his football boots.

They had a five-hour wait at King's Cross. By the time their train came in, Dave was exhausted. Dorothy managed to get a corner seat, but soon she had to have the little boy on her lap.

Over the next three days, while Dave skipped about 'helping', learning to call the returning masters 'Sir' and respond to cries of 'Hughes', Dorothy learnt that there was a great deal more to Matron's duties than mere health.

'Ordinarily your task, I fear.' Stanhope Edwards had prepared a list of dormitories and their occupants (he'd called her Matron from her arrival). Beds and little chests of drawers had to be assigned, each with its carefully written label. Seventy beds had to be made. The trunks had arrived and those of the junior boys had to be unpacked and checked against enclosed school clothing lists. Cubicles in the changing rooms had to be labelled. She mastered the mechanics of the laundry room and distributed dirty clothes bags.

In all this, and much more, she was supposed to have the assistance of Mrs Edgerley, the Housekeeper. Mrs Edgerley was a large, slow-moving, wheezing woman of about fifty-seven. Her back was bad. She had twinges and 'turns'. Only the kitchen, the catering, the cleaning girls from Ravenstonedale (the little village in the valley below the big grey house) really came into her sphere. This she made clear and Dorothy found it easier to acquiesce.

Fortunately Mrs Edgerley was also a garrulous and friendly woman, because Dorothy realised on her third day that they would have to spend much time together.

It was then, the day before the boys came back, that Mr Edwards introduced her formally to the rest of the staff. 'You are fully entitled to use the Staff Common Room whenever you like,' he said, leading her towards it. There was something about 'fully entitled', or perhaps it was his tone, which gave an air of ambiguity to the phrase. Dorothy realised its nature almost as soon as he opened the door and strode ahead of

105

her. 'Gentlemen, I would like you to meet your new colleague, the new Matron, Mrs Martel.'

It was a small hot room, so dense with pipe smoke that her eyes immediately began to smart. Seven battered easy chairs were placed, she felt in some sort of precedence, facing a large coal fire. From these, coughing, shaking, with a cracking of vertebrae and creaking of springs, the staff slowly became upright. Knobbly hands held pipes, spectacles, papers, books; moustaches straggled across wrinkled, mauve faces. Dorothy also had the impression of a pervading nicotine yellowness, as if a group of aged kippers stood swaying before her in their smokery, slowly tanning in pipe smoke.

At least, six kippers stood swaying; a seventh, oblivious, could just be discerned slumped in the chair nearest the fire.

Mr Edwards was introducing her. 'Mr Royds, Mrs Martel; Royds and I share English . . . Mr Bracken . . . Willis. . . .'

When he reached the still comatose figure by the fire, he stretched forth a hand, paused, and withdrew it. 'I think we won't disturb Mr Watson-Smith. He had a tiring journey.' And then, basely, Mr Edwards withdrew, 'sure they would all have plenty to discuss'.

There was a short embarrassed silence. Then one of the figures – Royds, Bracken, Willis, none of the names had impinged – croaked, 'Please, won't you sit down?' A quivering finger indicated what was clearly 'his' chair.

But Dorothy, her eyes actually streaming, declined. She had far too much to do. So nice to meet them all. Thank you so much.

'I can't possibly use that room of theirs,' she said to Mrs Edgerley.

'No dear, you'd best share my little sitting room,' said Mrs Edgerley. 'Miss Malster found that best. We'd always sit there of an evening.'

Mrs Edgerley had been at Danehurst Court twenty-seven years ('Mrs' was a courtesy title). She knew everyone, everything.

'Newman? He's a nice enough lad. Big for his age.' Newman was Dave's 'dorm captain'. Dorothy had given Dave a bed near the radiator, close to Newman. He could protect the new boy.

The boys arrived in the evening of the next day. As they burst down the dormitory corridors, the stairs, in and out of the classrooms, Dorothy thought it was like a huge flock of birds plummeting in – a million high-pitched sparrows with their upper-class squeaking and piping, fighting, flitting about filling the old house with noise and movement and life.

She was instantly bombarded. 'Matron, can I change with Rankin minor?' 'Matron, Hill jumped on my bed and the springs are broken.' 'Matron, I've lost the key to my trunk.' 'Matron, must I have my bath night the first night?' 'Matron, Matron, Matron. . . .'

It took Dorothy four weeks to master the position of Matron. By then her day was more organised, more tightly packed than it had been even in the Norwich General.

'Morning, Matron. Noticed a fair queue at surgery this morning. Is the mild weather bringing on colds – or do we have malingering?'

Mr Edwards always managed a few words. 'Nothing serious Mr Edwards.'

And indeed so far there had only been one crisis. For the rest it was colds, sore throats, bruises, cuts, eye infections, constipation.

When, exhausted at the end of the day, she sank into Mrs Edgerley's soft armchair, there was still a pile of mending to take onto her knee.

Mrs Edgerley would look across to her and say, with a mixture of admiration and relief, 'You'd do anything for those boys.' Dorothy didn't deny it.

Dave's troubles had come quickly, but been quickly solved. Three days after the boys had returned, he complained that they were teasing him about the way he spoke.

It was their 'last thing' time in front of her fire. Dorothy held him in her arms. 'There's no harm in the way you speak, darling,' she said, but she drew out her own vowels in the way that had become habitual with her.

She was amazed how quickly he adapted. Within three weeks he was 'talking posh' so's you could hardly tell the difference. Dorothy saw nothing to be ashamed of in this, either for him or her.

But his real acceptance came in true Tom Brown style.

Murray was a bit bigger than Dave and inclined to bully the other boys in dormitory four. Dave, toughened by countless battles on the hard asphalt of his Norwich primary school, wouldn't stand for it. He worsted Murray in fair fight, cheered on by the rest of the dorm.

Two days later, Newman came politely up to Dorothy in the corridor. 'Excuse me Matron, but is it true that Hughes's father was a flight lieutenant and got shot down and got a medal?'

With hardly a pause, Dorothy said, 'Quite true. He was a very brave man. And Newman,' she added, 'come to evening surgery and I'll have a look at that face of yours.'

Newman occasioned her first recourse to *Green's Encyclopaedia of Medicine and Surgery*. Acne had not been a problem at the Norwich General, nor did it feature in her manual of first aid. *Green's* had been published in 1906 and presented in 1924. The entry under acne was extremely long and complicated. Eventually Dorothy decided that a sulphur lotion would help.

The large pot of pale cream arrived two days later. Holding Newman's head back under the light that evening while she gently applied it Dorothy could hardly help but take in the face so close to her. Newman had an olive skin and restless, slippery black eyes; there was, in his thinness, his quickness, his wide thin mouth and close-together eyes, something vixenish about him, but a vixen already becoming a fox. Five foot five herself, he must have been at least five foot two, the tallest boy in the school. To hide this, he stooped when he walked, which gave him a furtive, slinking-about appearance.

'Now you're to come back every evening till we've cleared that up,' said Dorothy. And as he slipped, bent, from the surgery, she called out, 'And pull yourself up, Newman. You should be proud, a big chap like you.'

'Yes, Matron.'

The second time she used *Green's* was at the first real crisis. Mr Watson-Smith, whom she often glimpsed limping like a battered crow lopsidedly about the school, the whole left half of him useless, had suddenly keeled over in class and gone clattering down with the blackboard in a cloud of chalk.

Brought running by a panic-stricken pupil, Dorothy had

108

loosened collar and tie, and had the unconscious, stertorously breathing old man carried to bed.

Then she flew to *Green's*. It was not an epileptic fit. It was another stroke. *Green's* was lengthy. She seemed to have done the right thing but it was at any rate quite clear that here was a case in which she was justified in calling Dr Knightley.

Dr Knightley was an elderly, impolite, deaf northcountryman. He had arrived at the beginning of term to say he could no longer get the petrol to make his regular fortnightly visits. She could ring him in an emergency. He'd called her 'Nurse' from the start.

At her first 'emergency' – twenty boys with temperatures of 102 and 'nasty' throats – he'd barked, 'Good God woman, I can't come out for the common cold. There's a war on. Keep them in bed, aspirin, fluids. They'll recover.'

Even now, with poor Mr Watson-Smith poised for oblivion, he said, 'I'll come soon as I can. I've a case first at Riverdale,' and had added gratuitously, 'I'm glad to see tha's learnt when it's worth calling me out.'

Spring came very early that year. Climbing the stone walls down onto sheep-mown turf, or scrambling down to the beck which dashed noisily in peaty swirls over the grey boulders, Dorothy wondered if it was the spring that was making her so restless.

Whereas before she had felt, and sought, a terrible exhaustion – purposefully piling onto the exhaustion of her grief hour after hour at the Norwich General in the hope, often almost realised, of complete unconsciousness – now the life in her would not be stifled. She was possessed by a trembling hair-feather energy. She woke each morning thinking something momentous was going to happen, that she was preparing herself for a really dramatic sacrifice or adventure, and the disappointment that it was just the same hectic day of urgent trivia was gradually replaced during the evening, tired as she was, by anticipation that something extraordinary was stirring in the day to come.

And this restlessness invaded her sleep, causing tumultuous dreams. These both amazed and embarrassed her. She would lie for a moment holding to the longing. By the time she had run the cold baths, the dream would have vanished. Had it been put to her to identify she would have denied it.

The second crisis, and far greater challenge to her medical skills, came three weeks after half term.

It was a Saturday afternoon. The boys were allowed to do what they liked, and Dorothy had thought she'd take Dave for a walk on the fells.

She searched everywhere, but he seemed, along with his particular friends, to have vanished. No one had seen them go out.

Passing his dormitory on her way to collect her mac from her room, Dorothy decided on impulse to look there. Strictly speaking, dormitories were out of bounds during the day, but such things tended to relax at weekends. Dave and the rest could be up to something in there.

She opened the door and stepped briskly through. There in front of her, not fifteen feet away in the middle of the floor, she saw the most astonishing scene.

The six little boys, totally absorbed, were staring down at the seventh, who was lying on his back on the floor. This was Newman. His knees were bent up and splayed apart and his trousers and pants were pulled down round his ankles. From between his legs there rose, and which Newman was gripping with both hands and violently agitating, there stuck rigidly up. . . . Dorothy turned her head hurriedly away, but then, fascinated, horrified, turned it slowly back.

At her entry, the six little boys had scattered guiltily to their beds. But Newman, in a delirium, could not stop. Teeth clenched, face congested, eyes shut, he arched up, hands moving with incredible rapidity. The approaching moment of crisis was marked by his arching up still further, convulsively opening and closing his thighs, upon which Dorothy, with a sudden feeling of recovering her senses, turned abruptly round and ran from the dormitory, shutting the door sharply behind her.

She ran down the corridor into the surgery and hurried through the door that led to her adjoining bedroom.

What should she do? Was what Newman had been doing wrong? If so, in what way? Was it a medical matter, or one

110

for the Headmaster, or just something that boys did? Perhaps it wasn't wrong at all.

Dorothy's knowledge of sex was intense but limited. Her parents had never mentioned it. It was not that they disapproved of it. For them, it simply appeared not to exist. The evening before her marriage, Dorothy's mother had said, 'You'll be sharing your husband's bed from tomorrow, Dorothy. I just have this to say on that subject – whatever Jack Martel do there is right.'

Dorothy had been amazed at what Jack had done. And then amazed at the pleasure he gave her. She thought about it doing the washing up with her mother-in-law, hoping he might return, as sometimes happened, unexpectedly in the afternoon.

But whatever they did, whenever they did it, summer or winter, only by mistake did they see each other naked. Dorothy was always in bed first, the lights off, waiting inside the thrilling Bedouin tent of the bedclothes, waiting for him to slide her nightie up under her armpits or gently off over her head.

In the afternoons, they pulled the blackout blind and the thick velveteen curtains. Jack put his hand over her mouth in case old Mrs Martel heard her cry out.

Yet she seemed to remember him saying something once about the peculiar thing she'd seen Newman doing, though she couldn't even remember what he'd called it. She stared out of the window across Langdale Fell to the distant bulk of the Boar, gradually vanishing as the always-moist air thickened into rain. It would have been too wet for a walk.

That evening, instead of the bedtime story, she questioned Dave closely about the incident.

He was perfectly open and clearly saw nothing wrong in it. Did it happen often? Yes – he didn't always go and watch. Why did he watch? The others did, it was funny to see him make the white stuff come. Did he do it himself? 'What'd be the point in that, Aunt Dolly?'

It was later that night that the full, appalling import of what she had discovered was suddenly and swiftly unfolded to her in an hour of increasingly terrified reading in the grim volumes of *Green's Encyclopaedia*.

She found her first clue under '*Penis*'. Thence she was directed to the main heading that dealt with the subject. It was the cross-references at the base of this – before she had even read the main article itself – that came as a series of violent hammer blows. *See also*, intoned *Green's*, *see also: Adolescent Insanity; General Insanity; Impotence; Scrotum and Testicles, diseases of; Vice.*

But it was the main section, the long article *on* what it was, that led Dorothy, now truly horrified, into all these sinister ramifications. Newman was identified – 'shifty, unstraightforward appearance . . . creeps about'. The symptoms in their active form were graphically and lengthily described. Finally came the consequences: 'When the habit is persisted in and allowed to dominate the individual, moral and mental degeneration inevitably follow and progress, slowly it may be but surely, to mental dissolution.'

Nor was it just mental – though the progress to dissolution and 'drivelling idiocy' was described in the sections on insanity; it was also a physical scourge. It led, almost in passing, to lifelong impotence; the frame shrank and withered, eyes were affected, the skin grew pallid and developed acne, the scrotum and testicles were in the end virtually destroyed.

Dorothy suddenly felt her mother in her. Something long-dormant, violently agitated, fluttering, and yet imperative.

It was – poor Newman – a *disease*, and a very serious one. The sufferer was clearly referred to as the 'patient' throughout. She suddenly saw the whole scene sharply in her mind again, the boy in agony arched back, frenziedly gripping what was monstrously swollen, out of all proportion, about to burst, his trying to burst it himself as one would a boil, the distended bulb inflamed purple, red, angry. It would haunt her dreams.

But it wasn't just a disease. There was a moral element, as the long entry under '*Vice*' made clear. However, 'when the patient comes with a frank confession and a sincere desire for reform the battle is half-won'. She would seek help on both fronts.

Her interview with Mr Edwards was almost entirely unsatisfactory. For a long time he couldn't grasp what the woman was getting at. She'd come across something, some vice ring was it? Pinching in the dorms? Not entirely, some infection it seemed, serious judging from her anxiety.

When finally, blushing deeply, head lowered, Dorothy managed to murmur the embarrassing word itself, Mr Edwards's lined, wise old face cleared. Ah – *that*. No, he was absolutely sure there was none of *that* in the school. The fact was, you just didn't get it in a prep school. Public school – yes. A fearful problem sometimes. But that was later on. These were just puppies.

Dorothy, blushing continuously, demurred. She was certain. *How* was she certain, asked Mr Edwards, beginning to feel a faint impatience. She hadn't seemed the hysterical sort. Dorothy found she simply couldn't bring herself to describe, in all its lurid detail, the scene in the dormitory – especially as it might inculpate Dave. She fell back on physical symptoms – pasty-faced, furtive, spots.

'There's this one boy, you say – who is he by the way? Ah yes, splendid chappie – this boy, is he "going through" satisfactorily?' asked Mr Edwards keenly. 'It's that, I'll be bound. They often tick the chart – but you question him. Dose him hard whatever he says.'

'Look Matron,' a kindly arm on her shoulder, he led her to the door, 'I've been looking after boys now for over fifty years. You can take it from me you simply don't *get* that in a prep school. Why don't you consult Dr Knightley? I'm sure he'll tell you the same.'

Back in her surgery, Dorothy once again took down the heavy, dull red volumes. The encyclopaedia had warned her in advance. 'We affirm, without fear of refutation, that the great majority of boarding schools in this country are infested with this pernicious and dangerous habit. The evidence of masters, and especially head masters, is of the least possible value in this connection.'

Nor could she possibly ring Dr Knightley. She imagined whispering the dreaded word, Dr Knightley bawling, 'Speak up woman. Can't hear a damned word you say.' Having, perhaps, to shout the word. His scornful reaction. . . .

She settled to read in earnest. The reason the disease was so harmful was that it was 'the satisfaction of an animal instinct in an irregular and unnatural manner'. 'In certain primitive societies, principally in New Guinea,' she read on with surprise, 'it is not unknown for young adolescents of thirteen or fourteen or even younger to indulge in indiscriminate physical intercourse together. Such a solution to this grave problem is clearly unthinkable in a civilised society.'

The author of the article on '*Adolescent Insanity*' went on to give the treatments that were possible in a civilised society. He advised 'active exercise in the open air for as many hours as possible. In boys at school it is also a good plan to sew up the trouser pockets'. But the principal treatment was dietary. Porridge, soup, cod liver oil and milk: 'Milk in large quantities and as often as possible. It is, I think, certain that the habit, which is so frequent and deleterious, is less practised, and in a relatively short space of time, by patients on this diet.'

For really serious cases he advised that 'a counter-irritant or strong antimonial ointment can be applied to the patient's foreskin, though there is always the risk of fresh irritation being set up'.

After her evening surgery, Dorothy sent for Newman.

When he came through the door, slouched, eyes on the ground, she could see that the malady had progressed even in the two days since her discovery. He was sickly pale, with dark stains under his close-set, moist black eyes. She couldn't understand, now, how she hadn't noticed his condition weeks before.

She led him to the table and gently sat him down. 'Now, I expect you know why I've asked you here, Newman.' He nodded, eyes down, blushing. 'Yes, it's to do with what happened on Saturday afternoon. Now Newman, I wonder if you realise that what you were doing was very very naughty?' Newman nodded his head miserably. 'Yes,' said Dorothy, 'but it is far worse than just naughty. It is very very dangerous.'

She told him, in measured tones, just how serious the disease was. She explained that this was why he had acne. She even read a few passages from *Green's*, to show it wasn't just Matron fussing. Newman, miserable and guilty enough when he'd come in, began to look actually terrified – as well he might, thought Dorothy, as well he should. Nevertheless her heart went out to the silent, foxy-faced, sad, thin and hungry-looking youth crouched in his chair before her.

114

'Don't worry,' she said, putting her hand comfortingly on his arm. 'It hasn't reached that stage by a long chalk yet. We'll soon have you well again, you see.' No time like the present. She fetched the bottle of cod liver oil and gave him two tablespoonfuls. Then some final, brief questions to see how serious it had, in fact, got.

Once a week? Newman shook his head. Twice? Again, a guilty shake. Dorothy was alarmed to discover it was every night, and sometimes two or three times a night.

'But why do you have to do it so often?' she asked. She was quite sure *Green's* would have considered this the disease in a dangerously advanced state. She would order the antimonial ointment straight away.

Newman, blushing again, muttered something.

'What?' asked Dorothy again, bending her head close to his.

'I like the feeling.'

Dorothy stood up briskly. 'Now, there's to be no repetition of what happened on Saturday. None. If I hear of anything like that, it's straight to the Headmaster. Is that clear?'

Newman nodded.

'Otherwise we'll keep this just between ourselves. We'll soon have you well again.' As Newman, with bent head, left the surgery, Dorothy called after him, 'And bring me all your pairs of trousers, will you Newman?'

The pile of sewing was high that night, but she put the three pairs of shorts on the top.

'Your work!' said Mrs Edgerley relaxedly, looking at the pile. 'What you do for those boys! I wish I could help.'

'There is something you could do,' said Dorothy. 'I'm worried about young Newman. I'd like him put on the extra milk roster.'

'What, that great lad?' said Mrs Edgerley. 'What's he need extra milk for then?'

'It's just that,' said Dorothy, studying the insides of Newman's shorts, 'he's outgrown his strength.'

The instructions concerning the pockets had seemed inexplicable, but she saw now that the linings of Newman's shorts, at the front, were heavily stained.

Over the next three weeks, Newman's disease was

Dorothy's central preoccupation. A second, less severe outbreak of colds and temperatures swept the school and both san dorms filled up. But of all her patients, Newman – with the prospect of his eventual 'mental dissolution', his certain, already evident physical deterioration – was by far the most serious. It weighed the heavier, since she now knew she ought to report it to Dr Knightley. This she still couldn't face, prefering to await the outcome of the dietary treatment.

Not knowing what a 'strong antimonial ointment' was, she simply put it down as that in the weekly list and hoped the chemist himself would understand. She decided, however, as with Dr Knightley, to see if the dietary moves had any effect first. *Green's* had promised that results were swift. The ointment and the doctor would be kept as last resorts, in case of a relapse.

But there was no relapse. There was no improvement from which a relapse might take place. On the contrary, the disease seemed to grow worse. Or perhaps it was just that Newman, under uncensorious, gentle but persistent questioning, remembered attacks which in the first examination he had forgotten. Dorothy discovered they took place not just at night, but during the day – in break; before prep; once, it seemed, a crisis had occurred in the middle of a Latin lesson. Newman had raised his hand to be excused to the bog. . . .

Towards the end of the second week of treatment it was clear the situation was far more dangerous than at the start.

Spring came rolling down over the high Westmoreland fells in moist warm waves of wind or sweeps of gentle, fertilising rain. Daffodils appeared. The clear air was full of the sound of sheep and running water. Walking on the mossy turf Dorothy wondered if it was the restlessness of spring that was making her so anxious.

What was needed was a proper physical method. Something to counteract what had been brought so vividly home to her by Newman's muttered 'I like the feeling'. That contorted face, that arched and trembling young body had been in the grip of ecstasy, not, as she had supposed, in agony – but it was a poisonous ecstasy, the pleasure beguiling him to destruction. There had been a series of warning lectures given to all the staff at the Norwich General on the danger

116

of morphine addiction from continuous injections in cases with severe wounds.

It was the Monday three weeks before the end of term. After his nightly cod liver oil, Dorothy told Newman to come back to the surgery after 6th Form lights out. She did not want him to be embarrassed by someone or other, perhaps a junior, dashing in after surgery, as quite often happened.

Newman was already in the surgery when she came in from her bedroom. He was wearing his regulation blue dressing gown and striped pyjamas. Both were too small for him and Dorothy found him a touching sight standing, almost as tall as she was, apprehensively in front of her, bony ankles and wrists protruding.

She explained that she was going to apply an ointment specially recommended for his disease. It would not hurt at all; on the contrary, he would find it soothing.

It was true it would not hurt, but Dorothy could only trust to *Green's* that it would soothe. She had tested a little of the pale jelly on the soft inner flesh of her forearm and felt quite soon a warm, even fiery glow as the 'counter-irritant' became active.

She opened his dressing gown and told him without embarrassment to lower his pyjamas. Although she and Jack had hardly seen each other naked, it had been this very invisibility that had given their love its power; secrecy, darkness had become the ingredients necessary to passion just as the silence of her parents until the last instant had given whatever they had done its licence. Light, on the other hand, removed all such feelings, and Dorothy had often washed the private parts of unconscious or sedated soldiers without the slightest qualm.

Yet she had never studied them quite as she did Newman's now. It was, obviously as a result or even part cause of his malady, very badly enlarged. It looked, with its small eyebrow of angry black hairs, almost grotesque when you considered the unfortunate boy's age and even his size. She held the disease-swollen member, plump and surprisingly heavy, as delicately as she could with the fingers of her small left hand.

Newman had been circumcised and there did not appear to be any foreskin left. Dorothy therefore began to apply the

117

antimonial ointment carefully all over the tip itself – no doubt one of the seats of the trouble.

At her first touch, she felt Newman quiver. 'Don't worry. I won't hurt you,' she said. But as she gently massaged the infected area she felt the fingers of her left hand forced to open wider; the diseased organ was enlarging before her eyes. It forced its way through until, painfully swollen, it stuck out rigidly a good three and a half inches through her encircling hand.

Dorothy, with some vague comparison in her head to a hot poultice drawing forth poison, hurriedly applied another dollop of the translucent jelly, massaging it with the palm of her hand into the spongy resilience of the now darkening and dangerously distended bulb.

At this poor Newman reached both hands to hers – either to assist or stop her – and at the same time gave a convulsive thrust so that Dorothy was suddenly aware that an attack had been brought on. Not just brought on, and violently, but that it was approaching crisis and that, unless she acted very fast, it would quite soon come to its unnatural resolution.

It was hardly a decision. Almost by instinct (partly, perhaps, because such things had always in her experience taken place in the dark) she led Newman briskly through the still half-open door of her bedroom.

Five minutes later Newman was back in his dormitory and Dorothy was washing her hands in the surgery basin.

She felt too agitated to join Mrs Edgerley that night. Had she done right? She did not mean morally but medically. Morally there seemed no distinction between what she had just done and the lancing of a boil or the staunching of a wound. The place was more intimate, that was all. There had been wounds in such places in the Norwich General.

But medically? Anxiously consulting *Green's* again, there seemed no essential difference between what she had done and what Newman did to himself. There must, she supposed, be an element of *forcing* which was disastrous in so sensitive and complicated an area.

It was now that the fleeting reference to New Guinea struck with sudden force. 'Such a solution to this grave problem is clearly unthinkable in a civilised society.' Dorothy rose and paced the little surgery. Clearly, clearly. Yet – what other solution was open to her? Continue the dieting, the anti-monial, and, if all failed, finally Dr Knightley. But for her, here and now, what else?

For a week she agonised. Immoral in the eyes of many it would no doubt seem – him so young, so unknowing. And her elderly parents had been exceedingly moral, even stern. Yet because these matters had never been mentioned they seemed somehow outside morality – or to have their own morality.

And in this matter the morality was one, almost, of life and death. Against the decision to do nothing, Dorothy had to set the dreadful certainty of *Green's:* ' . . . moral and mental degeneration inevitably follow and progress, slowly it may be, but surely to mental dissolution.'

She could not rid herself of the sight of Newman in the grip of his seizure, teeth clenched, eyes shut, thighs working convulsively. She was tortured by the memory of his diseased member, so hot and heavy, swelling as the fluids welled up, inexorably forcing her fingers apart.

These painful visions, the anxiety, the indecision, still further exacerbated the restlessness already provoked by the onset of spring. It drove Dorothy – on her Wednesday half-day, the Wednesday after the antimonial – out onto the fells flowing with the almost sensual ripple and run of the warm wet westerlies.

It was here, breasting their caresses, she had her revelation. Jack's death had been a sacrifice; a sacrifice for his country but, because in all the country it had been her he had loved, a sacrifice in particular for her. The one thing that had held her back, put her in a dither, was that the step she contem-plated was wrong. It was, quite plainly, sinful. Now, suddenly, she saw that was the point. *She too was to make a sacrifice.* In a way, a greater one than Jack.

The way was now open – yet still she held back. She told Newman – faced with his usual, miserable recital of attacks – that they'd try the antimonial again next evening. (She'd discontinued it after the first disastrous application.)

Dorothy had had to break up a pillow fight in dorm seven, and Newman had therefore been kept waiting. When she got

119

back to the surgery she saw at once – a mere glance at his pyjama trousers – that he was already in the throes of an attack. He was bent almost double in a pathetic attempt to hide the symptoms, his face piteous, his hands clenched behind his back.

It was a question of acting at once. Without speaking, she led the trembling youth gently but firmly through to her bedroom.

It was oddly easy, even natural. Newman responded silently – though with surprising strength – to her guidance. Later, in the darkness of the Bedouin tent, holding his thin body still filmed with a feverish sweat, Dorothy explained this was another treatment. They would continue it for the last ten days of term. Newman returned silently to his dormitory. Or almost silently. As he left, Dorothy asked if he felt better. 'Yes, Matron,' said Newman.

That evening there was an enormous pile of mending to be completed prior to the last laundry. As usual Mrs Edgerley looked up and gave her sympathetic sigh. 'What they do to their clothes!' she exclaimed, and added automatically, 'You'd do anything for those boys, anything.'

For once, Dorothy found herself unable to reply and bent to her work. She was blushing.

During the holidays, she hardly gave the problem a thought. Jessie was overjoyed to see her son, and though Dorothy had sent detailed letters, Jessie insisted on every detail over again. She marvelled at his progress. 'Don't he speak nice?' she said.

She also confessed to Dorothy, halfway through the hols, how bitterly she missed the little boy. 'I sometimes wonder if I can stand it,' she said. 'Do you suppose I could manage all that work?'

'I don't know,' said Dorothy, looking at the frail form of her sister-in-law. 'Some of it.' She ran her mind over the last crowded days at Danehurst Court. 'Not all of it.' It had occurred to her, during those last days of the term, that she might become impregnated. She had dismissed the idea. The discharge, though copious – extraordinarily copious – was surely not that of a man. It must be sterile, surely, more in the nature of the fluid generated by exasperated joints or wrenched ligaments.

But the next day, happening quite by chance to pass the unobstrusive opening of the street in Norwich which contained the Marie Stopes clinic she found herself, almost without thinking, you never know, better safe than sorry, turning down into it.

There was – a pooling of coupons – the summer uniform to buy. Jessie bought Dave a cricket bat.

Once again, they were all together at Norwich Station. Jessie held Dave in her arms, her eyes full of tears. 'It seems like yesterday,' she whispered. His arms round her neck, Dave was waving his bat behind her back.

'Matron – why can't mice fly?'

'I don't know, David. Go and get undressed.'

'Because it wouldn't be fair on the cat.'

'Matron – my trunk hasn't arrived.'

The usual first-day-of-term pandemonium continuing until well after 6th Form lights out made it impossible to do more than give Newman his cod-liver oil.

'I want to see you after lights out tomorrow, Newman. With your chart.'

'Yes, Matron.'

He had grown. It was with a slight sense of shock that she realised this fourteen-year-old boy – now in his final term – was almost as tall as she was.

'Let me see the chart.' She had given him a 'going through' chart, with instructions to put a tick whenever he had an attack. One glance showed her that, far from abating, the disease still raged unchecked. Or almost unchecked. It seemed, like malaria, to come in bouts; a two- or occasionally three-day remission, then a storm of ticks. She had given him a letter to his mother about the diet. Clearly it had been useless.

The boy stood silently before her, head a little bent, his eyes lowered. Dorothy was about to put out her hand and murmur a word of comfort and hope when, following the direction of his eyes, she looked down at his pyjamas. Now still more obviously too small for him, the thin material was, at the critical point, stretched taut. At that moment, Newman

121

raised his head and looked at her with an expression of despairing appeal, the moist eyes feverish, almost desperate.

Dorothy turned without a word and walked towards her bedroom door, followed by the lanky and now bent-over figure of her patient. She found that her mouth was dry and that she was trembling.

As she battled through that long, hectic term with the tempest of his symptoms, Dorothy became convinced that in some ways the disease had worsened during the holidays. And she wondered, since his growth was uniform (that eyebrow tuffet of black hair was now a tangled and ferocious forest), whether this was something to do with it.

It had also taken a more complete possession of him. Where at first she had had to guide the frenzied boy as to the correct process of his treatment, increasingly he took control. Quite soon it was total, so much so indeed, and so strongly did the fever rage in him sometimes that one night, in an excess of sacrificial assistance, Dorothy heard herself cry out.

At once – at least nearly at once, shortly afterwards – Newman said, 'Are you all right, Matron?'

'Yes,' whispered Dorothy. 'I hit my head on the back of the bed.'

It was a lie, but she could not possibly admit to him that she felt any pleasure. She could hardly admit it to herself. And this was easier because of the rigidly functional nature of the operation.

Yet this in itself was surprising – that something so functional, so detachedly physical, so *medical*, should be able to cause pleasure. She had always thought that love-making, above all other activities, was one which required sharing, whose essence was jointness. But it was clear that for Newman it was as it had been on the dormitory floor – an urgent, desperate relief. It was an act solitary and without tenderness. They hardly spoke. When it was over, he left.

In fact, without this detachment she doubted she could have allowed herself to experience any pleasure at all. It would have been too close to Jack. Jack banished, she could enjoy the arduous therapeutic process to the full, but the pleasure took on the same detached quality as that accompanying other impersonal physical actions – such as drinking a whole glass of cold water when very thirsty, or taking the weight off her feet at the end of the day.

There were other anxieties, however. Medical anxieties. Dorothy felt that really all she was doing clinically was relieving symptoms. She deeply regretted not having informed Dr Knightley at first. The embarrassment would have been great, but bearable; now – and she had a sense, sometimes, things had somehow got out of hand – it was totally impossible to consult him.

She searched and re-searched *Green's* for further enlightenment. Soon she knew the sombre phrases off by heart. ' . . . patient's intellect becomes sluggish and enfeebled . . . end in becoming a drivelling idiot . . . mental dissolution . . . lifelong impotence . . .' But despite the very considerable space devoted to the disease, there was a curious lack of precision where it mattered most.

Dorothy evolved her own theories. She had always supposed that the development of men as regards this sort of thing to be like that of women – that is, like her own. It was more or less completely quiescent until they were eighteen or nineteen. Then they met the person they were to marry, fell in love, and the whole thing was set off.

The nature of this male disease was suddenly to slap these huge inflamed organs onto a recipient far too young. The result was the dormitory scene, which was deadly because 'unnatural' – like horses being sick.

Her role, in an elaboration of this, was gradually to introduce what was regular – a sort of 'natural' antibody. In this respect she resembled a vaccination.

Or, as she'd deduced from the chart, it was an infection, a malarial-type fever, coming in uncontrollable bouts. And certainly, as she succumbed to the violently agitated boy above her, she could feel the fever burning in his body.

Her favoured theory (though they became mixed in her mind sometimes) was the inflamed wound/over-stimulated gland one. Partly she was drawing off excess fluid, like expressing milk from an over-productive breast. Yet this was the most frightening of them. She knew from her experience of wounds that there was nothing static about them. Either they cleared up – or they worsened. Over-full breasts became infected. By the fourth week of term Newman's disease showed no signs of 'clearing up'.

She decided she must risk what she had hitherto shrunk from – trying if repeated applications of the powerful antimonial ointment might not effect a 'complete evacuation'.

Newman usually left after one treatment. This night, Dorothy restrained him and gently applied a second generous portion of antimonial. The irritant and her ever-so-delicate finger-tip massage soon brought on a second attack. But now Dorothy realised that a good deal of the fiery jelly had spread itself upon her, inducing a fierce glow that was part pleasurable, part maddening.

She found her usual clinical restraint suddenly impossible to retain as repeated applications of the antimonial whipped Newman close to frenzy. Writhing uncontrollably beneath him, Dorothy had to grind her teeth upon the pillow. In a short pause while they lay breathless she thought, I've caught the disease myself. Then, once more hugely swollen, the fluid erupting up from within, possessed from it of a demonic strength, Newman was swept by a fresh, much more prolonged attack. Eleven times the fever reached a crisis before it finally died away and left them in peace.

It was the next evening that Dorothy, searching desperately through *Green's*, came upon the last piece of information she was to find on the disease. It was under '*Glands, diseases of*': 'Little is known about other effects of adrenal over-activity. It is suspected it may cause the condition known as Infant Hercules. Infant Hercules is the term applied to young male children with precocious sexual development of an extreme form. This may be due to a virilizing adrenocortical disorder.'

Infant Hercules. Dorothy stood up and slowly replaced the volume of *Green's*. Her mind was quite blank, but catching sight of her face in the surgery mirror she was disconcerted – and a little embarrassed – to see that she was, very faintly, smiling.

From that day she stopped using the antimonial ointment. It seemed only to worsen the condition. She had clearly achieved a complete evacuation, yet the next night he was almost as bad as ever.

She supposed there must be remedies. How did the public

schools cope? She thought of writing to one, but felt too shy to phrase the letter. She also ceased to give Newman cod liver oil.

It was not that she had given up. The disease was as deadly as ever. But she realised she could not cure it; she could only contain it.

And here she was successful. Newman's appearance had improved beyond recognition. He stood straight and strong. He continued to 'fill out'. His acne had gone.

The success of her treatment – however temporary – gave Dorothy great satisfaction. Indeed she herself had never felt better. She seemed to have endless energy to cope with the incessant hither and thither of her life with the boys, their jokes, attacks of pink eye and athlete's foot, the cuts and bruises which the summer multiplied.

She went for walks on the fells whenever she could find the time. She would take Dave and his friends. She was endlessly amazed at the turbulent uprearing landscape in its soft damp air, so different from Norfolk, yet with odd, minute correspondences. One such were the rushes. In Norfolk they grew by the wide meandering rivers; here amongst the moss beside the road, in patches on the fields. Dorothy showed Dave how to peel away the hard shiny green outer skin to be left with the resilient pithy shaft within.

She never took Newman on these walks. She seldom encountered him during the day. Very occasionally, across the starling chatter of the dining hall, she would suddenly look up and find his eyes on her; or, watching him cross the drive from the surgery window, he would look up and their eyes would meet. At these moments she would feel an odd complicity between them.

The predicament of someone so young becoming a victim to a dangerous disease had initially touched her deeply. But it had been tempered by her confidence in a cure. The knowledge that she had not found the cure infused a new tenderness into her feelings for him.

She lost the need for darkness. Sometimes, after a particularly prolonged attack, he would fall asleep. Dorothy would quietly let rise the blackout blind until the evening light fell on his sleeping face. He had very long lashes, like a girl.

Warm in her arms, she could see the tracery of hairbell-blue veins through the clear, faintly tanned skin of his young neck. Impossible to believe that not ten minutes ago adrenocortical fever had raged in these delicate channels.

One night she awoke to find his pyjamas at the bottom of her bed. Standing beside him in the sleeping dormitory she had a sudden urge to wake him. She contented herself with resting her cool palm for a moment on his hot, narrow forehead. He did not stir.

Toward the end she spoke to him very seriously about the danger he would be in at his public school. On no account whatsoever was he to return to the irregular practices of the past. She made him read and re-read the relevant passages in *Green's*. If he found it impossible, he was to speak to the Matron. Public schools would certainly have special remedies. Much frightened, Newman promised.

The end of term ran out as silently and as unsatisfactorily as the last grains of sand from an hourglass. As usual, he left her room without saying a word. The next morning he had gone in the second coach. She was too busy to say goodbye.

During the long summer holiday, Dorothy found Newman constantly occurring to her. When she had known she would continue treating him, it had been possible to put him from her mind. Now she would wake in the hot night, that first terrible scene suddenly vivid before her again. Random phrases from *Green's* repeated themselves endlessly in her head: 'mental dissolution – disease of the testicles – adult impotence – pallid appearance – sluggish and enfeebled – total degeneration. . . .'

Her worries did not lessen when she was fully occupied at Danehurst Court again. In fact the familiar surroundings – the surgery where she had spoken so earnestly, the volumes of *Green's*, his old dormitory, his cubicle in the changing rooms – repeatedly reminded her of him and intensified her anxiety.

She found her work increasingly unsatisfying. Her battle with Newman's disease had had an heroic quality. Her sacrifice for him – the supreme sacrifice – had somehow symbolised and been the jewel of her whole life of sacrifice at the school. Now it was all monochrome, drab and trivial.

There was no longer that rich certainty and satisfaction at the core to soothe the many exasperations.

Not that she had less energy. On the contrary, all her old restlessness returned, and she once more woke early each morning spurred by a hectic but vague expectation that something momentous was going to happen.

The first letter arrived in the fourth week of term.

'Dear Matron, how are you. I am not very well. You know my illness, it has got much worse. I try and try to stop it but I can't. Once I did but it happened by itself in the night. I'm so frightened that all those other things will happen. Please what shall I do.'

This piteous cry, which wrung her heart with its anxiety clear in every ink-blotched line, was signed S.M.Newman.

She wrote back at once. It was serious, and he must try as hard as he possibly could. He must go *at once* to the Matron there and explain his trouble.

Over the next few weeks it became clear that Newman wasn't receiving her letters or was ignoring them. He wrote again, and then again. Dorothy grew increasingly worried and finally, when a letter came which seemed to suggest he was planning to run away, frantic.

She couldn't sleep. She could imagine him swollen with the disease, the maddened excesses that were destroying him. It was scandalous. Obviously, from *Green's* and Mr Edwards, this was a fairly common illness at public schools. They would have not just medicines, but ointments, drugs such as she'd seen used to calm patients at the Norwich General.

She would write to the Matron herself. No, better still, she would pretend Jessie was ill and go herself. It would be easier to explain than to write. She would stay at a nearby hotel. She would see Newman. . . .

And then, on the very morning she was about to go to Mr Edwards, another letter arrived from Newman.

He couldn't speak to his own Matron because she'd left. The school Matron was very strict . . .

At once – it was as though the sky had split across, soaring open, letting in light, a feeling of lightness – Dorothy saw everything clear. She would apply for the post of a matron there herself! Jessie could take her place at Danehurst.

It solved everything. Newman's disease. Jessie's unhappiness. Dave's future. She and Jessie had often wondered how they would afford a public school. Mr Edwards had said a scholarship was unlikely. Now she saw they could get him to public school the same way they'd got him to Danehurst Court.

Jessie's reply came a week later. She'd do it. She felt she could. It would be a relief to get away from the doodlebugs. But above all, she'd do anything to be near Dave. And old Mrs Martel was getting to be so *difficult*.

The moment she'd read it, Dorothy flew to her table. No sense in burning her bridges behind her till she was sure of those in front. Carefully she penned a letter rehearsed all week to the bursar of Sherborne. Understood there were vacancies . . . well qualified . . . experience . . . husband in the RAF. . . .

If she hurried she'd catch the afternoon post. There were some envelopes in her pigeon hole and she shoved them into her mac pocket as she hurried through the side door.

The post box was a mile uphill, where the school drive met the road to Ravenstonedale. In her impatience, she almost ran.

It was a cold blustery day, the sky all grey but with big energetic clouds discernible, thrusting south. Dorothy felt calmer than for weeks, yet also a yearning to resume her service. South, south, the song of her sacrifice was carrying her south. At the post box, her hair blowing, looking out over the deep beck-cut valley, across the wildness of Langdale Fell to the distant bulk of the Boar, she felt something that was almost exultation.

She reached into her pocket and pulled out the letter, and with it came the others from her pigeon hole. One was from Norwich about her coupon entitlement. The second was from her mother. The last was from Newman.

'Dear Matron, it's all right now you needn't worry after all. A new Matron arrived and I told her about my illness. I told her how you cured it and she was really kind. She is doing the same cure so at last I'm all right again. I am also in the Junior XV for my house which is quite good.'

Dorothy read the letter and then very slowly put it back

in her pocket. She looked across to the Boar, its blunt top swept by the clouds as they came lower. Without looking at it, she tore up her letter to the bursar and let the pieces fall into the wind, which carried the fluttering fragments away over the beck far below.

As she walked back down to the bleak square grey school-house, she suddenly heard, as though it were someone else, someone just behind her, the high sound of her sobs, they too instantly torn away from her by the wind.

The Centre of the Universe is 18 Baedekerstrasse

[1]

Dr Heinrich Gottlieb eased himself through the door of his flat, crossed the narrow hall and stepped into the private lift which opened automatically to receive him. In his right hand he held eight flimsy sheets of paper covered in a wavery script.

He always felt he was escaping from a refrigerator when he left his flat. How would his American friends put it – 'Fleeing the ice-box'.

His mouth began to water as the lift door closed. Breakfast had been a postage stamp of dry rye crispbread and a glass of ice-cold lemon juice, but it was fear as much as hunger that caused the involuntary spasm of his large empty stomach as the lift fell nineteen storeys. 'My test will come at height,' he used to say.

There were only two security guards waiting for him, a fact which confirmed what the Terrorist Bureau had recently predicted – a temporary decline in world terrorist activity. The car, however, showed that the relaxation was in reality slight. It was the large armour-plated 15.6-litre Hover Mercedes, with its dome of mauve-tinted bullet-proof glass. Heinrich Gottlieb settled his 152.6 kilos luxuriously into the green leather back seat. At fifty-six, his great size made him appear younger, lines and wrinkles finding little purchase on his face; it also conferred anonymity. All fat men look alike, and the plump stereotype of cheeks and chins had frequently, in earlier years, allowed Dr Gottlieb (cunningly avoiding the

131

VIP lounge) to pass unrecognised through an airport seething with aroused reporters.

As the car moved forward, he looked for a moment, expressionless, at the limp sheets still gripped in his hand. Then he thrust them into his inside pocket and swung over his knees the walnut wood panel crowded with his breakfast. Gottlieb inspected this closely. Some days before, a new cook at the Centre, for some reason not fully briefed as to his tastes, had served *a boiled egg!* Gottlieb had almost thrown it out of the window. The cook's superior had been severely reprimanded. Eggs were his Achilles' heel as an eater. As a baby a positive allergy had been diagnosed after weeks of inexplicable screaming and diarrhoea. He had not, except by accident, had an egg since. But, just in case he couldn't resist the Béarnaise, as sometimes happened, he always carried a box of large, almost golf-ball sized cow-bile pills, which usually seemed, as the English put it, 'to do the trick'.

Today all was well: liver sausage, salami, cervelat sausage, bierwurst, cheese, a pot of cherry jam, a honeycomb, a dozen fresh warm rolls, butter still glistening with dew, a pint of cream and the large white jug of hot coffee.

Few people were up in Lucerne at seven o'clock on that early April morning. The Mercedes moved swiftly and massively down nearly empty streets while Gottlieb munched and noted the delicate but slightly decadent discolouring of the cherry blossom through the armour of the dome.

Inside the Mercedes looking out at tinted Lucerne; Lucerne looking down on the gliding black blob; Lucerne to the Confederation, to the state of Europe, and back again. Car total, car relative; Lucerne total, Lucerne relative; back and forth flipped masticating Gottlieb in a series of almost instantaneously alternating stereoscopic perspectives that could be compared to the effect of looking at a rectangle three-dimensionally drawn and bringing the centre corner now forward, now back. Forward, back, forward. It was something Gottlieb had discovered at the age of four, and which, with gurgling pleasure, the already plump little fellow had extended to hexagon, decahedron and eventually to several skeletal polyhedral playthings lovingly supplied by his mathematically inclined papa.

132

Soon they were on the Autobahn which skirts the city, and ten minutes later were being checked through Gate 4 in the ten-metre high perimeter fence – third in the screen of five defences which ringed the World Computer Control Centre, although the first visible one. Almost at once they came upon the latest addition to the WCCC – the vast new buildings which would house the stretched version of the Aries 3000. This was capable of over a billion computations in parallel, each in a billionth of a second, and with memory bank facilities which meant, once they were harnessed, that the Centre's storage and retrieval potential would be approaching infinity. This was the twelfth new computer complex which had become necessary since Gottlieb had taken over fifteen years before in 2007, and he was pleased to see that workmen were already arriving. It was important that the stretched version of the Aries 3000 should come on stream within the next seven months. From outside, the dome of the speeding Merc-edes was an impenetrable blank, but guessing it might contain their Director-General, several workmen waved. Invisible, Gottlieb waved back.

And then, as they came over the lip of the valley, there was the Centre itself. Familiar as it was (or perhaps partly because it was so familiar) Gottlieb could never suppress a slight lift of the heart at this view, a feeling of elation, even love. So must have felt some German Count or Herzog in the eighteenth century when, descending the Harz mountains towards Brunswick, he first glimpsed his domains spread out below him. The World Computer Control Centre already rivalled in size the vast United Nations Organisation at Addis Ababa. In terms of power and prestige there might appear to be no comparison. The Director-General of the United Nations, his good friend Sven Haarlem, the brilliant Swedish negro, was one with presidents and popes, a man of world stature; the fat figure in the Mercedes received the attention equivalent perhaps to that given a moderately well-estab-lished millionaire. Yet a single morning in Lucerne could result in more effective action than a whole year at Addis. Every departure Dr Heinrich Gottlieb made from the WCCC's private airport – unheralded, untelevised, unremembered – was potentially momentous. Those who understood the realities of the international balance knew that he had become, in the last fifteen years, one of the three or four most powerful men in the world.

For this reason, however confident the Terrorist Bureau, security never relaxed at the Centre. The Mercedes had already been screened three times since entering the perimeter fence by ground radar which required three different response signals, changed each day, before the car could proceed.

Only once, in 2006, had terrorists come close to penetrating the defence systems. Then three low-flying, Mach 4 bombers had passed the first barrier 2000 kilometres from Lucerne. They had been destroyed by rockets seven minutes later as they approached the 500-kilometre defence ring. So now, entering his *Schloss*, Count Gottlieb had to present his identity wrist panel before the glass doors would part; and present it again at the lift.

'*Guten Morgen, Herr Doktor.*'

Gottlieb smiled at the chief of his three private secretaries. Frau Schmidt had worked with him for twenty years. Like him, she was large, a mountain of calm competence and loyalty.

'I will see if the Council has assembled,' she said, walking to the door. She spoke German as they usually did together.

'One moment, Frau Schmidt.' Heinrich put his hand into his breast pocket and withdrew the eight flimsy sheets of paper he had distastefully thrust there earlier in the morning. At the sight of his wife's handwriting – at once precise and distracted – he felt for an instant the touch of an ice cube at his heart. 'I would like you to file this please.'

Frau Schmidt had noticed, and for once misinterpreted, his expression. '*Ausserordentlich?*' she asked.

Dr Gottlieb smiled a little painfully, and then to show he was not unduly disturbed by this latest manifestation of his wife's madness, and also to indicate that the instruction was a joke, he answered in English. '*Most* sensitive,' he said.

Unfortunately Frau Schmidt missed the humorous nuance – although it was an habitual one with Dr Gottlieb. An unhappy suspicion that her eldest son, adored sixteen-year-old Adolph, was homosexual had been abruptly confirmed the evening before by an appalling scene glimpsed through the small gap left by his indiscreetly unfastened door. Her normal calm and acumen were temporarily suspended. On her way to the Council Chamber she filed the eight pieces of paper '*Most Sensitive*' and not, as Heinrich had intended, '*Personal*'. By such tiny errors, worlds are destroyed.

[2]

When she had gone, Heinrich settled himself behind his desk. This moment, waiting for the problems of the day, confident in his strength to solve them, was one he enjoyed.

He stretched out his hand and moved the large ebony blotter a millimetre to the left. His desk was rather cluttered: on the right, next to the blotter, there was a large green box of the luscious Swiss mint *glaçons;* resting on the square of green leather in the middle was the pile of plain white paper for notes, also the silver fountain pen for making them (both old-fashioned luxuries he allowed himself as an alternative to voice input); on the left a row of heat sensor buttons which, touched, would bring into view a variety of electronic aids; a pile of digests from various bureaux; the small round crystal ball he had had since Leipzig days.

Suddenly, immersed in these objects, Heinrich had the hallucinatory sensation that he was actually down among them. For an instant it was as though, a centimetre high, he walked between them – the gap between the *glaçons* and blotter a road, the box of mints itself a cliff, a building, the soft green leather a field. He was acutely aware of the size and the architecture of the structures on his desk, of the changing views and perspectives, the altering relationships, as he passed by them.

The next instant he was back, his normal size. It was an experience he had had many times as a child (out in imagination running beside the train, into the tunnel in the pattern of the nursery rug, the cars on his eiderdown); but it was one which, middle-aged, he could still repeat at will. No doubt it derived from his childhood in a more profound way, this ability to put himself on a level with things, to see their significance in their own terms and also, through himself, their significance in relation to other quite different objects or events. An only child, born when his mother was forty, he had had the concentrated devotion of both his parents. From the start, the world had fallen into a well-ordered, interconnected whole with himself at its centre (well-ordered, interconnected – also clean. After Heinrich, Frau Gottlieb's passion was the scrubbing brush). And it was a living, friendly, personal world: potatoes on the plate clamoured to be eaten, but had to share the privilege with equally eager meat; flowers, trees, insects could all be talked to; even the lonely grains of earth were rescued from the hall and lovingly reunited with their brothers in the flower beds outside.

Probably this is all common enough. But in Gottlieb it developed into a phenomenal ability to relate the apparently unrelateable. At Harvard, Cambridge, Massachusetts, he read History, Psychology and Philosophy, getting Honours in each. One answer in his History Finals alone (an interesting explanation of the breakdown of order after war; Gottlieb analysed the interlocking love relationships in an armed force and predicted, on its dissolution, the usual mayhem, but on a vast scale, which follows the end of an affair) so struck the long-sterile professor who corrected his paper that he purloined the idea and made it the subject of his last and most successful book. Heinrich (something of a teenage prodigy) was seventeen at the time. Nor was his grasp confined to this planet – already he was reaching towards the stars. At Leipzig (now twenty), where he read Quantum Physics and Astronomy, and was later Professor of Mathematics for three years, his paper on sunspots and their effect on birth-rate was revolutionary; its implications have still not been fully worked through. In some respects those years of speculation and discovery were, intellectually, the most exciting of his life.

It was his enormous spread of knowledge, as well as an international reputation (if a discreet one) which made Dr Gottlieb, now aged thirty-three and at Cambridge, England, a natural choice in 1999 for the Head of the Cultural and Scientific Council at the UN in Addis Ababa. No sooner had he arrived there, however, than his interest, like that of the rest of the world, was focussed onto an old problem suddenly become catastrophic.

Five events signalled and then became the catastrophe. For some time high altitude sub- and supersonic transport, together with the atmospheric concentration of propellants used in the humble aerosol (the deadly chlorofluoromethanes), had been thinning the protective ozone layer which cocoons the earth. The consequent rise in cancers, particularly of the skin, had somehow been tolerated – perhaps because they primarily attacked the pale-skinned Anglo-Saxon women sunbathing in South Africa, Australia and New Zealand. But by mid-1999 a new and terrifying effect of the vanishing cocoon manifested itself: thousands of babies – now scattered at random across the planet – were born revoltingly mutated.

At about the same time, radiation at lethal levels was detected in the Gulf Stream. Its origin – the enormous and unstable stores of nuclear waste down the eastern seaboard of the United States.

A new study in America (but rapidly confirmed for all the world's major cities) showed that the heavy metals – cadmium, beryllium, antimony, mercury and lead – were implicated in over half the deaths in New York. Another study published that same year revealed that cancer was increasing across middle America at an annual rate of ten per cent.

And for the first time since 1945 the world witnessed nuclear warfare – albeit only on a 'tactical' scale. The Sino-Russian war broke out in January; followed swiftly in February by the nuclear conflagration, long-predicted, in the Middle East. The results were so devastating that both wars ended within a month – but the radiation effects were to remain for years.

The thinning ozone, now much intensified by nuclear-spawned nitrogen oxides in the stratosphere, brought heat problems. The effects had been felt before, but once again it was the scale that changed. Three years' drought had led to famine across the entire Indian sub-continent. In 1999 the famine riots (now reaching appalling proportions) were complicated by sudden floods. Cholera-carrying sewage swirled in the cities, and the disease spread out into the villages. Transport broke down. Disease- and hunger-crazed

137

mobs – impervious to small-arms fire – broke into the great silos which had been painstakingly erected at strategic points to store seed grain. The grain had been dressed with mercury. Deaths – hideous, painful, lingering – were estimated at one and a half million.

The world reacted in a spontaneous, frenzied spasm of revulsion. It was not the first time it had united to fight its own filth, but it was the most determined. In the mighty act of purgation all high-altitude supersonic transport was banned and the flight of other planes severely restricted. Aerosols were banned. The thousands of mutated monsters were painlessly put to sleep and their families compensated (though many survived, concealed by a mindless mother love). National armies were banned and nuclear stockpiles destroyed (the swift rise of terrorist groups and small mercenary armies, often nationally supported, made this a move of mixed worth). All forms of nuclear power plant down the eastern US were closed down while, at a cost of billions of dollars, their waste was re-stored.

But it was clear that something more permanent was necessary. During the late eighties there had been considerable progress in pollution control. National Computer Control Centres, made possible by the still-evolving micro-electronics, had been set up to co-ordinate and evaluate highly efficient national monitoring systems. National was, of course, the trouble. Where the stakes were sufficiently high, warnings could be ignored. Most of the large airline countries had been well aware of the dispersion of the ozone layer; as had the US of the radiation leaks; both had grounds for hoping the problems would disappear. And in fact Mother Ocean, tolerating even the worst excesses of her children, did just in time allow the polluted waters of the Gulf Stream to dissipate into the vasty deep.

The ozone layer, alas, took a good deal longer to reform; but it was the continued appearance of mutated foetuses, combined with a great many other minor, and often not so minor eco-disasters, which proved the spur and provided the authority for the World Computer Control Centre.

This was started early in 2001. By 2002 it was the automatic recipient of anything registered and recorded by the National

Computer Control Centre monitoring systems – the recipient, indeed, of facts obtained on pollution in any way at all. By radar, super-conducting cable and laser through glass fibre, by word of mouth and diplomatic bag, from giant satellites out in space and massive walled balls of instruments suspended six kilometres down in the ocean trenches, even to a humble thermometer bobbing on the banks of the river Wornitz, information poured in in an ever-swelling torrent – hundreds, then thousands, then tens of thousands, then billions of items a day – into the gobbling computers of Lucerne.

National governments, or the councils of great confeder-ations like Europe or South America, retained only one form of control. Where facts touched on areas close to their vital interests they were allowed the benefit of secrecy. Such infor-mation was codified and its real content could be revealed only to those with access to the various categories of secrecy – *Near Sensitive, Sensitive, More Sensitive, Most Sensitive*. Those so privileged were extremely few. *Most Sensitive*, for instance, was only for the eyes of the Director-General himself.

Very quickly the WCCC discovered something, always known, indeed obvious, but up till then insufficiently appreci-ated. The NCCCs' monitoring devices (upon which the WCCC to a large extent still relied) had been excellent (when not ignored) as warning systems: growth in river-acid content here, a rise in sulphur count or acid rain there, the gradual extinction of *Smerinthus occellatus* – the eyed hawk moth of Europe.

But by their nature, the NCCCs could not detect relation-ships more widely separated in space or time. Within a year the World Computer Control Centre at Lucerne, like some electronic Harvey, had begun to reveal the full extent of the circulatory system of the world. There was a sudden increase of polluted fish on the markets of Hong Kong. No cause could be found by the highly efficient Hong Kong Computer Control officers. But it was noticed at Lucerne that the rise exactly matched the rise in oil spillage off the Great Barrier Reef to the south. Research showed that the triglyceride compound exuded by the brain coral of the Reef absorbed the oil from the spillages, this compound in turn was eaten by the butterfly fish who flitted so prettily down the corridors and in and out the alcoves of that 2000-kilometre-long Versailles. Their lives were shortened, but not before their oily tissues had been absorbed by the (misnamed) migratory bream who only came to the Reef to breed, later returning to their feeding grounds far in the north-east, where they were trawled by Japanese fishing fleets, frozen, and sold in Hong Kong.

This was a problem easily solved. Expensive – but much less so than, say, the elimination of acid rain during the early 1990s. Yet often an outflow of mercury at one point, or the harvesting of seaweed at another, as well as affecting a country many thousands of kilometres away, was the life-blood of a whole community, an entire industry. It could be immensely costly to put right, despite access to a vast international fund set up for just this purpose. It could also be very difficult. If an industry knew its source of raw material was to be closed it could be troublesome. From the start the effectiveness of the WCCC depended on secrecy.

Secrecy – and, later, blackmail. At first, while nuclear and cosmic radiation levels remained high, while the memory of that terrible year, 1999, was still fresh, it was enough to threaten exposure to the world community. But as the ozono-sphere reformed, as the climate returned to normal, as the effects of fall-out over Russia, China and in the Middle East diminished, as the cancer and mutation figures stabilised, sterner measures became necessary to force governments to act.

Heinrich Gottlieb's position as Head of the Scientific and Cultural Council at the UN automatically qualified him for a seat on the five-man Executive Central Cabinet. For the first time in his life he had access to the levers of world power. It was during his years at Addis that Gottlieb revealed two qualities hitherto unsuspected. His enormous capacity for work, his skill as a negotiator, the great range and quickness of his mind – all these he had shown at Harvard, Leipzig and Cambridge. At Addis, however, he revealed an ability to be ruthless and, even more unexpected, a pleasure in the exercise of power. It was Gottlieb who, successfully, urged non-inter-ference on the International Monetary Fund (by then long a

140

part of the UN) when the vast commercial empires of the Arab states began to totter in the mid-nineties, and was therefore largely instrumental in their collapse. There were other incidents (one could cite his attitude to minority groups in Asia, or the stand he took in the South African crisis of 2001).

Pleasure is perhaps too strong a word to use about his attitude to power. Any far-sighted and intelligent man is irked to see the wrong solutions applied to important problems; power allowed Gottlieb to apply the correct solution, and thus was no more than a necessary adjunct to his position. It was a sense of fitness he felt rather than an active enjoyment in the imposition of will.

Nevertheless, like most people in authority, his position occasionally allowed him to procure mundane improvements or concessions which would have been difficult for the ordinary citizen. Just recently, for example, although there was a more than adequate fire escape, he had asked the city council of Lucerne to fasten the drain pipes of their penthouse at the top of 18 Baedekerstrasse more securely to the walls and provide convenient hand grips. He had a fear that one day fire would cut him off from the regulation steel stairway and he would be consumed.

A trivial incident. But it was his ability to exercise power, together with his ruthlessness and courage, which, when the byzantine Dr Bjorg finally retired in 2007, gained Heinrich the supreme position of Director-General of the World Computer Control Centre.

These were not, however, the qualities which at first made the greatest impact. His contribution was unique and revolutionary. His predecessor, with apparent commonsense, had only computed the data which might, however remotely, be supposed to have some relevance to pollution; the data, that is to say, that had once been dealt with by the National Computer Control Centres. Recent developments in computer technology – where what could once be held on the surface of the old-fashioned 'silicon chip' could now be stored several thousand times over on a unit no larger than the point of a pin – made far more numerous and complex calculations possible. But Dr Gottlieb himself was the significant change.

141

He brought to bear the mind that had realised how in the most potent expression of its power to hate, in war, mankind also involved a signal expression of its power to love; the mind that could relate into architectural significance the haphazard arrangement of objects on a desk top. Gottlieb knew that everything was related to everything and that the apparently windy:

BURNAMDAH BURNAMIDAM BURNAD BURNAMUDACHYTE
BURNASYA BURNAMADAYA BURNAMEVA AVASHISHYADE

of the East was solid scientific fact.

Thus the WCCC, under its huge, imperturbable new Director-General, demanded and slowly began to get (slowly because there was considerable opposition and ridicule to overcome) every known fact and statistic, whether it was to do with pollution or not, from every country in the world: road casualties in Rumania, rainfall in Ireland, the height of the tides at Brighton, the depth of the sea off Cape Cod, moonquakes; failed BAs (Oxford, Cantab, England), successful suicides, button production in Detroit, confirmed alcoholics in Moscow, in Rhodes, in medicine, the daily mean temperature in the Kasbah of Tangier. And each fact, each figure, each item, was computed against every other fact, figure and item; those already received against those just arrived, and all re-fed and re-computed to eternity, so that fact begat fact begat fact, statistic spawned statistic, combination became theoretically infinite, and the whole recordable movement of the world, its every incident and interaction, more numerous than the particles in a cosmic dust cloud, were whirled and whirled together in the attempt to find significance, relevance and causality.

The work at the WCCC was rapidly increased by many hundreds of degrees of magnitude. Computer capacity was doubled, trebled, quadrupled; then multiplied itself by parallel orders of magnitude; it was in fact several years before it could start to cope adequately with even a fraction of the information deluge. Nor was the opposition and ridicule confined to the outside world. The Centre itself came near to revolt. There was talk of megalomania, even insanity. How on earth, asked overworked and exasperated scientists, could Kleenex consumption in Corsica be related to volcanic activity in Tierra del Fuego? Dr Gottlieb's great strength was that he knew it might be. In fact, in this instance, it was. A month after volcanic activity in Tierra del Fuego reached a peak, imports of tissues peaked in Corsica. A link was found in a newly reported stratospheric air flow, downthrusting in the Corsican area with its burden of fine volcanic dust. But the simple reporting to a single centre of world volcanic activity revealed for the first time a cyclic pattern to eruptions, conforming, it was assumed, to massive movements in the magma. Thus whole new spheres of activity were opened to the Centre, new levers of power revealed. It became, within rough limits, possible to give warnings of volcanic activity all round the world, warnings which, compared to the Corsican situation, were often of life-saving importance to those living on the slopes of an imminent explosion – though, of course, the Kleenex importers of Corsica were grateful too.

It was the astonishing success of Gottlieb's move which ensured his survival. Even in the early years, dozens of similar instances appeared. Tornadoes in one country had an industrial source in another. Penguin deaths in the Arctic matched the earlier receding of winter ice around Archangel. Both could be traced to rising lead production in northern Russia.

Nor was the work of the Centre confined to the present or the future. Setting up a small section to indulge in something he called 'Hindsight Control', Gottlieb showed how much more effective a WCCC would have been in the past had his theories been followed. One example: had the disappearance of anchovy-supporting sea currents off South America been noted earlier the collapse of the fertiliser market in Europe might have been foreseen a year in advance, and steps could have been taken to prevent it.

Of course, like all successful intellectual movements, the seeds had been long planted. As early as the 1970s it had been observed that, despite enormous variations in the sun's heat output and drastic changes in the composition of the atmosphere, the earth's temperature had not varied by more than two or three degrees over three and a half billion years.

There was already a sense here of unity, of self-regulation – indeed of something almost alive.

Curiously enough, this spawned a 'heresy'. Interference was quite wrong. Pollution must be used. It was one of life's most ancient processes, the use of toxic wastes – as micro-organisms had evolved which could convert mercury and other poisonous elements to their volatile (and so harmlessly dispersing) methyl derivatives. Cow dung was another favourite example.

This nonsense was swept away by the 1999 catastrophes. But the philosophic ground had been prepared. Gottlieb brought a grasp intensely practical, graphic (even, almost, coarse. Naturally, the heresy revived. 'So?' replied Gottlieb, before embarking on more reasoned refutation. 'I ask you – imagine *Himalayas* of cow dung'). He brought also the extent of his intellectual reach. He did not even intend to confine himself to the world. Already he had plans afoot to feed information about the solar system and the stars. He was able to comprehend an eco-system of the universe.

And yet this grand design, Einstein-like in its scope, so very much of the two centuries he bridged as to subject, was basically an eighteenth-century one. At its heart were the concepts of *balance* and *harmony;* the eighteenth-century assumptions, derived from Plato, that everyone and every-thing had a proper function and a proper sphere, and that provided the function was correctly performed, and the sphere kept to, all would be well.

'Man has put the world out of kilter,' Dr Gottlieb used to say, employing one of the esoteric (sometimes actually incorrect) Englishisms with which he liked, in the interest of humour, to sprinkle his conversation, 'it is up to us at the WCCC to put it right.'

[3]

It was to this giant and genial figure, now, in 2022, at the plenitude of his power, most of the events just described long years in the past, that Frau Schmidt shortly returned. Her mind still tortured by visions of her son's pumping posterior, she felt unable to indulge in their usual moment of chit-chat, and simply handed him the agenda and said the Council was ready.

Because its origins had been scientific, and because scientists are the reverse of formal, the sixteen-man Council made only a token gesture of rising when their Director-General came in.

'Good morning gentlemen.' Dr Gottlieb waved those who had half-risen back into their seats. 'I do not think this will detain us long.'

The agenda was certainly undemanding. The only codified matter a *Near Sensitive,* the rest routine: a report on the new computer complex he had passed that morning, a report on the progress being made with extending the WCCC's own monitoring systems (a subject dear to Gottlieb's heart), a discussion as to what profile the WCCC should adopt at the UN meeting on world terrorism next week.

The event which might have been tricky – the *Near Sensitive* – was also fairly simple. For twelve months the rainfall in Cambodia and Laos had been below average, while that in adjoining Vietnam had been high. This could happen naturally, but recently minute traces of silver nitrate had begun to show up in the river mouths of Vietnam. She had been seeding the rain clouds; in effect 'stealing' the rain from Laos and Cambodia, an action forbidden since 2002. A discreet visit from the WCCC seemed indicated.

Only one matter was in any way out of the ordinary. Over the last two months there had occurred a small group of incidents around the world which, though they looked as though they might be pollution-based, were as yet unexplained: some large oil slicks in the Pacific, increase in penguin mortality in the Arctic and Antarctic, cholera in Sicily, a small increase in cancer cases across middle America. Events of this order. The usual procedure in such cases was to extend the area of computerisation, activate more memory banks and so on. Gottlieb sanctioned this. It was only a speck on the horizon, a cloud no bigger than a man's hand, and he forgot it immediately.

He did so the more easily because he had decided to go to Vietnam himself. It was a matter which could easily have been handled by Ken Dunn, the pleasant Australian in charge of the Asian Bureau. But interfering with natural processes – rainfall, corn yield, the sea – upset most obviously that 'natural' balance which was at the heart of Gottlieb's philosophy. He often attended to matters of this sort himself. Also, as a once delicate trouble spot, both politically and ecologically speaking, he liked to put in an unexpected appearance there now and again.

There were more personal reasons. The *Pho* of the region was one of Dr Heinrich's favourite dishes. A light, transparent soup made from beef, a veal bone, onions, bay leaf, salt, pepper and a small teaspoon of muoc-mam – a fragrant concentrate of the brine exuding from decaying fish which, properly, took six years to reach maturity. At the mention of Vietnam, the rumble of his stomach had been audible half-way down the Council table. Finally, he felt the need – seldom indulged – to be away for a few days from his wife.

Heinrich's marriage. Briefly.

He had met Angela Parson while at Cambridge, England. Tall, spare, strong, she had then, a post-graduate of twenty-seven, the looks of a youth of eighteen; she reminded him of Tacitus' description of the Cimbri – tall in stature, with wild blue eyes, fair skin, flaming red hair. In her case, the hair was golden red and some of the flame had entered her cheeks in two glowing circles of pure health. Her quick tense English mind was as good as a man's in discussion; she enjoyed drinking, too (another characteristic Tacitus had noted in the Cimbri) and could sit downing pints for hours while Heinrich discoursed to his pupils in The Mill. She spoke fluent German, was an excellent cook, and, like his mother, meticulously clean (a tissue always at the ready). Above all, the pale sword of her boy-like body stirred the still almost virginal thirty-one-year-old Heinrich to his plump roots. They were married in the autumn of 1998.

Fairly soon things ceased to be idyllic. To concentrate only on the main issue, he soon found that her drinking was a great deal more than convivial, the message conveyed by cheeks the reverse of healthy. Marriage brought a swift relaxation of control, a handing over of responsibility, a desperate

146

bid for help. It was one summer morning, nine months after they were married; Angela was out of the room, the larder out of coffee, when Heinrich reached across the breakfast table for her teapot, poured himself a generous cup and found it full of sherry.

The course of the alcoholic has been so well charted it scarcely requires repetition. Heinrich followed his wife, pursued her along the path: Angela smelling incredibly of peppermint mid-morning; Angela abusive in restaurants, sliding under tables, unconscious in lavatories; Angela with neuritis, with delirium tremens; Angela hiding bottles, destroying medicines or drinking despite them (Angela vomiting); Angela drunk. They ceased to entertain and could hardly go out; whole areas of influence were denied him. It is an added tribute to Gottlieb's genius that during his rise to eminence at Cambridge and Addis he had, in place of an actively assisting wife, a totally destructive and hindering force as helpmate.

But after twelve years she was 'cured'. After twelve years of valium, librium, tryptizol, vitamin B12, hypnosis, aversion therapy, chromosome therapy, acupuncture and goodness knows how many other therapies, she reached the fragile security of total abstinence. Even a liqueur chocolate was fatal (this had been proved).

Heinrich's life became no easier. Neuroses and obsessions, for years buried in the sea of alcohol, began to emerge like jagged rocks as that sea subsided. Or not so much rocks, as phantoms from a dispersing fog; no sooner was one revealed than another appeared behind it and took its place. She became terrified of heights ('I shall throw myself out'). When Gottlieb, himself nervous four foot up a ladder, moved them to a commodious basement, she became claustrophobic; a fear she managed to combine with agoraphobia, refusing to go out. She heard voices. She imagined plots. Her dependence on Gottlieb, on his patience, his kindness, his listening ear, had over the years become total; yet her hatred had become total too. She would nag him, blame him, gradually inflame herself and at last embark on long raging attacks, screaming at him hysterically, blaming him for her mother, her childhood, shrieking at him with sustained fury, so that he would sometimes leave 18 Baedekerstrasse feeling that he had been steeped in some venomous fluid – his skin and brains glowing – and would sit fiercely in the Mercedes until, by a prodigious exercise of will, there would fall, like a thunderclap, an uncanny calm.

This was not the only talent marital adversity brought out. At first the repressed rage, the enforced control (no doubt half the trouble) had driven him to excel in the highly competitive worlds of the university and then international politics. But as the years passed he developed, as well as that unshakeable calm, an enormous patience, an adroitness in negotiation and discussion which no amount of bluster or anger could ruffle, and an ability to persuade and convince without angering his opponent. It had not escaped his attention that Socrates too, and no doubt for the same reason, shared some of these qualities.

With the years, the rages and obsessions diminished. Slowly, the icy indifference of the refrigerator settled about them. They seldom spoke; words, and finally thoughts and feelings – at any rate as far as Heinrich was concerned – dying, dead, in the cold air.

Why had he married her? Why did he stay with her? Sexual passions of the past, though acknowledged, often seem inexplicable. Angela Gottlieb's golden red hair was now grey and thinning, the blood vessels round the fiery blue eyes had been permanently damaged, the blade-like boyish beauty had been replaced by some haggard warrior on the fringes of the Bayeux tapestry. But the reason he stayed was simple. The strong were put on earth to help the weak, the sane to succour the insane. As well as that, the pain he had suffered in his marriage compensated for, indeed allowed him to have, the successes and satisfactions of his job. The concept of balance was as crucial a key to his private as to his public life.

It was a balance that had become increasingly difficult to keep of late. After years of failure, Angela at last appeared to have found a psychiatrist with whom she could make 'progress'. He was not one of the new chromosome- or chemico-therapists, but one of the few remaining old-fashioned 'analysts'. Dr Stephen Gabès, born and brought up in England, was the son of an Andalucian lawyer and an

Englishwoman. (His name was apparently pronounced 'Habeth', which for some reason Heinrich found irritating.)

Treatment had led to some rather distressing reactions in her behaviour. An old obsession had revived – one with housework and economy. She sacked all three servants including, to Heinrich's sadness, the cook, and insisted on doing the whole of 18 Baedekerstrasse herself. She accused him of accusing her of extravagance and that very morning had given him two months' shopping lists to keep and scrutinise. Worse than that, from Heinrich's point of view, was the stage Angela and Dr Gabès had reached in her analysis. Reliving, inch by inch, her entire development, they had arrived at the period of anorexia nervosa in her late teens (with sinking heart, Gottlieb seemed to remember that it was after that she had begun to drink). But, combining with her other economies (and actually contrary to a common pattern) the effect on her cooking had been most unpleasant. Dr Gottlieb's meals at home had become, quite frankly, absurd.

That night, as his plane and spirits soared above the lights of Lucerne, a well-stocked tray above his lap, he said to himself in his jocular English/American, 'Okay Saigon – here I come.' He almost fancied he could catch, across 8000 miles of land and sea, the beckoning, almost sexual scent rising from a steaming bowl of *Pho*.

[4]

During the spring the cloud no bigger than a man's hand grew slightly larger – say to the size of a single outstretched arm. The significance of what was happening went unrecognised, and this because of an as yet unnoticed peculiarity. A pattern of pollution-caused disaster was usually quickly discernible because it persisted until the cause was removed. But these recent disasters appeared to cease of their own accord – to be replaced by others. The cholera in Sicily, the small rise in cancer in middle America, the dead penguins in the Arctic, faded as abruptly as they had arrived. Instead, there was a flurry of high heavy metal counts in China, together with meningitis in Ethiopia, a further fall in the blue

149

whale count and a dozen other apparently unrelated but possibly man-caused events of a similar nature. Then these too were replaced. This continued throughout spring into summer.

The WCCC was not unduly worried, though perhaps there was some surprise that not one of the incidents could be pinned down hard and fast to any particular pollutant or band of pollutants. But as Dr Gottlieb often pointed out, since its initial purpose had been to save the earth from its own excreta, there was an inherent tendency at the Centre to assume all the world's ills were caused by pollution. This was not so. Nevertheless, he agreed it was odd no correspondences of any significant sort, including with non-pollutant data, had turned up. Since his own arrival, the WCCC had achieved as much in charting the overall pattern and inter-relatedness of the world events as it had in combating pollution and Dr Gottlieb privately regarded this task as equally important.

However, his own routine still continued unchanged. The frigid return to the ice box each night was relieved at week-ends by visits to his small estate over the border near Furtwangen. Here he liked to play the Count in retreat. Pottering ponderously about with clippers, he would snip off dead rose heads; or spend an afternoon, sometimes with a colleague or two invited from the WCCC – his friend the Under Director-General Van Diemen, or Sir Edward Evans, head of the Diplomatic Bureau – watching his forester blow out old pine roots with dynamite. Here, too, he could eat. Angela disliked Furtwangen and in any case refused to leave 18 Baedeker-strasse. Heinrich was able to retain his chef. He saw his weekends, in part, as calorific preparations for the siege conditions pertaining at his house.

They were conditions which some months before had begun to change for Angela herself. Finally, having 'lived out' her anorexia with Dr Gabès, she had started to eat again. With envy, and some alarm, Heinrich had noticed sporadic little forays, like someone testing a newly-mended limb, into stews and roasts and puddings; she took to breakfast and once had an egg for tea. The alarm was unfounded. He was almost certain she hadn't started drinking and a quick but expert search – bottles in the lavatory cistern, hanging from a long string down the rubbish chute, buried in a window box – confirmed it.

By the end of August, the cloud had grown darker and more menacing, beginning to reveal the lineaments of a giant. It was causing concern at ever higher levels in the WCCC. The events themselves remained of the same order as before – the same indeed which the Centre was continuing to deal with as successfully as ever (and this was the reason, no doubt, why the world press had so far remained mercifully unaware of what was going on). But now they suddenly increased in intensity and magnitude: oil slicks and islands of floating dead fish kilometres in area, lead in the environment soaring worldwide. And then, as inexplicably, the lead count declined, the slicks dissipated. It was as though the earth were being teased by some new god, the malignant spirit of pollution.

Gottlieb was one of the few who remained undisturbed. If he felt anything, it was interest. He set up a special bureau to concentrate entirely on the problem, and ordered that work should be increased round the clock on the huge new Aries 3000 computer complex. It should come on stream in a matter of weeks or days instead of the month and a half on the schedule. A week later, leaving behind a deeply uneasy and perplexed Centre, he flew to Addis for a week.

Apart from the delicious Gräddvaffler (Swedish waffles made with a pint of sour cream and snow) with which his friend always regaled him, he wished to further a pet scheme of long-term importance. While effective power in the world community had passed during the last fifteen to twenty years to the WCCC, there had, oddly enough, been a corresponding increase in the publicity received by the UN. Its debates were televised worldwide, it had become the chief forum for often dramatic propaganda statements and alliances, its resolutions were as resounding as they had ever been – and as ineffective. Dr Gottlieb believed that these developments in the two organisations were probably interconnected and should now become formalised. It would be much easier for him to persuade some country to take a costly pollution-eliminating step – the closure as it might be of some tidal-cleansed fifty million dollar metal works – if in return he could promise a spectacular triumph at the United Nations. But it was while he was in the middle of discussions on this with Sven Haarlem (and incidentally half-way through a plate of the delectable little Kräftor, Swedish crayfish specially flown from Stockholm) that the giant struck. Dr Gottlieb was summoned back to Lucerne by a 9 p.m. (Ethiopian time) telephone call.

Four days after he had left, cancer and mutation counts had risen across China and down through Malaysia and Borneo; at the same time radiation had once again been detected in the Gulf Stream. These, it will be remembered, were, precisely, some of the ingredients of the Great Pollution Catastrophe of 1999. And, just as any marked similarity on the Wall Streets and Bourses of the world to the slumps of 1929 or 1991-93 produced immediate economic terror, so any resemblance to 1999 could produce pollution panic. Gottlieb returned to find the presidents of Europe and the US, the chairman of the USSR and Chairman Li Pi of China all demanding to see him, the world's press just getting wind of the crisis, and a thoroughly rattled Council.

He took control at once. He had a series of lengthy talks with the four world leaders most concerned in the Audio-Visual Summit Room, and then issued a press statement summarising what he had told them (' . . . in recent months a number of unexplained but possibly pollution-caused events . . . WCCC actively investigating . . . no resemblance to 1999 . . .').

Unfortunately this statement had the effect of inflaming world opinion, not calming it. Alerted to a 'number of possibly pollution-caused events', and helped by some leaks from the Centre itself, a few journalists discovered that the situation had in fact begun seven months before and had been increasing in seriousness ever since. The Centre was forced to reveal more details. The cancer, mutation and radiation counts inexplicably rose again (and, far more ominous, there were indications they might be about to appear in the US too). Within a week Gottlieb found himself the centre of a prairie fire.

Old wars revived. Although his genius for negotiation had enabled him to win over world leaders, he had been unable to charm whole congresses and parliaments. National (and continental) institutions had frequently resented the billions of dollars which the WCCC cost annually; and they had disliked even more the fact that responsibility for national monitoring systems, with their vast potential power, had passed to a body totally outside their control. Calls for the disbanding of the WCCC became violent again.

The world press and television (soon followed by the public itself, in marches, protests and mass meetings) became, with one or two exceptions, hysterical. There were rumours that the pollution came from outer space and was being used in this erratic way deliberately, to create chaos prior to invasion. Rival terrorist groups accused each other (there had recently been a large-scale theft of a cancer-causing virus – so far unused). Violence flared in the usual trouble spots.

Gottlieb remained completely unperturbed. The louder the cries from outside, the calmer he became. Nevertheless, after ten days, he decided he would leave 18 Baedekerstrasse for a while and stay permanently at the Centre. This was to a considerable extent because, for the first time ever, Baedeker-strasse was now besieged, night and day, by reporters and cameras. It was entirely against Gottlieb's principles either to receive publicity or usurp the function of his extremely competent press office. The vast concourse of reporters horrified the Terrorist Bureau. It had also upset Angela.

She herself was a minor reason for leaving. Two changes had taken place in her recently. The first, which he thought he welcomed, was that she had begun to talk to him more frequently. The second he found more upsetting. She was eating prodigiously. This was, she explained, a good sign. Dr Gabès and she were now re-enacting the long years of alcoholism; Gabès had, however, with great skill managed to substitute food for drink. Although this was certainly an improvement on that terrible and vanished period (and it had even begun to improve her appearance – the haggard lines were filling out, wind in the Bayeux sails), Heinrich thought he detected an element of aggression. He was able, gently, to suggest this. While she ate more and more his own meals grew, if possible, smaller. There was of course the usual cloak of his diet (both knew he had no intention of following it), but Angela agreed frankly he might well be right. Gabès wanted her, during this period, to turn her aggression

153

outward (alcoholism, self-destruction, had been aggression directed inward); unfortunately, apart from Gabès himself, Heinrich was the only outlet open to her. Heinrich saw the logic but, despite his concept of balance, found that this was a particularly trying time to watch his wife consume mountains of strudel or slabs of tender beef while, stomach rumbling, he had cabbage on toast or a saucer of old olives.

There were, however, two far more compelling reasons for the move.

The first was that Gottlieb found the problem absolutely fascinating. There had often been warnings that if the entire eco-system were thrown off balance then reactions could take place which might at first seem quite inexplicable (Johannson had recently published an interesting paper on *Spontaneous Pollution*). The gigantic new computer complex, the stretched Aries 3000, came on stream and was hurled into the fray – at a stroke raising the computing power of the WCCC by 1000 orders of magnitude. Now literally billions upon billions of facts could be computed against each other, against past patterns and future extrapolations, in a matter of seconds. Working continually, the scientists sleeping in relays, there were thousands of coincidences to be studied. Quite definite patterns had emerged in the sequence of apparently causeless catastrophes and every conceivable hypothesis had to be considered. Gottlieb felt he should be available at any moment. He hadn't enjoyed himself so much since Leipzig days.

But the final reason was the most serious. As terrorist violence increased (there were four attacks on the Centre itself, all repulsed at the 2000 km defence ring), as, despite the efforts of his friend Sven Haarlem, the attacks in the UN became more furious, as the world's press and people howled and screamed – even joined now by the people of Lucerne; as, in fact, events began to reach explosion point, the Centre itself began to disintegrate. Gottlieb found himself with a revolt on his hands.

In essence the problem was one he had faced when he first became Director-General. Since he insisted that every known fact, event, statistic in the world should be computed together, and their patterns computed, and these patterns stored to be

154

extrapolated back into the past and forward into the future, and spun out in envelope curves, and since this was in practice impossible, it meant, so the anti-Gottlieb faction contended, that certain factors relevant to pollution would escape or be insufficiently dealt with. If certain methods of screening were employed then vast numbers of facts which couldn't *possibly* have any bearing on anything could be excluded and the computers could be allowed to cope more effectively with what remained. In theory the argument was simple and philosophic. In fact, it was highly technical, concerning the capacity of the giant computers and memory banks, the methods of screening, what was meant by effective computerisation and how much in reality escaped it and so on.

Gottlieb remained adamant. The world was bound together as a totality. It was a delicate balance of billions, trillions, an infinity of different weights and balances. It was a whole which attempts at division and categorisation had always falsified and would always falsify. The record of the WCCC had proved this many times. These terrible events, distressing as they were, were world (or conceivably cosmic) events. Something was causing them. In the end the WCCC would discover what it was.

And, just in time, Gottlieb was proved right.

At six o'clock on the morning of 20 September 2022, Frau Schmidt woke him from a deep, untroubled sleep in the comfortable apartment which adjoined his office. Her eyes glistening with pride and excitement, emotions strong enough to master for a moment her immense guilt, she handed him a piece of plastic.

'*Herr Doktor, es ist gefunden! Ausserordentlich.*'

'Good,' said Gottlieb, sitting up.

'There has been one error,' apologised Frau Schmidt. 'In his excitement, Dr Mancroft released the news to the Press Office. The world knows that a possible *Most Sensitive* source has been discovered.'

'That is certainly most irregular,' said Gottlieb. 'Though in the circumstances understandable. Now. . . .'

He rose from his bed, put on his dressing-gown, and walked calmly across the carpeted floor of his office to his desk. He felt a sense of triumph.

155

Arrived at his desk, he activated the monitor screen and then slipped the plastic disc into its slot. It had stamped upon it the code and index of the relevant material and he would now see the correspondences which had led the computers and his scientists to assume causal relationships.

For ten minutes Gottlieb watched while the parameters of the disastrous events over the past eight months were played against the parameters of the still codified *Most Sensitive* material. The result was uncanny. The relationship was not just tenable – it was undeniable. Practically every single unexplained event which they had been studying was matched, both as to time and to intensity, on the codified material. Of course there were variations, time lags, quantitive differences, one or two contradictions – without them the coincidence would have been suspect; but to all intents and purposes the two were identical. Gottlieb, his method, the WCCC had been entirely vindicated.

Trembling a little now, with excitement, Gottlieb turned to activate the codifying monitor. This, in the case of *Most Sensitive* material, was a little complicated. A series of digits, known only to him, had first to be pressed out. Next, he had to present his wrist identity panel to the correct sensor. Finally, the route was cleared by his voice print. *Most Sensitive* material was that considered by a nation (or confederation of nations) as vital to its interests. It could only be seen by the Director-General of the WCCC himself. Gottlieb spoke the appropriate words and then leant forward intently. Now he would see the original information from which the codified versions had derived.

The next moment he had thrown himself back in his chair and cried out in astonishment. Surely, he was hallucinating. There, flowing across the screen – pinched, spidery, mad – was the familiar sight of his wife's handwriting, set out in rigid little columns of commodities, quantities, prices. *Shopping lists*. For an instant, before his common sense reasserted itself, Gottlieb felt the clutch of ice at his heart.

It was theoretically impossible (and had proved so in practice) for the World Computer Control Centre to make a mistake of this size. Impossible because the operation of the fifteen huge complexes was independently monitored, and the monitors were themselves monitored. At the slightest malfunction, the tiniest error of input or output, the variation by a milliwatt of electrical energy, anything from a single circuit to an entire complex was instantly stopped. The malfunction was located and rectified. But, apart from this, any significant result on one complex was instantly checked on another complex; if it was a categorised result, checked on more than one complex. Because it was *Most Sensitive*, Gottlieb knew that the results he had seen would have been independently checked by all fifteen computer complexes. That they should all have made the same error was inconceivable.

And yet they had all made the same error; an error which was tinged, Gottlieb had to admit with a wry smile, with an element of humour. Yet an error of this magnitude was alarming enough. No wonder they hadn't been able to discover the source, or sources, of pollution. What other errors had been committed? And such an error almost certainly meant sabotage; its nature meant sabotage from within, motivated, as well as by terrorist sympathies of some sort, by personal spite against himself.

Gottlieb issued a series of orders. All software was to be checked immediately, every programme back for the last year. Then each computer complex with its attendant monitors was to be checked for faults. If the automatic checking operations revealed nothing, as he suspected they would, then each complex was to be inspected manually and completely. Every memory bank, every circuit, was to be opened and tested. This would be a lengthy business, and therefore each complex was to be taken off stream in turn; meanwhile, and notwithstanding the discovery of a possible *MS* source, the other fourteen computer complexes were to continue their search for a solution to the current pollution disasters with unabated vigour.

He spoke to the Terrorist Bureau (Ross C. Rather of Illinois in charge). He had strong reason to suspect saboteurs. Everyone was to be re-screened. Particular attention was to be paid to those engaged in solving the current crisis. If necessary, the Bureau could interrogate. No one was to be exempt, not the Council, not even his own personal staff.

It was to the chief pillar of this that he now turned his attention. When Frau Schmidt saw his eyes on her she stood up. She had prepared her short speech that morning, and had waited only until the *MS* source had been confirmed before delivering it.

'I will resign at once,' she said quietly. 'In a large part this is my responsibility.'

Dr Gottlieb too stood up and, dressing-gown swishing, came round his desk and pulled a chair up in front of her. He drew her down into her own chair. They had worked together for twenty years and he knew her in a lot of ways better than his wife. He had no desire to lose her, especially at this moment, unless it was absolutely essential.

'Tell me, Frau Schmidt,' he said gently, 'why was this material classified *Most Sensitive*?'

Frau Schmidt had not expected this question. 'You instructed it, Herr Doktor.'

By careful questioning Gottlieb elicited the fact that he had given the instruction *in English* – so, it was an error due to the subtlety of his famous English sense of humour. Some instinct stopped him saying he had in fact wanted the stuff filed *Personal,* and Frau Schmidt was already explaining the, to her, far more culpable course of her actions, the reason, that is, why not until now had she remembered to feed the material he had given her five months before into the computers.

She had, she explained, at that time been distracted by a family matter. Normally, once codified, *MS* material was fed straight into the computers; occasionally, however, the Director General would ask for this process to be delayed until he gave further instructions. He might, for instance, wish to confer first with the head of state concerned. For some reason, Frau Schmidt said, she must have imagined this was what Dr Gottlieb had wanted. Only today had chance association revealed her error. (She had woken abruptly at four o'clock to hear the stealthy exit from the bedroom across the hall of her son's middle-aged lover.) In a flash, the events of that April morning had returned to her. She suddenly realised that the *Most Sensitive* material had never been entered. Nor, as a result, had any of the subsequent lists which he had been handing her week by week been fed in either. She had immediately contacted the Centre, with the results he now saw. She would resign forthwith.

Dr Gottlieb was already behind his desk, his mind surging Napoleonically ahead.

'There will be no need, Frau Schmidt. No doubt I was unclear. You made a mistake. However, there is a strong possibility here of sabotage or computer malfunction. If you have revealed that, you have done a service.'

But there were stranger possibilities. Since the WCCC had started work a great deal had been learnt about chance. The laws of probability were undergoing, had undergone, fundamental revision. It had been discovered that non-significant coincidences were far more common than anyone had supposed. You stopped a man in the street and asked him for a light. It turned out he had the same name as yourself; not only that, his wife was also called Angela. And both your fathers had been doctors and had wives of the same name too! Once such events were the subject of superstitious amazement, credulous writers compiled books of them and even attempted slightly dotty explanation. A whole science of synchronicity had been proposed. But examples existed in the memory banks of chances as high as two billion to one occurring and then occurring again, when the 'chances against' had been raised by a factor of ten, and then *again*, when once more the 'chances against' had been raised by an order of magnitude.

So, though it was highly unlikely, it was theoretically possible, at any rate theoretically conceivable, that all the items on his wife's shopping lists had coincided by chance, over a period of months, with the terrible series of calamities the Centre was investigating. It was just possible – Gottlieb stretched a fat forefinger – that the amount of cherries she bought and the mercury count, the drop scones and the acid-rain, the veal and the oil slicks, had simply, but nonsignificantly, happened at the same time. The forefinger dropped. He couldn't be bothered even to activate the powerful Hero 4 calculator. He remembered the flowing parameters again, when list upon list, item upon item, kilo by kilo, date for date, had coincided precisely and again and again with world events. It was *not* possible. Even the most radical of the new theories of chance couldn't stretch that far. It was inconceivable, ridiculous, mad.

What else then, aside from error or sabotage? Was it possible that the computers had taken on a life of their own? Some of them, or parts of them, for a variety of reasons, had been given a certain bias or 'personality'; to the programmers never more than machines, to the uninitiated they could seem oddly alive, especially those with voice capability and large vocabularies. The pressure on the Centre – and therefore on the computers – had become extremely intense during the last few weeks, the motives for finding the cause of the disasters very strong. Under the press of failure, perhaps the computers had somehow combined to create success; the trillions of circuits, the memory banks, the whole city of electronics had become in some sense organic.

It was an extremely dated science fiction idea and Gottlieb knew that it was patently absurd. The malevolent 'human' computer had been the stuff of film and novel fifty years before. Also, the computers had received the *MS* material for the first time that morning. Though easily capable of such swift calculation, it argued a curiously rapid and unheralded metamorphosis. Nevertheless, he contacted the Technical Bureau again and asked them to check each complex against one of the great international computer centres. He believed facilities existed for doing this with the Centre at Brussels.

Now, although he had begun to be bothered by a longing for breakfast, Gottlieb realised he must talk to the Council. They would have been summoned, like him, upon the discovery of the *MS* source and had been waiting over an hour. It was while walking down the corridor to the Council Chamber that he took the first of two decisions which were to lead, in the end, to disaster. He decided not to tell the Council the true nature of the *MS* material.

Certainly there were sound reasons for this. Despite the

160

terror and horror resulting from the Great Pollution Catastrophe of 1999, national governments were extremely reluctant to allow the WCCC access to material they regarded as vital to them. The inviolability, sanctity almost, of *Most Sensitive* information was written into the constitution of the Centre; it was the third clause in his oath of office. Gottlieb, who prided himself on his English integrity, his ability to 'stick to the rules', was very reluctant to go against this. The saboteur, or saboteurs, if they had penetrated the Council itself, which seemed possible, would be more easily discovered if they did not know they had been detected. Finally, the discovery of a *possible MS* source had flashed (swiftly losing the qualification) round the world. The vast juggernaut of press, TV and radio, so recently attacking, had flung itself into reverse; bells were pealing, crowds cheering, telegrams and messages of congratulation and relief would already, he knew, be pouring into the Centre. To reverse this process, to say the answer had not after all been found, might produce a reaction of terrifying proportions.

Nevertheless, he would have done better to tell them. Saboteurs are as often rattled and reveal themselves when they are discovered, as made careless by thinking themselves safe. They would, as it was, be sufficiently alerted by what he was going to say. There would have been no need to let the information go beyond the Council Chamber, at any rate at first. If the world had to be told, it could have been done by degrees. It would probably have been unnecessary. Once the sabotage or malfunction had been discovered – and Gottlieb had no doubt this would happen swiftly – then the true sources of the pollution would be discovered and could be dealt with. And in fact, of course, the English ability lay in knowing when to break rules; it was a Germanic quality to obey. Had Gottlieb told them the true contents of the *MS* material they would have recognised at once the impossibility of the computer diagnosis being right. He would have had his Council behind him, whereas in the end, a crucial factor, they were against him.

They were certainly behind him when he strode massively into the Chamber at 7.45 on that fateful September morning. None of those who had tentatively challenged his authority earlier had liked doing so. He was both too formidable and too much liked. They were delighted that the Centre, their Director-General, they themselves, had all been vindicated. Murmurs of relief and congratulation – quiet echoes of the clamour in the macrocosm – greeted him as he appeared.

Dr Gottlieb quickly disabused them. The *MS* material provided almost conclusive evidence of sabotage, computer malfunction or both. The odds against it having anything to do with the events they were dealing with, even in a non-significant way, were too high for any other conclusion. As they knew, powerful forces existed outside who wanted to discredit the WCCC. They had no doubt seen the recent estimates of secret industrial funds dedicated to its destruction. He had taken all necessary steps to see that they would fail. It was a great pity that Dr Mancroft had released the news to the world. Indeed, it was surprising that a scientist of his experience should not have thought it suspicious that so many different calamities could have had their source in a single file of *Most Sensitive* information. But the damage was done and, in their various spheres, they must cope with it as best they could. For the rest, he wanted them to regard the problems as unsolved and to redouble their efforts to solve them. He himself would cope with the *MS* situation.

The faces round the table became grim. This was indeed appalling news. There were few questions. Some technical suggestions from Dr Manuel Diaz, the Mexican. A word in defence of Mancroft from Pierre Messemer, in whose department he worked. The Head of the Diplomatic Bureau, Sir Edward Evans, asking for guidance. Someone asked if there was no hope that the *MS* material might have some relevance? He had spoken of odds against; what were those odds? Gottlieb paused a moment before replying. Once more the parameters flowed together in his mind. Once more he relived the shock of discovery.

'They are cosmic,' he said sombrely. 'Cosmic'.

He dismissed the Council. They all had work to do. At least now – one advantage of Mancroft's indiscretion – they had a few days' grace. It was well known that an *MS* situation could take several days, or weeks, to resolve. In the great manganese nodule confrontation between Russia, China and the US in 2010, Gottlieb had done nothing for a week. Carefully he had planned and placed the various levers of blackmail and persuasion, promise and threat which he proposed to employ. But then neither the world nor the powers themselves were aware that the WCCC knew anything of the situation. Now he doubted world opinion would give them more than three days before expecting decisive action.

Back at his office he launched into a colossal breakfast and the developing situation. Reports were already arriving on initial tests as to computer malfunction (negative). He saw the Head of the Terrorist Bureau and the Head of Security. They were to get their departments working together on this. He outlined the sort of sabotage he suspected, where and what to look for. He would give them more information when he had studied the *MS* material in his possession more thoroughly. Once they had gone, he settled himself at his desk, linked his monitor system into the new *Aries 3000* and set to.

He worked all morning, through a delicious lunch and until mid-afternoon tea. He worked swiftly and well, focussing the clear beam of his tremendous concentration fiercely onto the problem. Even eating automatically, he scarcely noticed the passage of seven and a half hours. By the end of that time he had become entranced by the skill of the saboteurs. Here indeed was no ordinary terrorist set-up. He was looking at work of very high calibre indeed.

There was, for example, nothing simple about the correspondences – no element of sympathetic alignment, as it might be cooking oil for oil slicks or cheese for the terrible plagues of giant poison-resistant rat. The correspondences seemed completely haphazard, even bizarre (potatoes associated with the decline of the penguin for instance; those deadly clouds of chemical gas with certain sauces); but Gottlieb knew the hardest codes to break were those where the key was haphazard. The associations were, however, consistent as to effect and degree: cream involved the destruction of fish; currants equalled strontium 90. The more cream or the more currants, the more fish destroyed or strontium 90 released. But there were no patterns as to place; fish could die the length of the Rhône, or fill the harbour at Reykjavik. Nor did the patterns by any means coincide precisely with what was bought. Often there was a lapse of several days, and from this Gottlieb deduced it was the *eating* which produced the reaction. Indeed, in that sudden outbreak of meningitis in Ethiopia he thought he recognised one of the chill little dinners they had very occasionally served his colleagues. He remembered a particularly scrawny chicken.

Plainly, therefore, 18 Baedekerstrasse had been very effectively bugged; poor, unwitting Angela kept under close surveillance (another call here to the Head of Security). But there was a further peculiarity. Not only was it solely in the flat that food eaten had any effect; it seemed as though it was only himself and Angela eating which had any effect. The size of his own contributions, though detectable, could not have hurt a fly; nor did they. That was hardly surprising. But that meal of elderly chicken – the meningitis outbreak corresponded to his own meagre portion and Angela's vast one combined; a fact that could be compared to a much more recent and more terrible outbreak in Rumania on a day, he could remember, that they had dined alone and she had devoured an entire plump bird. (Poor Heinrich's meal that evening had been one small tomato on a stamp-hinge of Ryvita.) Indeed the steady crescendo of unexplained disasters during spring and summer matched exactly the burgeoning of her appetite as she came out of the analysis of her anorexia. And this fact at once implicated Dr Gabès. He would require instant and thorough rescreening. This second call to the Head of Security gave Gottlieb some satisfaction. Although he had had to pretend gratitude, he had never really taken to Stephen Gabès (a tricky relationship, that, between a husband and his wife's psychiatrist).

And there were subtleties within subtleties. With two notable exceptions (various pastas from the Italian quarter and apple strudel from the Austrian Jewish quarter), Angela seemed to have returned, in her new-found appetite, to the menus of her English childhood: rice pudding, cottage pie, plaice rolled up and cooked in milk. Cottage pie produced a nice balance of calamity. Beef equalled detergent, potatoes destroyed penguins, onions matched the decline of the panda, carrots a certain 'flu virus . . . and so on. The computers –

here as throughout – analysed correspondences down to the last milligram, fractions of a cubic centimetre, down to the very grains of salt. It was fascinating to observe the repercussions following quite minor variations in a pie's ingredients – a little more onion here, an extra cupful of stock there. Then quite a large number of items appeared to have no harmful effect – mustard, cauliflower, packet soup . . . the list was long. The saboteurs even had a sense of humour. One food and one food only had a palliative effect – eggs. One egg, two eggs, a yolk beaten into a sauce, could nullify or diminish (to a degree that could be precisely calculated) the evil effects of anything else. For a moment Gottlieb saw hope here; did it not restrict somewhat the possible suspects? But then – the whole Centre knew of his allergy, his horror of eggs. He was famous for it, and for the large, foil-wrapped cow-bile pills he always carried in case by chance he should eat one of the horrid things disguised in something else. It was a standing joke. Indeed, he had a delightful little joke he made about it himself. How did it go? 'I may be a Doctor of History, Science and Mathematics – but I'm certainly no "egg-head"!'

His preliminary work completed, Gottlieb chuckled as he stared out over the mid-afternoon haze above Lucerne. But the situation was grim enough. The possibility of computer malfunction now seemed extremely remote. Plainly, terrorist sabotage was much more likely. How would it go? A terrorist group – or more likely groups, since the resources required would be enormous – would keep a close watch on his wife (Gabès a key figure here). A pattern of pollutant-caused, or apparently pollutant-caused correspondences would be worked out and then put into effect worldwide. The resulting panic and chaos could easily be orchestrated. Then one of three things could happen. The WCCC would never discover the correspondences, nor find any other cause – it would be shown to be ineffective and discredited. Panic and chaos would reach epidemic, even world-war proportions, the very situation many terrorist groups wished to bring about and would benefit from. Or else the WCCC would discover the correspondences – and this too could have been arranged. A discreet hint from Gabès, and Angela would have given him the lists. These he would have filed and they would have been fed automatically into the system, in common with any information however trivial coming into the Centre. The WCCC might not have dared believe or publish the results – in which case the situation would be the same as though it had never found them in the first place. Or it would publish – and be even more effectively discredited. Shopping lists! It would be destroyed by ridicule. The Director-General himself would be implicated, not just his integrity but his very sanity called in question. But how on earth had they gained access to *Most Sensitive* material without the voice print and his identity panel? Of course, that was the cunning of it. They had no need to. They had access at source. Rapidly, Gottlieb dictated a series of instructions to the two Security Bureaux.

But the pollution itself – was there not more to look into here? How did the Gabès connection get their information so quickly – often, it must be, before the Centre itself? Given their resources, some crude interferences could be engineered directly – here an oil slick, there chlordane sprayed direct onto the feeding grounds of the Arctic penguin. But the bulk of the events were not of that order. No doubt they had observers, informers, stationed strategically, but there was a serious possibility that the ten-centimetres-thick, tens of thousands of kilometres-long fibre optic cables, whose laser pulses carried much of the information into the Centre, had somewhere been tapped – a feat which, though theoretically possible, had not hitherto been done successfully, even under laboratory conditions. And if tapped, then information could be fed in as well as taken out. It would not be the first time the Centre had received false reports in an attempt to stir things up. Once more Gottlieb dictated.

And yet . . . and yet . . . his mind working with superb calm swiftness, ranging the totality of the problem - was there not one final avenue to explore? The discipline of science has one curious aspect. Although it enshrines the rational principles of experiment and proof, it sometimes requires of its devotees acts of faith greater than those demanded by the most unreasonable of religions. If a cause has an effect, and the same cause always has the same effect – no matter how extraordinary or even fatuous cause or effect might be – then a scientist is of necessity compelled to assume the operation of some law which it is his duty to discover. Often such searches have been based on insufficient evidence or misinterpretation of the evidence. Scientists have devoted their whole lives to discovering a *cul de sac*. But, as Popper had shown so many years before, a scientist who discovered a *cul de sac* was only a little less important than one who hacked out the high road. Now, although Gottlieb was quite certain he knew the correct interpretation of the facts at his disposal, he was, by training, a scientist. And so he took the second decision which was to lead – swiftly and directly - to disaster. He decided, albeit in a spirit of complete disbelief, to experiment.

He set out from the Centre at 7.30, leaving instructions that he was to be informed at once by scrambler of any significant development. Stepping out of the lift after the usual mild anxiety of the nineteen-floor ascent at 18 Baedeker-strasse, he reflected that his witty Anglo-American metaphor of the ice box was no longer strictly accurate. Even in the small hall, the fragrant smell of cooking was plainly detectable. Perhaps 'oven' would be more appropriate.

Angela greeted him with some irritation. The flat had been filled the entire afternoon with men, poking and searching.

'I know, *mein Schatzle*,' said Heinrich gently. 'I tried to warn you. We have a crisis at the Centre. The entire establishment is having to be checked. I'm afraid it may happen again.' Whatever bugging devices they had found, and he had no doubt they had found a great many, visual, auditory, and tactile, Gottlieb had said they must be left in place. They were necessary for his initial experiment.

Next, as though engaged on some harmless, more or less aimless stroll round his flat, he wandered across and peered in at the kitchen door. What he saw rooted him to the spot.

On the table was the largest apple strudel he had ever seen in his life. It was enough for eight people – ten even. And, worse still, a great bag of flour stood open beside it, as though poised for further use.

For an instant Gottlieb stared in horror and then, without thinking, feeling almost as though he were impelled by some outside force, he gave a hoarse cry and hurled himself into the air and down upon the table.

His great chest crushed and obliterated the strudel. At the same time he managed to catch the bag of flour an enormous thwack with his fist, so that it was flung against the upright of the window and burst down into the sink. Almost at once the legs of the table broke under his weight and he was thrown violently to the floor and up against a pretty dresser of shelves Angela had bought in Cambridge. This tilted dangerously forward but then swayed back again, not, however, before most of its contents had come sliding out and smashed on to the floor. A particularly heavy jar, containing some condiment or other, fell on to Gottlieb's head, causing him to cry out again.

[6]

'Heinri – what happened? Are you all right?'

She had not used the diminutive for years. Shock brought it to her lips. Nothing like this had happened since – well, nothing like this had ever happened before. The kitchen looked as though a bomb had gone off in it.

'It is nothing, *mein Schatzle*,' said Gottlieb, getting unsteadily to his feet. 'I slipped.'

He was almost as astonished by what had happened as Angela. His jacket was covered in strudel. He could already feel a lump forming on his head. 'I will just change my clothes.'

Newly dressed, he returned to the kitchen, still determined to pursue his experiment.

'*Mein Schatzi*. I've ruined your supper. I'll just slip out and buy you something else.'

He had not offered to do this for years, simply because Angela would have refused. Now, however, distractedly beginning to clear up the mess, she merely said, 'Help me carry what's left of this table into the hall.' When she returned to the kitchen, he slipped into the lift.

It was not what he had done that had surprised him. That was rational enough. Pastry and all kinds of pasta meant cancer, apples corresponded to radiation from nuclear waste in the sea, currants to strontium 90. Since his first experiment

168

was to take place while the terrorist group's equipment was still in place, he was certainly not going to give them an excuse for unleashing more of that inflammatory suffering. Had it been the second experiment, done out of deference to the spirit of science, when the equipment had been removed, it would have been different. But he had been surprised at the violence of his reaction. Surely he could have just knocked the strudel and the flour to the floor with his elbow. He had been more affected than he realised by the events of the past months.

Down in Baedekerstrasse he realised he hadn't the faintest idea where the shops were, shops still much used in that food-conscious city in preference to the many home-based audio-televisual methods of buying food. One of the security guards, who accompanied him discreetly on any outside journey, directed him to Liechtensteinstrasse. Gottlieb then dismissed the guard. He wished to be alone.

He felt even more lost in the huge supermarket, seemingly arranged in no logical order whatever. A motherly attendant, seeing the huge harassed figure roaming the shelves, directed him to the meat counter. Gottlieb bought six large veal cutlets for Angela and cast a longing look at some kidneys for himself. But, however distracted, Angela would never 'stomach' that. He smiled appreciatively. At least he hadn't lost his sense of humour. He bought a kilo of bonbons to eat in his bedroom later that night.

At supper they talked more than they had for months. She was a trifle irritated that he had done the shopping (though she wolfed the cutlets) but was still amazed at the accident. Secretly, she wondered if it had been deliberate. She hoped so.

'I can't understand it, Heinrich. It was as though you had been stung.'

He said vaguely that he'd slipped, then twisted his ankle under and jumped. The work at the Centre was extremely intense at the moment.

'It's those huge lunches,' said Angela. 'It's pointless my helping you diet. You're grossly overweight.' She had cooked him a small boiled turnip.

However, she listened with some interest while he described

the delicate poise of the international situation at that moment.

He arrived early at the Centre to find news already flowing in. Complexes 1 to 4 were all functioning normally; 5 to 8 would be completed by tomorrow. Inexplicable but possibly pollution-caused incidents were continuing: lead count rising in cities of West Australia, a 1504.8-kilometre oil slick in mid-Atlantic, a further catastrophic decline in the penguin. Gottlieb activated the Aries 3000 to his desk monitor. A 1504.8-km. oil slick was exact to the milligram of veal. He was baffled by the lead count and the penguins, until he remembered that Angela had had a kilo of potatoes and a kilo of turnips (hers crisply fried) as well. He noticed that, as usual, his own pathetic turnip contribution had had virtually no effect.

But disturbing news came at nine o'clock, midway through his post-breakfast snack. First, an interim report on Gabès. Completely negative. It was only interim, of course, but it seemed unlikely anything further would emerge. Fifteen years before he had been one of eight resident psychiatrists at the UN. As Gottlieb knew, the screening facilities at Addis were among the finest in the world. Since that time he had prac-tised in Lucerne and had come under the normal, but intense, scrutiny awarded anyone who had even the remotest contact with the Centre. Grimly, Gottlieb had ordered that investi-gation should continue. No corner of Gabès's life was to be left unsearched.

But it was the second piece of news that was really shat-tering. The penthouse of 18 Baedekerstrasse was as clean as a whistle, not a bugging device to be found – visual, aural, tactile, not even paranormal, laughed the Head of Security.

Gottlieb held himself upright in his chair and stared at the Head of Security for ten seconds without speaking. Once more he felt ice at the heart, the sway of his reason. But reason reasserted itself swiftly. He leant forward. Just how thorough had the search been? The flats below? Had they examined Frau Gottlieb? Was it not possible to swallow a probe – accidentally of course, planted – which then attached itself to the lining of the stomach? She'd gone to the chiropodist some months before. He might have slipped something under a toenail.

The Head of Security was somewhat taken aback. He'd expected relief, not this – well, loss of calm wasn't the word quite, the DG was never anything but totally calm – but this intensity. Yes, the investigation had been extremely thorough. Of course, they hadn't done a medical, that was to say physical . . . he hadn't realised the Director expected a . . . but, hurrumphed the embarrassed Head of Security, so sensitive was their detecting equipment that it would have registered anything, no matter where it was concealed. In fact, it would have detected anything concealed within a kilometre of the flat, in any direction.

While the Head of Security was talking, Gottlieb was thinking – how on earth do they do it? Was the flat overlooked by powerful telescopes, radar, infra-red scanners, satellite surveillance on a new scale? Did they follow her to see what she bought? No, it was consumption they were interested in. Perhaps they monitored the sewage or stuffed minute probes into everything purchased. It could be those innocent-seeming women at the credit registers of that huge, baffling *Supermarkt*. Gottlieb wished he could have everyone screened, or the whole area around them cleared.

And the infuriating thing was, of course, that he could. In a world pollution crisis of this magnitude the powers of the Director-General of the World Computer Control Centre were virtually absolute. But to exercise them he would have had to reveal, in secrecy, at any rate something of the nature of the problem – either to the city fathers of Lucerne or more likely the government in Geneva. He could not be entirely arbitrary. And there lay the fiendish skill of the plot. He was hamstrung by the nature of the material, the powers of his position severely curtailed. He had to fight them virtually alone.

And so when the Head of Security hurried anxiously and a little bewildered from the room – with instructions (the most Gottlieb felt he could give) first to re-investigate any building overlooking 18 Baedekerstrasse, second to see whether Frau Gottlieb was followed on her shopping expeditions, third to 'have a look at' the sewage – Gottlieb himself got up and said he would have to go too.

'But *Herr Direktor*,' said Frau Schmidt, pointing an agitated finger at the neatly typed list on his desk, 'Sven Haarlem wishes to speak to you urgently. Russia and China are anxious for a consultation. The Head of the Press Bureau and the Head of the Diplomatic Bureau need guidance. The President of Europe. . . .'

'This is more important,' said Gottlieb. 'Tell Van Diemen to deal with them.'

But in the Mercedes, speeding back to Baedekerstrasse, he realised he had been a little hasty. He also wished he hadn't organised the Centre to revolve so completely around himself. Van Diemen was highly competent but he was not, to put it mildly, exactly *au fait* with the situation. Gottlieb switched on the audio-visual communication and dictated a series of instructions to Frau Schmidt. It was 10.45.

He arrived back just in time. Angela was in the living room. She herself not only used the old-fashioned shops, she also disliked the automatic home delivery systems and preferred actually to collect the food herself. Wheeled trolley bag was in one hand and (Gottlieb blanched inwardly) shopping list in the other.

'Angela – *mein Fräuli*.'

'Yes Heinrich? I'm just going shopping.'

They stood looking at each other. Heinrich found difficulty in expressing what he wanted to say; or, more exactly, in disguising what he wanted to express.

'*Mein Fräuli* – let me do the shopping for you today. I am deeply ashamed of what happened yesterday. Give me the list and you can "put your feet up" as they say.'

As he spoke, Heinrich realized that not for years had he asked Angela to do something for him. Perhaps he had never asked her for anything. Deep within him he had a curious sensation – a sense of reversal, as though a see-saw had tipped.

'I see,' said Angela. 'You've finally noticed. You think I'm wasting money. You think I'm extravagant. Well it's perfectly true – for the last three months I have made a practice of buying things at their most expensive. The quality is better.'

'You know *mein Schatzi,*' said Heinrich, 'I've never thought you extravagant. On the contrary. Of course you should buy the best quality. It is just I would like to help you. You've been looking tired recently.'

Angela stared at him. Small darts of excitement were going through her. At last, at last. Gabès was right.

'Heinrich. I can't understand, from what you said yesterday and what I read in the papers today, how you can possibly leave the Centre. As to my health, I'm feeling better than I have for ages.'

Heinrich looked at his wife, again more closely than he had for months, for years. She did look better, if, to him, not exactly attractive. The slender blade he'd loved as a young man was now very definitely blunted, swollen in fact, more like a bludgeon.

'Please,' said Heinrich.

'No,' said Angela, and stepping round him she walked out.

For a moment Heinrich stood irresolute. A small green light was winking above the door of his large bedroom-study. It meant the Centre was calling him urgently on the scrambler. But nothing was more urgent than this; whatever was urgent was so because of this. And time, precious time was passing.

Heinrich strode out into the hall. He took the green deerstalker hat he wore at Schloss Furtwangen and pulled it well down over his head, he wrapped a muffler round the lower part of his face and then draped his heavy fur-lined cape over his shoulders. There was little chance of anyone knowing who he was. The need for secrecy in his work, as well as personal aversion, had long caused him to avoid publicity. The press and TV were quite willing to respect this and most of the photographs taken during the recent trouble had been suppressed. One or two news programmes, however, reporting live, had carried some momentary shots of him thrusting to his car. Although it was still hot in September, too hot for the fur-lined cape, he did not want to be recognised.

He took a back entrance from 18 Baedekerstrasse and came out much further up the street itself just in time to see Angela turning into Liechtensteinstrasse. Already panting, Heinrich lumbered in pursuit.

She went into the *Supermarkt*. He waited a minute or two and then warily followed. It was packed.

And now his task became extremely difficult. Gottlieb cursed the day he had decided that, out of all Lucerne, the private purchases of WCCC personnel and their companions would not be automatically transmitted and recorded at the central bank. Angela's Credit Disc confined details of the transaction to the till, where they would later be destroyed; only the total sum went to the bank. It was a move made to protect privacy, something that had virtually vanished elsewhere. Here, once again, the saboteurs had an uncanny way of – how did it go? – 'bursting him with his own petard.'

He had to take note of what she bought but must not be seen. It was too dangerous to follow her directly and not really possible to see what she was buying from a distance through the jars and tins and tubes jam-packed upon the shelves. Heinrich, bending low, followed her passage up parallel avenues, peeping round the ends to try and see what she had in her trolley, whisking out of sight if she made a turn. Large women jostled him impatiently. Even when she was quite close it was difficult to distinguish what the items were: marmalade, milk, sugar; with a clutch at the heart he thought he saw mutation-causing parmesan. But most of the things she bought were meaningless to him. The trolley filled rapidly. He supposed she was replacing the contents of the dresser.

It was an extra brisk whisk that caused the hem of Heinrich's cape to strike the base of an enormous pyramid of tins. With the sound and appearance of an avalanche they poured down and rolled wildly in all directions. Turning hurriedly and bending low, Heinrich ran back down the avenue, dodging and pushing through the crowds of instantly furious and protesting *Hausfraus*.

He concealed himself, a highly conspicuous figure, behind a rack of some packeted product at the far side of the *Supermarkt*. From here he could watch the credit exits, and quite soon he saw Angela appear at one, present her special Credit Disc, transfer everything to her own trolley and walk out.

Wearily, feeling extremely hot, he followed. Already his plan was failing. And it had been a sound plan, if only

174

interim. Evidently some new crisis was brewing at the Centre, and he could guess what it was. If he could see what she bought then he could announce in advance precisely what new inexplicable disasters the world should expect. The WCCC would be seen to be getting a grip on events; prediction was the first step towards control. Almost as important, it would allow him to demonstrate to the Centre that he too had the situation in hand. He could have waited till Angela returned from shopping, but more time would have been lost; also, clearly, the further in advance the warnings the more impressive.

She was leading him into a part of Lucerne where he had never been before. It was an *Einkaufszentrum* – a vast labyrinth of arcades and walkways, each one lined with shops, boutiques, even 'stalls'. No vehicles. No moving pavements. She had gone into a fish shop. Patiently, Heinrich waited round the corner, getting his breath back, his head just visible, brim pulled well down. It was hot even standing still. The moment she came out he would go in: 'What was that delicious-looking fish bought by the lady who's just left?'

But the lady didn't leave. After eight minutes, Heinrich edged his way up to the doors and peeped in. There were a number of people buying fish, but not his wife. At the far end he saw another set of double doors. He rushed into the shop and then stood irresolute – should he pursue, or find what future catastrophe had just been sold? A girl serving one of the refrigerated units stood close by him.

'What was that delicious-looking fish bought by the lady who's just left?'

'Which lady, sir? There have been a number.'

Heinrich stared at her, and then without answering he ran to the far doors and out into the sun. There was a choice of three arcades and he took the middle one, since it seemed a continuation of the food section. He walked rapidly, twisting his head left and right. There was no sign of her. Now the arcade branched again; a series of electronic shops, pocket computers and the like to the left, clothes to the right. Heinrich broke into a panting run, choosing clothes. He was sweating profusely, the heavy furred cape impeding his legs. But now clothes had become an open walkway of furniture shops.

175

Heinrich turned round and, his breath labouring, forced into a walk, began to retrace his steps, but soon took a false turn and found himself among art galleries, bookshops, displays of sculpture.

He was lost. He was hungry. He was very hot. He lifted off the cape, its collar soaked with sweat, but judged it wise to keep on the hat and muffler. He leant against a pillar, chest heaving. He must get back, but he felt he'd walked half-way across Lucerne; he would take a taxi.

'Excuse me, *mein Herr*, could you direct me to the nearest. . . .'

It took him half an hour to escape from the maze. Again and again he had to ask the way, and when at last he stumbled out of the blur of boutiques, shop fronts, infinitely dividing arcades, he found he had in fact been directed right across the *Einkaufszentrum*. He must have walked kilometres. He sank into the taxi and thankfully took off the hat and muffler.

When he got back she was just finishing a vast dish of plaice rolled up and cooked in milk and butter, and a mountain – an Everest – of mashed potato. So he was too late. There was going to be an appalling outbreak of cholera somewhere; and it meant, to all intents and purposes, the end of the penguin. He thought she looked at him a little oddly as he stood watching her. He felt ravenous, starving. Angela gave him half a cucumber.

And so Heinrich Gottlieb entered on the final stages of his nightmare. And it is interesting to compare his tragedy to that, say, of Agamemnon. In Greek drama the fate of the hero, the great one, is supposedly the result of hubris, pride, arrogance – a fatal flaw in his nature. But Gottlieb's fall was due not to a flaw, but to the very qualities which had brought about his rise: his total and incorruptible integrity as a world servant; his refusal, as a scientist, to deny the validity of the scientific method. All that had happened was that events had so altered that these qualities, while remaining the same, took on the appearance, and had the effect of defects. And perhaps this is true of many human tragedies – and makes them the more tragic. The Greek heroes at least had the consolation of seeing in their downfall an element of rough, if capricious, justice. There is no consolation when it is the circumstances – and them alone – which are to blame.

Heinrich's lunch was soon over. Once again, he had the impression that Angela was watching him. But when she left him alone for a few moments he was able to hastily throw three largish bags of flour and a box of apples out of the kitchen window. Unfortunately, he heard her returning before he could throw five packs of spaghetti out as well and had to stuff them up his coat. At least he'd bought time from the most dangerous scourges. There was enough food in the flat to feed an army. She would hardly set out on a second shopping expedition just to replace the flour, the spaghetti and the apples. She would think she had left them behind by mistake.

The scrambler light was winking in the Mercedes. He contacted the Centre and said he was on his way. At once he felt calmer. In some ways his life had been very sheltered – universities, the UN, then the WCCC. This world of shopping, spaghetti arcades – he felt at sea, his powers had no scope. Now he was returning to a world he knew.

It was a world once more in a considerable state of agitation. Van Diemen, Sir Edward Evans of the Diplomatic Bureau, and the Head of the Conservation Bureau were all waiting for him in his office when he arrived. This was unusual, but Gottlieb merely raised an eyebrow and went over to his desk.

'Well?'

The world situation was developing exactly as he had expected, but it had only taken two days and not three. The moment the WCCC had announced a *Most Sensitive* situation, the heads of state had at once begun to confer with one another. Each, confidentially, said they had not been contacted, it was not their vital interests which were causing these terrible disasters. But then, instead of abating, *the pollution catastrophes continued with increased ferocity*. At once, every head of state believed that some or all the others were lying. Russia began to suspect China or America or Europe – even, since the WCCC apparently knew the cause but was powerless to stop it, an unholy alliance of all three. America suspected Russia or Brazil. Europe . . .

177

'The situation is getting intolerably tense,' said Van Diemen.

'And these events are continuing. Only this afternoon. . . .'

'Don't tell me,' interrupted Gottlieb. 'Cholera and penguins.'

'Oh, you were informed,' said Van Diemen. 'I was told no one could contact you.'

'I was not informed,' said Gottlieb. 'I could – but for an accident – have predicted them.'

'It's no ordinary cholera,' burst in the Head of Conservation. 'It's raging across most of Pakistan. And the report speaks of hectares of dead penguins.'

'At the moment,' said Sir Edward Evans, 'world opinion imagines consultations are going on, negotiations, pressures being exerted, measures discussed to stop what is happening. But if we get something really dangerous – more cancer cases across China, radiation in the Gulf Stream again, mutant births and cancer in America – we can expect anything. It could mean war.'

At the word cancer, Gottlieb suddenly remembered the spaghetti. He got up, his mind working furiously, and walked slowly round the desk.

There he opened his coat and let the five spaghetti packets fall into the waste paper basket. Van Diemen and Sir Edward Evans exchanged a look. Gottlieb sat down again and spoke decisively.

'I shall address the Council in half an hour. It will be a short meeting. After that, Sir Edward, I shall have a series of summits with all heads of state concerned. Perhaps you could arrange this. As many as possible. I shall be available for the rest of the day. Now, gentlemen, I have urgent matters to attend to.'

Amongst the list of people who had tried to contact him he had seen the name of the Head of Security. The moment he and Frau Schmidt were alone (she had silently placed before him a plate of freshly fried chips and a large *Wiener schnitzel*) he flicked through to him.

'Anything to report?'

'Yes, *Herr Direktor*,' the man's voice was full of pride and relief. 'Your wife is definitely being followed.'

'Ah,' Gottlieb chewed strongly and swallowed.

'At 11 o'clock this morning she left 18 Baedekerstrasse to go shopping. At 11.07 precisely my agent reports that a large man dressed in a deer stalker hat and a long cape. . . .'

Gottlieb felt a sudden surge of irritation. 'I know all about that,' he interrupted. 'I don't want to hear about that. Was she followed by anybody else?'

'Not as far as I know,' said the Head of Security. 'My agent reports that this large man. . . .'

'I don't want to hear about him,' said Gottlieb crossly. 'In fact,' he added, as an idea occurred to him, 'I want you to drop that line of enquiry entirely. What else have you done? What about the buildings overlooking the flat?'

'There are only three such buildings,' said the Head of Security. 'All have been checked. Negative.'

'Dr Gabès?'

'Nothing more so far,' said the Head of Security.

'Haven't you done anything else?' said Gottlieb, beginning to feel exasperated.

'What else could we do?' said the Head of Security.

'Why didn't you think of checking the sewage? I thought I suggested sewage,' snapped Gottlieb. He wondered why he had never noticed the extraordinary incompetence of the Head of Security before.

'The sewage?' said the Head of Security in a surprised voice.

'Yes, probes in the sewage, bugs in the sewage,' said Gottlieb impatiently. 'Check the sewers, the lavatories, the pipes.' He flicked the switch and cut off the Head of Security's agitated reply and then turned to the screen for reviewing graded material.

Quickly he ran through the shopping list parameters again and dictated to Frau Schmidt as he did so a list of every one of the things that had so far been harmless. He wanted these bought at once in large quantities and put in the Mercedes, ready for him to take home that evening. Finally, he asked her – completely confidentially – to find him the best firm of private detectives in Lucerne. He had decided to have Angela followed. Everything she bought would be reported to him immediately. He would also ask them to bug the flat with audio and visual probes. Everything she ate, the quantities would be relayed to him at once. He'd match the terrorists at their own game.

Fortified by his meal, he walked along to the Council. The meeting was not too difficult. They had been accustomed for too long to being dominated by him. He told them that, in the interests of total confidentiality, he had misled them about the *Most Sensitive* material. It did have some relevance. By tomorrow he, and the Centre, would be in a position to warn the world what disasters to expect, their magnitude, their duration. It was a subject of enormous complexity. He must beg them not to press him further. The Council did press him further. Van Diemen in particular. Gottlieb stood firm. It remained as essential as ever – now, indeed, more essential than ever - that *Most Sensitive* material should be the sole province of the Director-General.

He spent the rest of the day in consultation with world leaders. He did not leave the Audio-Visual Summit Room for six hours. By that time he had won. To all of them he explained it was a pollution problem and disturbance of the eco-system of vast complexity. There were, among many other things, indications that the long predicted, long feared carbon dioxide build-up was now involved. No single nation or federation was alone responsible. It was possible that the entire industrial, chemical and energy-producing activities of the world might have to be temporarily suspended – or at least reduced to essential life-support services only. Suspend them, reduce them, said some of the developing nations, delighted. If necessary, said Gottlieb, but that also involved calculations of staggering complexity. He cajoled, he threatened, he charmed, he reassured – never had he manipulated with such adroitness, blackmailed with such delicacy. Sven Haarlem agreed to arrange a number of diversions at the UN. He won – but there was one universal warning. They could hold their hands for a few more days provided, as Sir Edward Evans had predicted, there were no more key trigger incidents – cancer, mutations, nuclear radiation. If world opinion started to panic again it would be much harder, probably impossible, to resist the swift drift to war. Gottlieb could not promise, but he'd taken certain measures, he was eighty per cent sure. . . .

180

At 19.30 he returned to his office. Van Diemen, Ross C. Rather and Sir Edward Evans – the three senior members of the Council who formed a sort of unofficial cabinet – were there, together with Frau Schmidt, who handed him a small folded sheet of paper. He put it in his pocket and told them briefly what had happened. Then he descended to the Mercedes.

Eating his supper from the walnut panel while the big hover car sped towards the lights of Lucerne, he read Frau Schmidt's note: *'Privatdedektiv Ancliffein, 17b Berlinerstrasse'.*

At 18 Baedekerstrasse his chauffeur opened the great boot of the Mercedes. It contained three enormous cardboard crates with the groceries he had ordered. It was as much as the two security guards could do to lift one between them. Staggering, they followed Heinrich in and put the crates, as he directed, in the little vestibule beside the lift.

'Gute Nacht.'

'Gute Nacht Herr Direktor.'

He had the first whiff of suspicion as he stepped into the hall. He stood, nose uplifted, sniffing. *Donnerwetter!* His weariness vanished to be replaced by, not quite panic, but certainly fear. With beating heart, he pulled open the door, hurried across the living room, crossed the corridor and into the kitchen. There, once more, before his eyes, all his plans, all the long day's work, lay hurled into ruins.

Angela didn't even wait for him to speak. She informed him. Oh, she had had such a delicious supper. The largest, tastiest apple strudel she had ever made. Did he want anything to eat or had he eaten at the Centre? She sat looking at him, smiling.

Heinrich was suddenly filled with rage. So – she had deliberately gone out and replaced the flour and the apple. No doubt it had been pasta for – how did the English put it? – *starters*. A tureen of spaghetti. He wanted to strike his smiling wife, smash her, kick her, strangle her, pound her into a jelly, drop the body down the rubbish chute. It flashed across his mind – *does she know?* Then, from long habit, but with terrible effort, he mastered himself. And in the icy calm that followed, he realised he would have to face the penultimate gamble, the solution he had been fighting to avoid ever since the crisis had begun. However much he might dread it, he had work to do. Having not uttered a word, he turned and went to his room.

Well pleased with this reaction, which confirmed everything she had already noticed, Angela began to do the washing up.

Heinrich first called the Centre on the scrambler. He informed them of what would happen (was at that moment happening – it was too late to warn the world – the news no doubt already flowing into the Centre's computers). He called a Council meeting for 08.00, to be followed by a World Press Conference at 08.30. Then he turned on the small table computer beside his bed. It too could be linked by superconducting cable directly into any one of the Centre's complexes. Still a novelty, he chose the Aries 3000. He worked swiftly, covering a sheet of paper with figures in his small neat handwriting.

He must have dozed. It was 02.30. His light was still on, the eye on the computer glowed. Heinrich got up and began to walk slowly up and down his room. His earlier mood, highly uncharacteristic, almost unique, had gone; he was filled now with an iron determination to succeed, to win. The battle had become personal. He would still need some time in the morning; thank goodness he'd thought of a contingency plan to ensure this.

He took off his socks and shoes, turned off the light in his room and then tip-toed out into the living room. The apartment was silent, heavy with sleep. Light as a Zeppelin, Heinrich tip-toed silently across the parquet flooring and carefully opened the door at the far side. Angela was by nature a light sleeper, but she took powerful sleeping pills each night and he didn't think she'd wake. Also, between her and the kitchen, there were two doors, three counting her own, and the passage.

Once safely in the kitchen, all doors closed behind him. Heinrich moved with less circumspection. He opened the large metal flap of the rubbish chute, then, going over to the refrigerator, filled his arms with two kilos of butter, piles of ham and bacon, five cartons of milk, and emptied it all into the chute. It made, in the silence of the night, rather more noise than he'd expected – an echoing subdued reverberation. He stood for three minutes listening intently. Nothing stirred in the flat.

Now he proceeded to clear the kitchen and adjoining store-room (with the deep freeze) of food. It took him thirty minutes: armful after armful rumbled down, she'd laid in enough to withstand a siege. And what food: cherries, beef, veal, plums, turnips, carrots, chicken, rice, fish, pasta, apples, currants, parmesan. Heinrich's blood froze as he shovelled it in. There was enough destructive power here to decimate whole continents, oceans. He scooped out long ranks of tins and sent them hurtling into the blackness; unable to pull the glass top out of the big jar of raisins he flung it down intact. By the end he was panting but triumphant.

The flat was clean.

He slipped out of the kitchen and, practically on his points in the desire not to wake her, tip-toed silently across the parquet and out into the hall. He left the door open. There was a momentary flash of light as the lift doors opened, then darkness again as Heinrich descended.

He found the first crate of groceries almost more than he could manage; however the second was even heavier. But he was still a strong man and by bracing himself against the wall of the vestibule he managed to force himself upright, sweat starting on his forehead. He backed slowly into the lift, staggering a little. He had to bend his knees and nudge the button with the back of his head.

At the top, the few seconds' light from the lift doors gave him the line on the front door and he got through it safely. He was breathing hard, but moving silently, when all at once he lurched again and had to kick out violently to the right to prevent himself falling. Unfortunately his big bare toe struck, with blinding force, the sharp metal edge of the table leg in the middle of the room.

The pain was excruciating, appalling. Quite unable to stop himself, Heinrich let out a great bellow of wounded rage and dropped the crate of groceries. It burst with a crash on the parquet flooring and there was the sound of bouncing, rolling tins and packets, the noise of breaking glass.

No sleeping pill could have withstood it. Light flooded the

room. Dazed and somewhat alarmed, Angela stood at her door. Before her, in the midst of some devastation, surrounded by groceries, her husband stood on one foot, holding the other in both hands. Blood was pouring from his toe.

After several moments' silence, she spoke. 'Heinrich,' she said almost gently. 'Heinrich, I think you ought to go and see Dr Gabès. Quite soon.'

Heinrich glared at her, then, in a series of painfilled, ungainly hops, he made for his bedroom. He decided it was better to say nothing at all.

[7]

By the time Gottlieb limped into the Council chamber at eight o'clock next morning the atmosphere was close to despair. Their rising was less a movement of respect than of protest or appeal. Gottlieb gestured them firmly back into their seats.

When he spoke, it was to appeal first to their loyalty. They had worked a long time together, some of them had been with him many years. They had had crises before. They had conquered them. They would conquer this one. He wished to appeal to them not just as colleagues, but as friends.

'But Heinrich . . .' burst out Van Diemen, the mild formalities of Council procedure forgotten in the stress.

'Yes?' said Gottlieb.

'Yesterday you said . . .'

'Nothing I said yesterday has been in the slightest degree contradicted by what has happened since. I said I was eighty per cent sure there would be no incidents. I took certain precautions, but they were inadequate. Had I known what I know now they would not have taken place.'

There was a pause. 'Was there something else, Under Director-General?' said Gottlieb, looking at him.

What Van Diemen really wanted to say was something far simpler and yet something he found impossible to ask. He wanted to say things like – are you feeling all right, Heinrich? There had been rumours about the Director-General. They had been traced to one of the security guards. Van Diemen

184

had dismissed them. At a time of crisis there were always rumours. The work of the Centre had often involved cloak and dagger stuff, the laying of false trails. Nevertheless. . . . The Head of Security had complained to him. Van Diemen told him he should do exactly as ordered. Then Frau Schmidt, though far too loyal to say anything, was plainly worried about Gottlieb. Yesterday, the spaghetti. . . .

He could not do it. Not in Council. Gottlieb was a formidable man. There was in fact nothing illogical in what he had said. And Van Diemen had been moved by Gottlieb's appeal for loyalty. They had worked together for over twenty years.

'No, Director-General,' he said. 'Only this – what do we do now?'

Gottlieb stood up. 'We announce to the world that the WCCC has found the cause of the pollution-caused events,' he said, 'and we announce that from today no more will take place.'

'*What*?' Incredulity, delight, relief, anxiety, astonishment – in the faces before him Gottlieb read the extent of their trust and loyalty. It was only partially reassuring.

'But are you sure? Can you guarantee it?' Ross C. Rather,. who was certainly loyal, spoke for all of them.

'No,' said Gottlieb. 'It is a gamble. But it is the only thing we can do. If I am wrong, then within a week we will have a world war. If we do nothing, then we shall have the same result. But if I am right then we, the WCCC, and the world are saved. It is therefore a gamble we must take – or rather I must take, through the powers vested in me through our charter for dealing with *Most Sensitive* material, and which I must ask you to support. Will anyone who does not support it raise their hand.'

What could they do? No hand was raised.

His announcement to the world was made from the Audio-Visual Summit Room, which on these occasions doubled as studio. Gottlieb, almost alone in the small, intimate room except for two nervous and obsequious technicians, did not, for once, have his usual feeling that he was talking to no one at all. (Though usual is perhaps a misleading word. Only twice in fifteen years had he appeared in this way.) The terror

185

and fury outside – the fear of so many billions of watching and listening people – seemed to concentrate on him, menacing him, through the mouths of the cameras. He was not going out to them; they were pressing in on him. But he felt more than equal to the task. During his short speech he reasserted his dominance, forcing the rods of fear back into the cameras, turning them to eyes again, pouring out through them, calm, powerful, reassuring, certain.

But as he hurried through his office and down to the waiting Mercedes he prayed to God that she wasn't having a mid-morning veal cutlet or an onion pie. There had been a good deal of mess to clear up; also, before he'd left, he'd taken the two security guards up in the lift and made them spill the third crate all over the hall, stamping open the packets and breaking some jars. She hated mess. He thought he could risk one last effort – '*O my father, if it be possible, let this cup pass from me. . . .*'

His interview with Dr Gabès was short, maddening and also, subtly disturbing.

Stephen Gabès had a compassionate, lined, saturnine, good-looking face and a limp. They limped towards one another, shook hands and then sat in facing chairs. Dr Gabès said nothing. Gottlieb said nothing, waiting for Dr Gabès to ask him why he'd come. After three minutes, when it was clear he was not going to be asked this question, Gottlieb spoke.

'It's about my wife,' he said.

'?'

'I'm extremely worried about her eating.'

'?'

'Don't you think it dangerous?'

Dr Gabès looked at the huge man sitting in front of him. 'It depends what you mean by dangerous.'

'Well, dangerous. Compulsive. Excessive.' Gottlieb shifted uncomfortably in the chair, aware that, like all chairs, it was too small for him. He suddenly wanted to appeal to Dr Gabès. 'What shall I do?' he said.

'That depends on what you want to do. Why do you want to stop your wife eating?'

'I don't want to stop her eating,' said Gottlieb. 'I just want

186

her to, how do the English put it, "tone it down".' He forced a laugh. 'All that pasta and pastry and parmesan cheese. It's too much.' He was aware he wasn't putting a very cogent case, and yet how could he? Again he felt the desire to appeal. 'What shall I do?'

There was a pause, then Dr Gabès said, 'Psychoanalysis is a voyage, Dr Gottlieb.'

'A voyage?' said Gottlieb.

'A journey of self-discovery,' said Dr Gabès. 'One cannot tell what one may encounter, what one may do.'

Gottlieb lowered his head and muttered into his chin.

'What did you say?' asked Dr Gabès.

'I said,' said Gottlieb loudly and distinctly, 'that if it is a voyage then my wife is making it in a tank.' He was beginning to feel irritated and baulked. A voyage indeed. Romantic out-of-date clap-trap.

There was another long pause while Dr Gabès looked at him speculatively. Suddenly he leant forward and said, 'Dr Gottlieb, have you ever thought of consulting a psychiatrist yourself?'

'Me?' said Gottlieb, amazed. 'A psychiatrist?'

'Sometimes,' said Dr Gabès, 'when one partner is under-going therapy and the other is not, certain strains can spring up in a marriage. One partner is growing, changing; the other is not. The therapy is hard work, difficult. It is not pleasant, having someone look in at your bedroom all the time. The other partner may not appreciate this.'

'Are you suggesting,' said Gottlieb slowly, 'that I should go and see a psychiatrist? Is that the only solution you can suggest to this appalling predicament I am in?'

'I think it might be a good idea to consider it,' said Dr Gabès.

'You mean you think I am mad?' said Gottlieb.

Dr Gabès said nothing. He sat looking thoughtfully at Gottlieb.

Gottlieb felt a surge of fury. Gabès, Habeth indeed. The man was plainly a spy. It stuck out a mile. He rose to his feet, remembering just in time to press down on the arms of the chair so that it would not rise with him, turned and

walked without a word out of the room. A fascist, terrorist
spy.

The flat was empty when he returned to it. Hurrying
through to the kitchen he saw to his relief that the groceries
he had ordered were arranged upon the shelves and in the
refrigerator. No doubt she was out buying some less innocent
nourishment now, but at least he had allies. He went to his
bedroom and looked at the sheet of calculations, memorising
it. Then he lay down on his bed and relaxed, composing
himself, steeling himself.

She came in just before lunch, the shopping trolley, as he
had guessed, laden. He followed her into the kitchen. He
decided on one last appeal.

'Would you like to come out to lunch at a restaurant, *mein
Schatzi* – or we could drive out together tonight?'

'You know I don't like going out,' said Angela, briskly
unpacking. Oh, the strength of the weak; the weakness of the
strong.

'Angela,' said Heinrich. He did not dare face her. He stood
at the sink, looking out over Lucerne, over the glinting waters
of the Vierswaldstättersee. 'Angela, why don't we go away
together – a little holiday somewhere. Now. It's been so many
years. . . .'

There was a pause, then he heard her say lightly, 'Why
yes, I might like to do that. It would be nice. But it would
have to be after the *Apfelstrudel-Wettessen*.'

He gripped the sink and swayed forward. His stomach
contracted. 'What did you say?'

The *Apfelstrudel-Wettessen*, or Strudel-eating Contest, was
one of the least appetising features of Lucerne. The only
possible thing to compare it to was the Munich beer drinking
contests. But in Lucerne, in the Austrian Quarter, it was
the women who competed, consuming metre upon metre of
strudel, forcing it into huge stomachs, filling the entire intes-
tine, urged on, after blaring publicity and hideous eliminating
rounds, by husbands, lovers, fathers, families, teams of
cheering supporters. It was followed, he seemed to remember,
by the Spaghetti Gala in the Italian Quarter. But this, its
present significance apart, did not have the same unpleasant

element of competition and was, really, just a jolly eating orgy.

As in a dream, he heard Angela's voice, ' . . . and I saw one of the posters in the *Supermarkt,* it's in six days' time, and I thought I feel so much better now and I do love strudel so why not? And if I did well we could go to the Spaghetti Gala afterwards and then on holiday. Anyway, I've put my name forward.' So it had come at last, ' . . . *nevertheless, not as I will, but as thou wilt.*' The words of his childhood returned to him again.

'Angela, I went to see Dr Gabès this morning.'

'Oh really, what did he say?' She sounded interested.

'I have decided to eat more. To eat more at home.'

'Why?'

'Dr Gabès said I should try and do more of the things I want to do, let myself go more,' said Heinrich with a flash of brilliance.

This was certainly authentic Gabès. Angela said, 'I see. Well – what would you like for lunch?'

'I shall cook my own food.'

'Cook your own food? What are you going to cook?'

'Eggs.'

'But Heinrich, you hate eggs. You are seriously allergic to them. They have a terrible effect on you. Dr Bronstein expressly warned you years ago not to touch eggs. Don't you remember?'

'Sometimes one likes doing things one dislikes,' said Heinrich.

This too rang true. She and Dr Gabès had often discussed the possibility of Heinrich being a masochist. Not fully appreciating his concept of balance, she couldn't see any other explanation of how or why he had stood the first terrible years of their marriage. All its terrible years.

'Very well. If you like,' she said. 'There are some eggs in the fridge. I must be getting on.'

Heinrich prayed that it would be meat or perhaps a soup, but no – with staring eyes, noting the weight, he watched flour pour on to the scales. Then apples. He visualised the page of figures, then checked on his wrist calculator - *Scheisse! Eighteen eggs!* He took the hard, unpleasant objects, little white

189

bombs, out of the fridge and broke them convulsively into a bowl. Toad's eyes. Disgustedly, his large fat hand more like a flipper, loosely holding a wooden spoon, he vaguely stirred them together and then poured the mess into a saucepan. It gave forth a nauseous stench, looking like the aftermath of some evil birth. What did you do? Boil them? Fry them? He held the saucepan over the gas, shaking it distastefully, until the contents had gone solid, a yellow-orange block. Then, watched all the while by a now truly astounded Angela, he sat at the table and ate it straight out of the saucepan. It was like forcing down some foul old blanket, eating the solidified scum on a sewer, a raft of filth.

When he'd finished, already feeling dizzy, Heinrich swallowed fourteen cow-bile pills and went and lay down on his bed. His heart was beating and he was sweating; his stomach felt as though something large had got inside it and was trying to get out; he realised that he was not only gambling with the future of the WCCC, the future of the world, but with his own life. He reached out a shaking hand and threw down another four cow-bile pills. *Scheisse!*

After an hour, he rose unsteadily from his bed, the fury of an enraged *foie* fully on him, and rang the Centre. Anything to report? No, nothing. They were sure? No – nothing to report. No pollution catastrophes – unexplained that was – of any sort at all. So it had worked. He had won. But it was with a feeling of triumph rapidly being overwhelmed by horror and dread that Heinrich went and lay down on his bed again, fingertips resting lightly on his still churning gut.

And so the extraordinary last fight began. Angela, of course, had no intention of doing anything so ludicrous as entering the Strudel-eating Contest, or even attending the Spaghetti Gala. But she had noticed immediately, when Heinrich began what she took to be his nervous breakdown, that it was these two foods which stood out amidst his general obsession. Gabès was by no means sure it was a nervous breakdown. It was extremely significant that food played so important a part in her husband's life and psychology. It was possible he was trying to re-establish his dominance over her, to suppress, or evade and ignore again, her aggression, as he had in their early years. Food often represented sex. It was possible her eating suggested to him sexual advances, or was a symbolic 'play-act' of copulation (the erect spaghetti, limp after the orgasm of cooking) which terrified him. Either way, she must not give way, she must let the aggression flow. When Heinrich took to eggs (during the four days the battle raged she was in constant contact with Gabès) the psychology became more complicated. There seemed to be here an element of atonement. Subconsciously Heinrich could be aware that it was his dominance, combined with his fundamental indifference, that had so aggravated her condition. He was punishing himself; at the same time, perhaps, trying to elicit pity, to get her to stop from compassion. Arousing pity was another, subtler form of domination. Again, she must not give way.

Angela did not give way. The aggression did indeed flow, fiercely liberating her, making her grow – grow in several senses. Her appetite became incredible. She found she could eat 5, 8, 12 kilos of pasta without turning a hair; a strudel as long as the kitchen table, then two strudels that size. It gave her a ferocious pleasure - yes, Gabès was as usual right, there *was* something sexual in it – to tear into one of her long strudels or gollop down what amounted to spadefuls of spaghetti; a pleasure which grew even more intense when she realised that grimly, ashen-faced, silent, Heinrich was matching her, occasionally outpacing her, with eggs – larger and larger saucepans of eggs, huge sloppy bowls of eggs, then basins, finally he was violently smashing eggs up in the big sink itself. Fighting her. Or were they making love?

If so, it was an aspect which escaped Heinrich. To him the four days passed in an egg-crazed haze of pain, rage and nausea. (And yet, incredibly, he was never sick. Some instinct told him that he must keep it – them – down; and with iron will, however tumultuous the heaving, he did.) His character changed overnight. The very first morning, after that first dreadful day (five eggs swallowed raw for tea; a twenty-four-egg blockbuster for supper), he appeared at the Centre for twenty minutes. When he came in, walking with the aid of a stick, Frau Schmidt was terrified by the change in his appearance; even more so by the change in his behaviour. He sent at once for the Head of Security. What had they found in the sewage?

'What sewage?' said the Head of Security nervously.

Gottlieb began to tremble. Had they not, then, inspected the sewage? The Head of Security had started to explain that he hadn't quite followed what was meant – when Gottlieb exploded. He began to shriek at the Head of Security. Time after time he had specifically mentioned the sewage. The Head of Security was totally incompetent. He was criminally incompetent, little better than a common crook. He was probably entirely responsible for this terrible, this appalling suffering. He sacked him on the spot. He was fired. Get out. He called for his deputy and appointed him Head of Security. He wanted the entire sewage system beneath 18 Baedeker-strasse torn apart and inspected that very instant. He wanted Gabès re-screened. If necessary, tortured. Then Gottlieb dashed, or tried to dash, but at the door was gripped by a paralysing spasm of pain across the whole of his stomach round to his liver, clung to the door-side panting, then tottered, stumbled down to the Mercedes.

On the way back he stopped at a chemist and made his chauffeur buy a kilo of cow-bile pills.

And so it went on. He was in continual pain, swept by waves of nausea; he couldn't leave the flat, in case something was eaten; yet he also had to leave it. Whenever he came back he asked her what she had eaten. If she said nothing he didn't believe her. He'd swallow a couple of prophylactic eggs raw or make one of his revolting fried messes; then chew down four or five cow-bile pills and go to his room. But not to stay there. He would soon be out, spying on her. If she popped a morsel of whatever she was cooking into her mouth – as what cook doesn't? – he'd rush furiously in and repeat the process.

By the end of the second day, she began to worry. But Gabès strengthened her. Don't give in. Once more she let the aggression flow, stimulating her digestive juices, a fiery exhilarating tide. And also sanity. The more mad seemed Heinrich, the saner felt Angela; the see-saw was lifting her up into a clear cool sky while it plunged him deeper and deeper into a murky, noisesome hell, stinking of eggs.

He came continually to the Centre, calling in the members of the Council, random scientists, technicians, to harangue and shout at them. What were they doing? The *MS* material was quite irrelevant. They must find the cause. Regularly – and this was something which horrified Frau Schmidt perhaps most of all because Gottlieb, like many large men, had been fastidious, even dainty, in his personal habits – every twenty minutes or so he gave vent to loud farts. He even appeared in the complexes themselves, supported by his chauffeur, his face orange-yellow, the colour of egg yolk, and roared at the operators. He once made as though to strike Frau Schmidt with his stick. Yet - what could they do? It had plainly unhinged him, the strain of doing whatever it was he was doing (he refused even to indicate what it was) but whatever he was doing worked. The terrible torrent of pollution, of suffering and death, had stopped. They didn't dare confine him in case the whole catastrophe began again. Gottlieb raged unchecked.

Out and back, out and back. Out to the *Supermarkt* – your usual, Sir? – how's the restaurant going? – no answer – swaying back, the great sack of eggs over his shoulder.

He couldn't sleep. His nights were filled with groans and nightmares. The cow-bile pills seemed useless. They brought no relief. Indeed in the confusion of the night (hardly more confused than the day) he sometimes couldn't remember whether he was taking cow-bile pills to cure him of eggs or eggs to cure him of cow-bile pills, and several times, in the darkness, he had crawled to the kitchen and was halfway through another series of awful mouthfuls when he remembered it was the other way about and tottered back to his bedroom and the pills.

By the third day he was being almost perpetually shaken by terrible belches, ripped asunder by farts. His stomach rumbled unceasingly. His breath stank. He fought on.

The end came on the evening of the fourth day. It was the first dress rehearsal for her totally fictitious entry in the Strudel-eating Contest. The lengths of strudel were draped all over the kitchen. The second dress rehearsal was to be supper next day.

In the bathroom, Heinrich, slumped against the wall,

193

feeling close to death, was slowly stirring an enormous omelette of 450 eggs in the bath.

And then suddenly, monstrously, it was not eggs he was stirring but the turds of some strange aquatic bird, penguin turds; it was crocodile semen, eyeballs, intestines, the contents of burst wombs; the bath had become a writhing cauldron of glands and gonads and cauls, of whales' scrotums spilling their testicles – he was possessed by devils, by a sort of egg delirium tremens.

Instantly he was violently and continuously sick. The relief was immediate. He leant against the bathroom wall, pouring with sweat and breathing heavily. Then he looked into the bath, at the lake of penguin semen, the burst crocodile wombs and was at once very sick again. He swayed out of the bathroom, into his bedroom, on to his bed. He had been defeated. He fell almost at once into something close to a coma; yet through his coma – or in it, part of it – it seemed to him that the noise of eating went on all through the night.

When he became conscious again it was after four o'clock in the afternoon. He felt very weak, still wracked by pain, yet calm, sane. He wondered whether to call the Centre; then wondered why they had not called him. Perhaps they had. Or if not, then possibly some palace revolt was in motion. He did not call them.

Angela was in the kitchen when he came out, already preparing for the second dress rehearsal. He stood in the door watching her, then he said, 'Angela, this has got to stop.' She did not reply. 'I shall come back this evening and if necessary I shall stop you by force.' They were the first coherent words he had addressed to her in three days.

'We shall see,' said Angela.

There was no need to contact the Centre to see the results of the night's events. Gottlieb read them in the newspaper stands from the speeding Mercedes. *'World's Worst Pollution Crisis since 99'; 'Cancer mutations sweep China, US'; 'Entire Gulf Stream Nuclear Polluted':* and several times the stark question – *'WAR?'*

Frau Schmidt greeted him with obvious apprehension, almost fear. She tried to explain to him that the Council . . . Gottlieb motioned her to silence.

194

'I understand,' he said.

The Council was in session when he walked in, Van Diemen sitting in Gottlieb's chair. He noted that Dr Mancroft was present. There was an uneasy silence as he walked up to the Council table.

'Gentlemen,' he said, 'I have come to inform you of something I see you have already anticipated – my resignation. I shall send the formal note, which he will accept, to the Director-General of the UN this evening. I tried, I nearly succeeded, I have failed. Now it is up to you. One final thing: I cannot let you have the original of the *Most Sensitive* information. I have destroyed it. I have destroyed the memory of it.'

This brought instant expostulation.

'You had no right to do that.'

'The parameters fitted in every significant particular' (Dr Mancroft, this).

Then Pierre Messemer, no doubt one of the instigators of the revolt – and who could blame them? – stood up. 'We must ask all nations for copies of any *MS* material they have sent to the Centre over the last year. It must be sent sealed to Van Diemen.' No fool, Messemer.

'Why not do that?' said Heinrich gently. 'Goodbye, gentlemen.'

They were already talking hard as he left the Council chamber.

So, eclipsed entirely by the darkness of a world crisis, unnoticed by sixteen men in a state of panic, he deposed himself – few falls have been as complete, as swift and as disregarded.

Yet, as he descended in the lift to the hall and the Mercedes, Gottlieb was suffused by a peace such as he had never known before – the peace, joy even, of a man who was finally about to fulfil his destiny. He dismissed the two security guards and his chauffeur and drove the Mercedes himself to a spot some twelve kilometres outside Lucerne. In those days of incessant terrorist warfare it was possible to obtain almost any sort of device, provided you had the right contacts or were in a position of sufficient power. When he returned to 18 Baedekerstrasse, at seven o'clock in the evening, Gottlieb was

195

carrying a box the size of a medium suitcase attached to his wrist by a chain. He went up in the lift, stepped across the hall, and put his activating pass key to the door. It would not open. It had been secured from the inside. Gottlieb shook it hard and then stood thinking. He knew that the doors of the flat had been made exceptionally strong.

He went down in the lift and then into the street. Still very weak after his four-day ordeal, he did not feel equal to the task of climbing the indoor emergency stairs. He stopped a young boy, gave him ten Euro-dollars, and asked him to take his pass key and try it on the door at the top. If the door opened he was to close it quietly and return to Gottlieb.

As he suspected the door there was secured inside as well and did not respond to the pass key. So, he would after all have to prove equal to a climb. Walking very slowly to conserve his strength, he went round to the back of 18 Baedekerstrasse, now receiving the full flow of the evening sun, and over to the middle where the steel fire escape zig-zagged up the building. Hand on the rail, step by step, he began to climb it.

It took him twenty minutes, with frequent pauses to rest. There was a light breeze blowing, but Heinrich was soon pouring with sweat. He took off his jacket and left it on the steel step. The September sun could be hot in Lucerne.

When he reached the top he found the window onto the fire escape was shut. Behind it, steel shutters had been drawn and bolted. Trembling now, careful not to look down, but looking only at the wall or at what he was doing, Heinrich took the chain off his wrist and clipped the square box onto his braces at the back. He had always known his test would come at height and so it was. He must just pray she'd forgotten the strengthening of the drain-pipes and the fitting of hand stanchions. Staring at a patch of lichen twenty-five centimetres from his nose, he took hold of the first stanchion with both hands, swung one leg over the rail and put his foot down on to the drain-pipe; then gingerly he moved one hand to the next stanchion and swung his second leg over. The box bumped against his legs, trying to pull him backwards.

At once Heinrich was swept with such a wave of vertigo he thought he was going to fall. Although he was gripping

196

the stanchions with all his strength, his hands were so wet with sweat he thought he'd slither free. He was trembling violently.

Slowly he forced himself to become calm. He must go on. He opened one eye and reached for the next stanchion, grabbed it and without thinking glanced down.

Immediately he was swept with vertigo again. Far, far below he'd seen the tiny people, the concrete, the endless metres of the fall. He began to tremble furiously, causing the box to bang against his legs, dragging him back. He could hear himself panting hoarsely, as though it were someone else.

Centimetre by centimetre Heinrich pulled himself along the pipe. He had to fight a terrible and elemental fear. At one stage, in the middle, he thought he felt the drain pipe starting to buckle under his 152.6 kilos. He had a clear vision of sagging pipe sagging further, tearing itself out by the roots. Instantly, his hands locked onto the stanchion. For ten minutes he couldn't unclench them. He clung terrified, while huge drops of sweat rolled down his face and fell, to smash into pieces on the concrete below.

When he reached the end, after three quarters of an hour, he knew that he couldn't make the return journey. If she had barred the window, then he would just have to hang there until he was noticed (but the sun was now low); hang there until he dropped.

Very slowly he raised his head and opened his eyes. The window was open. She had forgotten. He put his hand on the sill and pulled himself up. He heaved himself onto the sill, adjusted the box behind him, and fell forward onto the bed of the little spare room at the end of the flat.

At 20.30 the Lucerne emergency services received an anonymous telephone call in an obviously disguised voice. The voice said that a terrorist organisation (the Contrade Gabès) had taken 18 Baedekerstrasse and that it would be destroyed in half an hour. Anyone within one and a half kilometres of the building was in extreme danger. Any attempt to bomb or attack 18 Baedekerstrasse would immediately set off the device. The voice gave one of the codes used to authenticate such messages, a code known only to certain terrorist organisations, the emergency services, and one or two people in high positions in the city. Then the line went dead. The wires had been cut.

At once the Lucerne authorities went into swift, long-prac-tised action. Police cars raced through the streets broadcast-ing, the terrorist alert sirens wailed (causing anyone near a radio to turn it to the terrorist wave band), frightened shop-pers and inhabitants were herded from the danger zone. All radio and television programmes were interrupted for continuous warnings.

By 20.50 the task was complete. An uncanny calm surrounded 18 Baedekerstrasse, the streets deserted, the traffic silent.

At 21.00 hours precisely, through their binoculars, obser-vers suddenly saw that the building had begun to swell. For an instant it looked as though it was just inflating, then with a searing white flash, followed seconds later by a deep roar, it exploded violently outwards and upwards, sending swiftly into the sky the familiar stemmed mushroom of a limited nuclear device.

One and a half kilometres had been a generous warning. Buildings within 600 metres were badly damaged (the *Super-markt* in particular). 18 Baedekerstrasse was, of course, completely destroyed, no trace remaining. But the nuclear device had been a small one, and in fact the mushroom cloud stopped rising at 4500 metres.

And now observers saw a strange and rather beautiful sight. The cloud began to assume a shape; indeed, with its stem blown away by the breeze that had failed to cool Hein-rich, its upthrust centre caught and turned orange by the last rays of the setting sun, the outer fringes of the cloud remaining white, it seemed for quite a while that there floated high above Lucerne something which resembled, from a distance, an enormous fried egg.

And what was perhaps stranger still – though there can be no doubt it was just one of those extraordinary chances, those non-significant coincidences whose discovery had been one of the WCCC's most interesting contributions to world science – what was really quite odd was that as the cloud itself slowly dispersed in the wind, so the terrible and inexplicable pollution-caused disasters came to an end, never to reappear. The world was clean again.